ELLE GRAY

THE LEGEND OF THE FALLS

The Legend of the Falls

PROLOGUE

"How you holdin' up?" Gene asked. "Should we turn back? Don't want to overdo it."

Hal frowned. "I'm fine. I don't need to be coddled."

"All right, all right. Keep your shirt on."

Shafts of early morning sunlight stabbed through breaks in the thick canopy overhead, casting small pools of light around them, leaving much of the forest floor still cloaked in gloomy shadow. The woods around them were silent. It was the kind of quiet that had a physical pressure to it. The kind of quiet that seemed to precede the man in the human skin mask jumping out from behind a tree with a chainsaw, ready to go to work on his unsuspecting victims. Although, to be fair, that kind of guy's victims were usually impossibly attractive teenagers out in the woods drinking, smoking, and having sex, and not a pair of middle-aged men traipsing through the trees who were ostensibly hunting.

Hal Westmark grinned to himself. His wife, Martha, always teased him about his love of horror movies. She said those kinds of movies, combined with his overactive imagination, never led to anything good. She was probably right. But Hal had grown up with Jason, Freddy, and Michael. The screams of their terrified victims and the ring of the killer's blades had been the soundtrack of his youth. They were terrible movies. They were campy with terrible visual effects, bad acting, worse writing, and few redeeming qualities. But he'd always enjoyed them all the same. In fact, he still enjoyed them.

"Been out here two hours already and we ain't seen a stinkin' thing," Gene complained.

In truth, they hadn't seen anything in weeks. Hal couldn't recall the last time they'd actually brought anything down. But that wasn't the point. At least, not for him. Gene, his best friend for the last forty years, was frustrated by the scarcity of game these days, but he still enjoyed the hunt. However, Hal didn't care whether they ran across anything or not. In truth, he wasn't looking all that hard for it. For him, it was simply a matter of getting out and enjoying a walk in the fresh air with his best friend a few mornings a week. And Gene was a good sport about it all, always agreeing to go with Hal, despite the lack of actual hunting.

Feeling a little winded, Hal stopped and pulled his water bottle out of his pack. He took a long swallow, taking a minute to catch his breath as he admired his surroundings. He had cancer and had resigned himself to the fact that there would come a day, probably sooner than later, when his body would start to break down and he wouldn't be able to get out to do this physically. Hal had resigned himself to his fate. Nothing he could do about it. But he dreaded the future and what was to come. He'd always been active, and the idea of being bedridden and unable to do the things he loved… it was equal parts terrifying and depressing. It's why he was determined to take advantage of it for as long as he could.

"Where should we go?" Gene asked.

Hal turned his face up to the canopy above, breathing the musky scent of the earth and pines all around them as the river's burbling echoed in his ears. It was beautiful. It was peaceful. Relaxing. The air was pure and crisp there and he savored every lungful he drew. He could never understand people who preferred living in a big city with all its noise and pollution to a place like Sweetwater Falls with its pristine natural beauty. He'd been born there, and he was going to die there. And he wouldn't have it any other way.

"Let's head up around the bend," Hal replied. "I remember seeing a lot of rabbits livin' up around there a while back."

"Rabbits?"

"Deer are too smart to live close to town anymore," Hal said with a shrug. "If you want to shoot somethin', rabbits are probably gonna have to do."

"Those little suckers are fast."

"Guess you're gonna have to be faster."

They shared a laugh as they continued on down the path. They rounded a bend and walked beside the river for a bit, eventually coming upon a spot in the woods that was popular with campers. As they drew near, however, Hal immediately saw that something was off.

"What is that?" he muttered.

They stood at the edge of the campsite for several long moments, silently surveying the scene before them as they tried to comprehend the destruction they were witnessing. Hal tried to understand what he was seeing for almost two full minutes "What the hell happened here?" Gene broke the silence in a hushed whisper.

"I have no idea."

Gene stepped forward and reached for something on the ground, but Hal stopped him.

"No, don't touch nothin'," he said. "You don't want your fingerprints on anything."

"Yeah. Smart. That's smart."

Wisps of smoke drifted from the pit, the fire having already been banked. The ground was littered with food and bottles, some of them half full, some half empty, most of them crushed. Hal saw that some of the food—bags of chips and cookies—had been ransacked by hungry wildlife. Raccoons probably. But coons, no matter how hungry they were, couldn't have reduced the tent to the heap of twisted metal and shredded fabric that stood in the middle of the campground. The metal frame had bent in places, snapped in others, and someone had slashed the nylon material on the sides, as if they had cut their way in.

His grip on his rifle tightening, Hal walked around the campsite and looked through the gaping holes in the sides of the tent. Like the tent itself, the pair of sleeping bags inside, were also slashed and shredded. Hal saw crimson smears and drops of scarlet all around the interior of the tent's ragged remains. He was no expert, but it seemed to be far less than he'd been expecting from what looked like such a brutal and violent attack.

"Bear?" Gene asked.

Hal shook his head. "It wasn't no bear. There's no bodies."

"Maybe it carried off whoever was here."

"Hasn't been a bear attack around here in the last hundred years."

"Not that we've heard about," Gene responded. "If somebody got killed and eaten by a bear, they ain't going to be around to report it, huh?"

The corner of Hal's mouth quirked upward. "Pretty sure somebody woulda noticed one of their loved ones missing. Believe me, if there was a bear attack, we'd have heard about it."

"Yeah. I suppose so."

Walking gingerly around the site, Hal clutched his rifle tightly as he searched the ground around them carefully and shook his head.

"I don't see any bear tracks," he said, pointing to the tree line. "Lots of footprints—looks like somebody ran off in that direction. These here look like somebody was dragged. But no bear tracks. No animal tracks at all."

"Well, somethin' bad happened here," Gene said.

"No question about that."

"What are we gonna do?"

"Not sure yet," Hal said.

But as the words passed his lips, Hal was already walking toward the tree line, following what looked like footsteps and drag marks in the dirt. Their weapons at the ready, and sweat beading on his brow, Hal walked through the trees, doing his best to keep the trail. But the undergrowth quickly grew too thick, and he lost it. Cursing under his breath, he looked around.

"What do you think?" Gene called.

"I'm thinkin' we're going to need to go talk to the sheriff."

"Yeah. Maybe."

Hal turned to him. "Maybe?"

His rifle cradled in his arms, Hal's lifelong friend shuffled his feet and looked around, his posture distinctly uncomfortable.

"What is it?" Hal asked.

"I just... I mean... we both know what did this. And it ain't somethin' the sheriff is going to be able to do nothin' about."

"You're not saying—"

"I am."

"Don't be ridiculous. That's just a kid's story, man."

"Is it?" Gene asked. "That campsite back there looks like a hell of a lot more than a kid's story. If it wasn't no bear that did that, then what was it? What slashed up the tent like that? If it wasn't no bear, what else is big and strong enough to carry two people off into the woods?"

Hal shook his head. His love of horror movies was one thing. But believing in urban legends and monster myths was something else entirely.

"It was the Okasha, Hal," Gene said in a low whisper as if afraid it would hear him. "It couldn't have been nothin' else but the Okasha."

CHAPTER ONE

Spenser grimaced as she sat down in the chair against the wall and closed her eyes. When she did, though, images of her fight with Alex Ricci flashed through her mind. Her body rang with every punch, slap, and kick all over again. His screams of rage echoed in her ears, and she saw that maniacal glint in his eyes as his long knife sunk into her flesh. The scene playing out in her mind changed, and she watched his body twitch and jerk as her bullets punched through him. She watched him fall. Heard him begging her to end him. Spenser was consumed by that almost overwhelming temptation to pull the trigger one last time all over again.

The memory made her wince.

Tears spilled down her cheeks and she quickly wiped them away. She'd come so close to executing Alex Ricci. The pain of having been forced to watch Alex murder her husband had fueled the rage she'd carried since that night, and she had been within a hair's breadth of killing him. Ryker had talked her down. Thankfully. Alex ultimately hadn't survived the wounds, dying on the operating table at the hospital. But she'd come so very close to ending him there on the driveway in front of her cabin. In cold blood.

Taking a life was never easy—not even the life of a piece of garbage like Alex Ricci—and she still carried a bit of residual guilt about it. But it was fading a lot faster than the pain that still gripped her, courtesy of Ricci's brutal attack. She'd get over the guilt a lot faster than she was healing from her physical wounds.

"He was a rabid animal that needed to be put down," she muttered to herself.

Steeling herself, Spenser took a deep breath and tried to ignore the lightning bolts of pain that tore through as she leaned down and tied her boots. Moving around was an exercise in agony. She was sure medieval torture didn't hurt half as much as the pain she was currently in. But Spenser was tired of lying in that bed. It was time to get on her feet and return to her life.

"What's going on here? What do you imagine you're doing?"

Spenser jumped, then looked up as Marley walked into the hospital room, a disapproving scowl on her face.

Her cheeks flushed as guilt gripped her again, as if someone had just caught her with her hand in the cookie jar. Marley put her hands on her hips and looked at Spenser with a frown.

"Hey, Mar. I was told you didn't come on shift until later," Spenser said brightly.

"I'd say it's a good thing I came on early then," she replied. "Otherwise, I would have missed you trying to sneak out."

"I'm not trying to sneak out."

"Slipping out when you assumed I wasn't on shift? That kind of sounds like you're trying to sneak out," Marley said.

A nervous chuckle passed Spenser's lips. "Fine. I was trying to slip out. In my defense, it was only so you didn't have a chance to guilt me into staying."

"Girl, I've never been able to guilt you into anything."

"And yet, it's never stopped you from trying."

"That's very true," Marley replied. "So, how about this time, instead of guilt, I try to appeal to your common sense?"

"I don't feel great about your chances."

"Spense, it's only been like, a week—"

"It's been nine days."

"Regardless," Marley said testily. "You suffered major trauma to your body. You were stabbed, for God's sake—"

"But nothing vital was injured."

Marley frowned. "Perhaps not. But you lost a hell of a lot of blood. And oh yeah, he beat the snot out of you. You had come in with a pretty severe concussion—"

"*Had* is the key word in that sentence. You guys have been testing me every which way I can be tested. My concussion symptoms have cleared up—"

"But with trauma to your brain like that, you can't take anything for granted. The best thing you can do is rest and allow us to keep monitoring you."

"Mar, I've been on my back for more than a week now. I'm tired of it. I want to get out. I want to walk. I want to see my dog," Spenser said.

"I get that, but if something happens to you while you're out, if you have some unforeseen neurological episode, or if you break your stitches and start to bleed, or God forbid, if there's some complication and you develop a clot or bleed internally—"

"Then I'll get help immediately."

"It might not be soon enough," she argued. "But if you're here, letting us monitor you, we can catch any issues before they become serious problems."

The look on Marley's face said she knew she was fighting a losing battle but was determined to go down swinging anyway. It was coming from a good place. It was because Marley loved her and was worried about her. The fact that Spenser agreed to stay in the hospital for more than a week without complaint spoke to the fact that she'd been a bit worried herself. But enough was enough. Other than the physical discomfort, her other symptoms had cleared up. She was feeling good… relatively speaking. As far as she was concerned, it was time to get up and start moving again.

"You're a grown woman and, obviously, I can't stop you from checking yourself out, if that's what you want to do, but I can't stress enough just how big of a mistake I think you're making."

"Noted. And don't think for a second that I don't appreciate your concern. I know it's because you love me," Spenser said. "But you also know me. I don't do idle time very well."

"Yeah, and also, you're stubborn and don't properly take care of yourself."

"What? I eat right, exercise regularly, and get plenty of sleep."

Marley pulled a face. "That's not what I mean. Being snarky and sarcastic isn't going to make me get off your back, lady."

"But I'm going to keep trying anyway."

Ryker paused in the doorway to the room, his eyes flicking back and forth between Spenser and Marley. It was as if he sensed the tension in the room.

"How are we doing today, ladies?"

"Talk to your woman," Marley said. "She's checking herself out."

"And you think I can make her stay?"

"I think you might have a better chance than I do."

Ryker laughed. "You've met her, right? I'm pretty sure once she makes up her mind about something, neither God nor act of Congress can change it."

"I really wish that wasn't such a true statement," Marley groused.

"Are you two done?" Spenser asked.

"Have you decided to smarten up and stay a few more days?" Marley retorted.

"No."

"Then no, we're not done."

A chuckle drifted from Spenser's mouth, and she looked to Ryker for help. He shrugged.

"Don't look at me," he said. "I agree with Marley. You should stay in the hospital for a few more days. You went through a lot and need to heal up, Spenser."

"Thanks, Benedict Arnold."

Ryker turned to Marley. "See?"

"Yeah, I see. She's always been this way," she replied. "I guess I was just hoping she'd start to mellow with age."

"You'd be better off trying to keep the sun from rising in the east than trying to get this one to change," Ryker said.

"Tell me about it."

"Still in the room," Spenser said. "Still right here."

Marley turned to Spenser, the displeasure on her face abundantly clear. "For the official record, it is your right to check yourself out, but you are doing so against medical advice. And you'll have to sign the AMA form when you discharge."

"Understood."

"Ryker, will you be able to keep an eye on her?"

"Of course."

"Okay, I assume you're okay with changing bandages?"

"Changed plenty when I was in the military."

"Good. Then you'll need to change that bandage on her torso wound every twelve hours," Marley said. "She's also got some prescriptions she needs to stay up with. The instructions are on the bottles, but you can call me any time, day or night, if you have any questions."

"Feel free to talk to me directly. I mean, this all seems kind of like you're giving instructions to my mom," Spenser said.

"Well, if you weren't acting like such an impatient and unruly child, I probably would talk to you directly," Marley said curtly.

"Wow. Shots fired," Spenser said.

Ryker's lips twitched and Spenser could tell he was trying to hold back a laugh, so she cast a withering glare at him. That broke the dam, and he couldn't hold it back after that, guffawing loud and long. Spenser punched him in the arm, then grimaced as pain ripped through her.

"Dammit," she muttered and when Marley opened her mouth to speak, she held up a finger. "Don't say it. Just don't."

"Don't have to," she replied, then handed Ryker a couple sheets of paper. "These are her prescriptions. I'll call them in, so you just need to go and pick them up."

Ryker gave her a quick salute. "Yes, ma'am."

"Okay, I need to get to my rounds," Marley said with a strained smile. "I'll check in with you later. Are you going to be at the cabin or—"

"I'm going to get her set up in the main house," Ryker said. "It'll make it easier to keep an eye on her and keep her out of trouble."

"Okay, good," Marley said. "But listen, I'm resigned to the fact that I'm not going to be able to keep you from doing—anything, really—but please, please, please, if you have to do something, do the bare minimum, Spenser. Take it as easy as you can. I worry about you."

"I promise. I'll do as little as I can."

"I'll make sure to hold her to that," Ryker said.

Marley frowned but nodded, seeming to accept the inevitable. "Okay, the discharge nurse will be by soon, then. I'm going to call you later and you better answer your phone."

"Yes, ma'am," Spenser said. "Love you, Mar."

"Yeah, love you, too, you stubborn idiot."

It took a little more than an hour to get her prescriptions and pick up some things Ryker insisted were necessary for an extended stay on the sofa. Pretzels, popcorn, cookies, Cheetos—the puffy kind—and a host of other junk food. Clearly, Ryker intended to get her so fat and ungainly, she wouldn't be able to get off the couch even if she tried.

By the time they got home, Spenser was wrung out. She was exhausted and reasonably sure she wouldn't be able to get into trouble even if she'd wanted to. She leaned heavily against him as he helped her into the house and Spenser had a flash of what life might be like fifty years from now, when they were both elderly, leaning on one another to get around. Other than the whole being old and feeble thing, the image itself wasn't entirely objectionable. It surprised her just how comfortable she'd gotten with the idea of growing old with him.

Ryker walked her over to the sofa and helped her lie down. Annabelle excitedly wagged her tail, looking at Spenser with those wide, soulful brown eyes, waiting for her to get settled. It was as if the big dog was aware she was hurting. She probably did. Annabelle was unusually intuitive.

"Hey, girl. We haven't been apart that many days before, huh?" Spenser said.

"She missed you. A lot. Just laid on the couch sad and depressed," Ryker said.

"My poor girl."

Ryker propped Spenser up on the sofa, gently placing a couple of pillows behind her back, then stepped away. Annabelle immediately pranced over to the couch and laid her big, blocky head on Spenser's lap with a heavy sigh of contentment and a soft whine. Ryker watched them for a moment, then scratched Annabelle's head for a minute before turning and walking out of the room.

"That's my sweet girl," Spenser said as she scratched the big dog behind her ears.

Annabelle was gentle and didn't try to force her way onto the couch to sit beside her like she normally would. Instead, she licked Spenser's hand and nuzzled her. Ryker walked into the room with a bottle of water and a small glass bowl, handing both to her. Spenser looked at the three small pills in the bowl and frowned.

"Time for pills," he said.

"I hate pills."

"Well, you can either take them or I can call Marley and she can come over and make you take them," he said. "Honestly, I'm having visions of a vet force-feeding pills to a cat, and while that might be amusing to watch, I'd rather you not have to go through that."

Spenser laughed softly. "I would much rather not go through that either."

"Then, bottoms up."

"Yes, sir."

Spenser tipped the pills into her mouth, then chased them with a long swallow of water. Ryker took the bottle and set it down on the coffee table, then took the small bowl from her. Spenser looked up at him.

"Thank you," she said.

"For what?"

"For always taking such good care of me."

He perched lightly on the edge of the sofa and took her hand, giving it a gentle squeeze. Ryker wasn't a man who typically showed his emotions. Stoic wasn't a strong enough word to describe the man. He sometimes reminded her of the blank, stony faces of the statues on Easter Island that way. But the emotions that flashed across his face as he looked at her were so intense and so pained, Spenser couldn't breathe for a moment.

"When I found you out at the cabin—I was terrified, Spenser. I was terrified that I was going to lose you," he said softly.

"You're not going to lose me."

"I almost did. Alex Ricci almost killed you."

"But he didn't," she said, squeezing his hand in return. "I'm still here."

"I have no idea what I'd do if something ever happened to you," he said softly. "Spenser, you mean the world to me."

"And you mean the world to me. You really do."

"Then I need you to do something for me."

Spenser's stomach bottomed out, and a ripple of fear passed through her heart. She wasn't sure what he was about to ask, but something in the tone of his voice gave her the notion that she wasn't going to like it. There was agony on his face as all the emotions surrounding the murder of his fiancée rose up within him. It was so thick, she couldn't ignore it.

"What is it?" she asked slowly.

"I need you to stop taking so many chances," he said.

"I'm a cop, Ryker. Risk is an inherent part of the job."

"And I understand that. But you seem to go out of your way to put yourself in the riskiest positions possible," he said. "I just… I need you to stop being so reckless. If something happened to you, I… I can't go through that again."

"Reckless? I don't—I'm not reckless."

"Sometimes, yeah, you are."

Spenser opened her mouth to respond, but as his words rattled around inside her skull, she had to admit it was possible he wasn't entirely wrong. She wouldn't have gone so far as to call herself reckless, but she could admit that she sometimes pushed the envelope and could be a little careless when it came to her personal safety. Rushing headlong into a situation when lives were on the line was just the kind of cop she was. That she'd always been.

But that was because she would rather be the one put in a dangerous situation than somebody under her command. Most of her deputies had families and the last thing she wanted was to have to go to their loved ones to inform them their husband or wife, father, or sister had been killed in the line of duty. That they'd been killed because she'd ordered them into a dangerous situation. Spenser knew what that was like. She knew it all too well and wanted to spare them that pain.

At the same time, though, she supposed she had to consider she now had somebody at home waiting for her. Somebody who dreaded getting that knock on the door in the middle of the night informing him that she'd been killed in the line of duty. And having been there herself, Spenser understood the fear and the pain that went along with it all too well.

She also knew that Ryker, having already lost one person he loved, might not recover from losing somebody else he cared for. He'd done so much work and had come so far in overcoming the mental and emotional wounds his time overseas as well as the murder of his fiancée had inflicted upon him, if something happened to her, all that work would be undone in an instant. He would withdraw from the world, and she wasn't sure he would ever reemerge.

"I'm sorry that I scared you," Spenser said.

"You didn't mean to."

"And I promise I will stop taking so many chances. I'll learn to delegate more," she told him. "After all, I've got a lot to live for."

"We both do," he said.

Ryker's dark eyes smoldered and she could see the same depth of emotion in them that was reflected in hers. They had danced around their feelings for each other for so long, it just seemed like a natural part of their relationship. But Ryker cared for her every bit as deeply as she cared for him, whether they gave voice to those feelings or not. Their shared history of loss and pain had made enjoying their time together the focus of their relationship rather than labels or expectations. They had been content to just be what they were.

As Spenser looked into Ryker's eyes, though, she realized that no longer seemed to be true. If it ever truly was. It seemed that something had changed. As she held his gaze, Spenser realized that she did want more from him, and judging by the way he was looking at her, he was on the same page. He'd probably gotten to it before she did. Reaching up, Spenser laid her hand gently upon his cheek.

"Is the offer to move into the house still open?" she asked quietly.

He stared at her blankly for a long moment, seeming to be unsure what she'd just asked. She could see him replay it in his mind and when he came to the conclusion that he'd indeed heard what he thought he'd heard, Ryker looked at her, his full lips curling upward.

"Are you serious?" he asked.

"I am."

"Then, of course, the offer is still open," he replied. "But are you ready for that kind of step forward? I mean, this isn't some guilty knee-jerk reaction or something, is it?"

"It's not," she told him. "Are you ready for that sort of step forward?"

"I've been ready."

"Good. Then I am, too," she said. "I'm just sorry it took me so long to get here."

"You're here now. That's all that matters."

He leaned forward and gave her a gentle kiss on the lips, and Spenser's heart swelled until it seemed three sizes too large for her chest. After Trevor had been killed, Spenser never believed she'd find herself in a place where she was sharing not just a home but these kinds of feelings with another man. But there she was.

And surprising as it was, she couldn't have possibly been happier.

CHAPTER TWO

"FOR THE RECORD, I'M NOT A BIG FAN OF THIS," RYKER said as he helped her out of his truck.

"Noted," Spenser replied and held up the cane he had given her that morning. "And for the record, I'm not a big fan of this."

Black with ghost flames outlined in neon blue that appeared to be shooting out of the rubber tip, the cane had a question mark-shaped curve with a grinning, silver skull ornament at the end of the handle. It was also built for Ryker, who was about five inches taller than her, so it was a little awkward to use. But Spenser was determined to be off the cane as soon as possible, so there didn't seem to be much sense in going shopping for a new one.

"What? That cane is fantastic. It's a historical artifact," he replied. "My team got it for me when I sprained my ankle on a job overseas."

"Well, I appreciate you letting me use your family heirloom."

"Mi cane es su cane."

"You're such a gentleman."

"Yes, I am," he chirped.

She turned to him. "I appreciate you being here. But really, I'm sure you have better things to do. I mean, you're building a new cider business—"

"A cider business I can't do much about until my apple orchards grow, so I've got a few years of relatively free time on my hands," he responded. "So, I'm not letting you out of my sight. You might as well get used to it."

"Well, I'm grateful for your help."

"Oh, I'm not doing it for you," he said. "If I let you get all out of pocket like you tend to do, Marley will one hundred percent murder me. I'm looking out for myself, lady. This is all about me."

Spenser guffawed. "Your sense of self-preservation is admirable."

"Damn right."

Leaning heavily on the cane, Spenser moved slowly but deliberately to the office doors. Ryker held the door open for her and she gave him a quiet word of thanks as they walked in. She'd been on the couch for a full day, consuming a bag of pretzels and half the bag of cheese puffs before she decided she was done with it. Ryker had objected, of course, but she'd told him she was going into the office whether he liked it or not. He didn't. But he also didn't try to stop her, which she appreciated.

"Sheriff," Alice said, beaming. "What in the world are you doing here?"

"Last I checked, I still work here. Did that change?"

Alice laughed. "Of course not. It's lovely to see you, Sheriff Song."

"Thanks, Alice. It's good to be here."

Most of the deputies were out on patrol, so Spenser was able to move through the office with minimal fanfare, which she was thankful for. The last thing she wanted was to be a spectacle. With

Ryker shadowing her, Spenser greeted the few deputies in the bullpen who welcomed her back, then walked into her office. As she dropped into the chair behind her desk, Ryker sat down in one of the chairs that sat in front of it. Spenser looked up.

"Are you really going to sit here while I do paperwork?" she asked.

"I am."

"Why would you waste your time like that?"

"How else am I going to make sure you don't give in to your natural impulse to go kick in doors?"

Amusement glittered in Spenser's eyes. "Trust me, I'm in no shape to go running and gunning on the streets. I am aware of my limits."

"Are you, though?" he replied.

"I am."

"Well, in my experience, you often view those limits as suggestions and like to push beyond them."

"You think you know me so well, don't you?"

"Oh, trust me, I do."

Amused, Spenser started going through all the paperwork that had been collecting on her desk while she'd been out. There was a lot of it. She was usually so on top of it all and up to date with her paperwork that she normally didn't even realize how much there was. But having been away from the office for the last, almost two weeks, she was a little overwhelmed. The towering stacks of paperwork that surrounded her were suffocating.

"I need to put this in some sort of order," she muttered to herself.

As Ryker scrolled his phone, Spenser put all the papers and files that had accumulated in her absence in date order, figuring it would be best to go through it chronologically.

"I'm going to go get us some food," Ryker said. "Can I trust you not to run out and do something silly while I'm out?"

"I'm really not in a position to run anywhere. But if it makes you feel better, I promise not to try. Scout's honor," she told him.

The truth of the matter was Spenser was already a little tired. She was definitely not in shape to be out there running and gunning no matter how much she might want to.

"All right," she said. "Any preferences?"

"Surprise me."

"I can do that."

Ryker got to his feet and walked out of the office as Spenser turned her attention to the mountain of paperwork sitting on the desk in front of her. The first stack were incident reports from the last couple of weeks. It was the thinnest stack, thankfully. There hadn't been a whole lot going on while she was laid up in the hospital. For that, she was thankful. Amanda had been in charge while she was out, and Spenser hadn't liked the idea of putting her through a trial by fire. The younger woman would one day be sitting in Spenser's chair, but that day was still a long way off.

"Hey, what are you doing here?"

Spenser looked up to see Amanda standing in the doorway of her office, hands on her hips, disapproval on her face.

"Not that I'm not glad to see you up and about," Amanda said in a slightly chastising tone. "But you should still be in the hospital."

"I got bored and tired of lying on my back staring at the ceiling, so I signed myself out."

"Sheriff—"

Spenser held up a hand, cutting her off. "You don't need to say it. And don't worry, on Marley's orders Ryker is attached to my hip making sure I don't do anything too crazy."

She pursed her lips. "That's good and all, but it'd be a lot better if you were at home resting until you were actually healed."

"I'm healed enough for paperwork."

"Fair enough, I suppose," she said then looked pointedly around Spenser's office. "But if he's keeping an eye on you, I'd say he's falling down on the job."

"He went to go get us some food."

"Okay, that's a good excuse."

Spenser's chair squeaked as she leaned back in it. The bolt of pain that tore through her told Spenser she'd moved a little too quick, making her wince. Amanda was good enough to let it pass without comment. Spenser gave herself a moment to let the throbbing in her side subside before she went on.

"So, how have things been while I've been out?"

Amanda gestured to the stack of incident reports. "Quiet, for the most part, as you can see."

"And how have things been here? How are the deputies treating you?"

"Fine. Good, actually," Amanda replied, sounding genuinely surprised. "They seem to be getting used to me being in charge while you're gone."

"That's good, Amanda. They need to get used to it because one day—"

"One day far in the future," she interrupted. "I'm not even close to being ready, Sheriff. I've still got so much more to learn about doing this job."

"You're a good cop, Amanda."

"I'm learning and getting better at that part of the job. But I'm not a great leader. I've still got to earn the respect of some of the old guard. They treat me well for the most part, but a lot of them still see me as a kid."

"Well, to be fair, you are still a kid. At least to some of the old timers," Spenser teased.

"I need them to see me as a competent leader. Not a kid."

"And they will. They'll get there. The biggest thing you need to work on is your confidence. You're good at the job," Spenser told her then gestured to her desk. "You just need to work on believing you're good at the job and more to the point, that you can be the kind of leader I see in you. Belief in yourself and confidence is everything."

"It's everything, but it's also the most elusive thing."

"True. But the longer you do this, the better you get at this, the more you'll learn to see in yourself the way I see you."

Amanda paused for a moment and sat back in her chair, crossing one leg over the other. She seemed to be gathering herself and reining in her emotions.

"I'm still not sure why you picked me to mentor out of everybody here, but I'm grateful, Sheriff. I'm grateful for the opportunity you're giving me."

"No need to thank me. And I'm not giving you anything. You've earned every opportunity."

The smell of fried food preceded Ryker into the office. He had a smile on his face as he stepped in and set the box he was carrying down on the edge of Spenser's desk.

"You went to Smashed," Spenser said.

"I did," he replied.

"Bless you. I officially recommend you for sainthood."

Amanda pulled a face. "I might have to consider my vote."

"So, I guess you don't want the burger and fries I picked up for you?" Ryker asked as he held up a bag, which Amanda snatched out of his hand.

"I can be bought," she teased. "But how'd you know I was here? You clairvoyant?"

"I might be," he teased her back.

Amanda frowned but then laughed. "Seriously, how'd you know?

"I saw you pulling in as I was pulling out. Figured you'd be hungry."

Amanda looked at Spenser. "He's definitely a saint."

"He is."

Spenser rolled her eyes and groaned in pleasure as she bit into the bacon cheeseburger he'd gotten for her, then stuffed a crispy onion ring into her mouth and chewed. Despite swearing off food after her gluttony-fest on the couch yesterday, Spenser indulged. They ate in silence for a few minutes before Ryker pulled a newspaper out of his bag and set it down on Spenser's desk.

"You might want to see this," he said.

Spenser looked at the headline: *Former FBI Agent Guilty On All Counts.* She read it several times, wrestling with the complex emotions churning inside of her.

"Well, it looks like it's really over," Spenser said slowly. "For better or worse, the Ricci saga in my life is finally done."

"Yeah, about that."

Spenser looked up to see Mayor Maggie Dent standing in the doorway, an incredulous expression on her face that set Spenser on edge.

"What's up?" she asked.

The mayor regarded her calmly, her face grim. "I received a call from a man named Clyde Rea, who said he's the—"

"The section chief of the Organized Crime division in the New York field office," Spenser finished.

"Yeah, that's him," Maggie said.

"What does he want?"

"He said he's going to come out. He wants to talk to you about Alex Ricci's death," Maggie responded.

"What's there to talk about? It was self-defense," Ryker objected.

"Of course, it was. But Rea said they just have a few questions they need answered. I'm sure it's just a formality," Maggie replied, trying to sound encouraging.

"Nothing is just a formality with these people," Spenser said and dropped the onion ring she was holding. "I guess the Ricci saga isn't quite over after all."

"It will be. You were in the right," Ryker said.

"I guess we'll see," she replied.

Spenser was skeptical. She knew Rea a little and nothing was just a formality with that guy. If he was sniffing around Ricci's death, she feared that he was looking at opening an investigation into her… an investigation that could lead to charges if he wasn't satisfied with her answers. She was suddenly very concerned.

"Excuse me, Sheriff," Alice said as she stepped into the doorway. "Hal Westmark and Gene Ulster just came in and asked to speak with you. They said they might have found a murder."

"Might have?"

Alice shrugged. "They said they're not sure what they found exactly. But they're pretty rattled and would really like to speak with you."

"Okay, put them in the conference room, please," Spenser said, thankful for having a distraction to take her mind off the suddenly ongoing Ricci saga.

Spenser held up a finger when Ryker and Amanda opened their mouths simultaneously, likely to object to her doing anything resembling work.

"It's just a conversation," she said. "I can have a conversation."

CHAPTER THREE

HAL WESTMARK AND GENE ULSTER WERE WHITE AS sheets and couldn't meet her eyes. They shifted in their seats and wrung their hands, unable to sit still. They looked absolutely terrified. It was to be expected. In Spenser's experience, most people who had no practical experience with police work tended to have that shell shocked-slash-horrified expression when they stumbled across a body or a crime scene. It just wasn't something civilians were used to, and they were often left trying to process the unprocessable.

"Thank you both for coming in," Spenser said. "You mentioned to Alice you witnessed a murder?"

"No, no, we didn't witness a murder or nothin' like that," Hal replied.

"But we found somethin' that might have been where a couple of people were murdered," Gene replied.

"And what makes you say that, Mr. Ulster?" Amanda asked.

"Just call me Gene. And I say that because when we was out huntin' this mornin', we ran across a campsite that was torn to hell," he said gruffly.

"The tent was shredded like somebody took a razor blade to it. The metal frame was bent and snapped, and I saw blood on the sleepin' bags and in what was left of that tent," Hal added.

Spenser sat back in her chair, a sharp pain stabbing in her side, and struggled to keep the grimace from her face. The last thing she wanted was to make herself look weak in front of the two men who were coming to her for help. Amanda shot her a look of concern, but Spenser shook her head.

"And you didn't see anybody—"

"They was gone, Sheriff. They done got carried off."

"Carried off?" she asked.

The two men exchanged a nervous glance and shifted in their seats again. It gave Spenser the idea that there was more to this story that they weren't sharing with her. She looked at them closely, watched the silent interaction between them and couldn't shake the idea there was some sort of embarrassment or perhaps shame in their eyes. It was curious. These men had a story to tell, but they were both antsy and looked like they were on the verge of bolting, so Spenser settled in and didn't push, letting them tell it in their own time.

"Yeah," Hal said. "It looked like somebody was dragged away—"

"What makes you say that?" Amanda asked.

"I been huntin' and trackin' in the woods around this town since long before you were born, Amanda," he said. "I've seen what it looks like when somebody gets dragged off."

"And where was this?" Spenser asked.

"It was out in Mossy Flats," Gene answered.

Spenser turned to Amanda, not knowing where that was. As familiar with the town as she was getting, there were still a lot of "local" places and town characters she was still trying to get acquainted with. Amanda, having been born and raised in Sweetwater Falls, was a valuable reference source for her.

"Mossy Flats is a popular camping area east of here that sits off Crystal Creek, which is a branch of the Sweetwater River," Amanda translated.

"Got it," Spenser said then turned back to the men. "And you found this scene this morning, correct?"

They both nodded. "Yeah," Hal said. "We figured somethin' had happened out there, so we came here right after findin' it."

"Okay, good. That's really good," Spenser said. "Amanda, get Summers and Bustos out there to secure the scene. Tell them to drop what they're doing and get out there right away. We need to make sure there's no other foot traffic and preserve the site."

"On it, Sheriff."

The younger woman hustled out of the conference room to carry out her orders. Spenser turned back to the two men sitting across from her, neither of whom seemed willing to meet her gaze. They looked shaken. It only deepened her curiosity about what they weren't saying.

"Are you all right, gentlemen?" she asked.

Hal sucked in a breath. "Yeah, uhh … fine. We're fine."

Gene moved around in his seat, appearing so uncomfortable he could well be sitting on a bed of broken glass. And his face was such a deep shade of scarlet, it was like he was choking on whatever he wasn't letting himself spit out. She'd been giving them time to relay the story in their own time and trying to avoid forcing the issue, but Spenser could see they weren't going to get there on their own. They needed some prompting after all.

"What is it, fellas?" Spenser asked.

"What do you mean?" Gene responded.

"I don't have to be clairvoyant to see there is something you both want to tell me but won't let yourselves actually say it," she pressed. "So? What is it?"

Their uneasiness grew and a sour expression crossed Hal's face. He leaned back in his chair and blew out a long breath, something akin to embarrassment on his face.

"All right, I already know how crazy this is going to sound. Hell, I'm livin' it and it sounds crazy to me," he started. "But have you heard of the Okasha?"

Spenser shook her head. "I'm afraid I haven't."

"Well, a lot of people around here believe there's a creature out there in the woods—"

"A creature?" Spenser asked incredulously.

"Well… yeah. A creature," Hal said.

"It's been around forever, Sheriff. It usually runs off with somebody's animals or livestock," Gene jumped in. "But every now and then, some hiker or camper goes missin'. That's what happened here. It's got to be."

"I see," Spenser said.

"I know how it sounds. But the Okasha is real," Gene argued.

"So, you've seen it?"

Gene's mouth puckered. "Well, I ain't seen it personally. But I've talked to some folk who have. You may want to write me off as some crackpot and I wouldn't blame you, but the Okasha's real, Sheriff. It's as real as you and me."

"What about you, Mr. Westmark? Have you seen this… creature?"

He looked over at his friend and shook his head. "No. I ain't never seen it myself."

Hal looked away, near mortification on his face. He obviously didn't fully subscribe to the belief in this mysterious, man-eating creature. Or, at least, not as much as his friend. But it was easy to see there was some small piece of him that did.

"Okay, let's start simple. What makes you believe what you found out there at the campsite was this Okasha?" Spenser asked.

"The condition of the campsite," Gene said like it was the most obvious thing in the world. "The place was trashed, and everything was ripped to shreds. Like literal shreds, Sheriff."

"All right, so, did you find footprints or anything that—"

"The drag marks we found obliterated most of the footprints," Hal offered. "We followed the trail until it disappeared into the undergrowth in the forest."

"And you really believe it's this mythical creature?" Spenser asked.

"I do," Gene replied. "What else could it be?"

A thousand things it could have been other than some magic monster flashed through Spenser's mind, but not wanting to offend or ridicule the men, she held her tongue. Amanda walked back into the conference room and perhaps, sensing the awkward tension, looked from Spenser to the men and back again.

"What did I miss?" she asked.

"Mr. Westmark and Mr. Ulster were just telling me that a monster is responsible for the scene they found out at the campsite this morning," Spenser said, grimacing at how mocking that sounded.

Amanda's eyes widened and the corners of her mouth curled upward. The excitement crackled off her like a Tesla Coil.

"You don't mean the Okasha, do you?" she gasped.

Gene nodded and Hal frowned while Spenser scrubbed her face with her hands.

"Sheriff, I grew up with stories about the Okasha. I remember me and my friends used to go out looking for it all the time. My friend's cousin even saw it once," she said.

"That's all they were, though. Stories," Spenser said, trying to rein in her exasperation. "I guarantee you, what these gentlemen found was caused by a very real, very human being. Possibly an animal. Not some… monster."

"Not everything in this world can be explained, Sheriff," Gene said, obviously emboldened by Amanda's reaction.

Spenser grimaced as she got to her feet. "All right. Thank you for coming in, gentlemen. We'll check it out and if we have any questions, we'll be in touch," she said then turned to Amanda. "Come on. Let's go see if we can figure out if it's man or myth out there."

CHAPTER FOUR

"YOU PROBABLY SHOULDN'T BE OUT HERE, SHERIFF," Amanda said.

"Your objection is noted," Spenser replied then held up a finger and glanced at Ryker. "Your objections are noted, too."

"I didn't say anything," he objected.

"You were about to."

"All I was going to say is this goes a little beyond paperwork and a conversation," he said.

"This is just a little stroll in the woods. It's no big deal," Spenser countered.

Ryker and Amanda shared a glance, their frustration with her obvious. Spenser limped along on her cane while leaning heavily on Ryker's shoulder to walk. Yeah, it was probably a bit bigger of a deal than she was willing to admit but she wasn't going to give them the satisfaction. Amanda shifted the bag on her shoulder and walked ahead of them on the trail. Ryker leaned so close to Spenser, his lips brushed her ear, sending a surprisingly delicious chill along her spine.

"Didn't you promise you were going to delegate more?" he asked.

"I promised I'd stop being as reckless and putting myself in dangerous positions. This is just surveying a possible crime scene. Nothing dangerous about it," she countered.

"Wow. With your ability to parse words and find loopholes, you probably should have been a lawyer, not a cop. You missed your true calling," he groused.

Spenser stuck her tongue out at him then winced as she hit an unsteady patch of ground. Ryker held her up and shook his head.

"Nope. Don't want to hear a word," she said.

"You're one of the most frustratingly stubborn people in the universe," he grumbled.

"Which is yet another trait most lawyers have," Amanda called back over her shoulder.

"Shut it," Spenser said.

Amanda giggled as they walked on. It was slow going over unsteady ground, but they eventually found their way down to the trail that ran alongside Crystal Creek. Just up ahead, Spenser saw the yellow tape marking off the crime scene then spotted Deputy Lane Summers standing guard. Deputy Miguel Bustos emerged from a bush and was buckling his belt. When he spotted Spenser and her entourage, his cheeks flushed.

"I really hope you didn't pee on my crime scene, Bustos," Spenser said, rolling her eyes.

"No, ma'am. I uhh … no, I didn't. Sorry," he stammered.

Spenser turned to Ryker. "I need you to stay outside the tape line. I'm sorry."

"I understand," he replied. "Just be careful and take it easy."

"Aye, aye, Captain," Spenser replied with a snappy salute.

Amanda helped lead Spenser under the tape. They paused and silently surveyed the wreckage before them. The scene at the campsite was every bit as bad as the two older men had described. If anything, they might have undersold the utter destruction.

"What in the world did this?" Amanda gasped.

"Well, I'm pretty sure it wasn't some mythical monster," Spenser replied.

Ryker chuckled. "Are they telling you it was the Okasha?"

"Why do you assume it wasn't?" Amanda asked then turned to Summers. "Lane, you grew up hearing all the stories about the Okasha, right?"

The younger woman nodded. "I did. I've even talked to a few people who've seen it."

Bustos scoffed and walked to the other side of the campsite, clearly in Spenser's camp of skeptics unlike Lane and Amanda who were on the side of the believers. Spenser chalked it up to their youth. In her experience, younger people tended to have more of a willingness to embrace the outlandish and unbelievable.

"You know what I find funny?" Spenser asked.

"What's that, Sheriff?" Lane responded.

"What I find funny is that nobody has ever actually laid eyes on this Okasha thing," she said. "Everybody knows somebody who knows somebody who knows somebody else who's seen it. But nobody has ever really seen it themselves. Kind of weird, right?"

Amanda and Summers exchanged a glance, both of them looking a little sheepish, as if they hadn't considered that before. Ryker covered his mouth, trying to stifle a chuckle. Summers, though, looked around at the campsite then turned back to Spenser, seemingly unwilling to let it go.

"Then what could have done this, Sheriff?" she asked. "I mean, what could have slashed through the tent like that?"

"A man with a box cutter, perhaps. Or a machete. It could have been any number of edged weapons that slashed through that nylon tent, really," Spenser responded. "And before you say anything, the tent frame could have easily been busted up by a man, rather than a monster. It's thin aluminum tubing, not cold rolled steel."

Lane frowned, obviously disappointed that this scene wasn't confirmation of the legend she seemed to want to believe in so badly. It might have been funny if it hadn't been such a serious situation.

"Yeah. I guess so," she said.

Moving slowly and gingerly around the campsite, Spenser studied the scene. She could see why Hal and Gene had been so shaken by what they'd found. The violence in the campsite was extreme. Whoever had done it had come through with bad intentions. As Spenser ambled around the site, studying it from every angle, she became convinced of one thing.

"This isn't a murder scene," Spenser said.

"Are you sure? The sleeping bags are shredded and there's blood in the tent," Amanda pointed out.

"Not nearly enough. If somebody had been killed here, there would be a lot more blood in the tent or the ground around it," Spenser countered.

"There are drag marks over here," Lane said. "It looks like somebody was dragged off into the woods in this direction."

It jibed with what Hal and Gene had described. Moving clumsily and laboriously with Amanda at her side, Spenser leaned heavily on her cane as they made their way along the trail the two older men had followed earlier that morning. There was a clear trail of drag marks in the carpet of the forest floor as well as small branches that looked to have been snapped by somebody's passing. They weren't too far into the forest line when the trail disappeared into the undergrowth. Spenser noticed something else, though.

"These look like shoe prints to you?" she asked, pointing to them with the tip of her cane.

Amanda squatted down and looked. "Yeah. They do, actually."

Spenser studied them closely for a minute. "They look like men's shoes to me. Size eleven or twelve maybe, and wider than a woman's foot."

"It's possible, yeah."

"Okay, so we've got one person being dragged and one walking alongside," Spenser mused.

"If these footprints were made at the same time. It's possible these are older, or possibly from somebody else who found the scene before Lane and Miguel were able to lock it down."

"That's possible, too. But there were two sleeping bags in the tent, so I'm going to assume we've got two missing people," Spenser said.

"That's fair."

"Come on."

Amanda walked alongside Spenser as they stepped out of the forest and back into the campsite. Ryker, Bustos, and Lane chatted quietly off to the side as they waited at the tape line. Ryker glanced at Spenser when they stepped out of the woods and gave her a small smile then turned back to his conversation with the deputies.

"That man has the patience of a saint," Amanda whispered.

"He really does," Spenser replied.

"You do understand that you try that patience, right?"

Spenser snickered. "I really do. And yes, before you say it, I am well aware that I don't deserve the man."

"I wouldn't go that far. You two complement each other really well. You guys just seem to fit. Honestly, you're both good for each other."

"Yeah?"

Amanda nodded. "Yeah. You are each other's people."

Her gaze lingered on the big man, quietly reflecting on how far they'd come in their respective journeys... and how far they'd come together. Nobody was more surprised than Spenser that she was in this position. That she was open to loving again. After Trevor's murder, she'd closed and shuttered that section of her heart. Ryker, though, had somehow managed to unlock that door and step right through. She was happier than she'd been in a long time. At the same time, though, she was terrified. The complex brew of emotions was thick and intense, and while tentative, Spenser felt more alive than she had in a very long time.

"Yeah. We are," she finally murmured.

Spenser snapped on a pair of black nitrile gloves then tore her gaze away from Ryker and surveyed the scene around her. Amanda followed her lead and, together, they poked through the debris that littered the campsite. Spenser noticed prepackaged food containers from Pickton Farms, one of the upscale grocery stores in town. The sunlight raining down from above glittered off the jagged shards of glass that lay in the dirt all around the tent. She also noticed a couple of discarded joints and a small baggie of loose weed lying among the rest of the debris.

"We're definitely looking for a couple," Spenser said.

"How do you know?"

Spenser gestured to the food containers and the jagged bottom of one of the several wine bottles that had been smashed in the destructive frenzy.

"This was a romantic setting," she said.

"How do you figure?"

"The high-end, fancy meal containers, the wine ... it's not the kind of thing you bring to hang out in the woods with your boys," Spenser explained. "It's the sort of thing you bring to a romantic picnic. It was definitely a couple staying here."

"Okay, I can get behind that. But what does that mean?"

"Maybe nothing. But maybe something. We can't be sure until we analyze the rest of the scene and identify the missing couple."

Amanda squatted down and started looking at the glass and containers Spenser had pointed out, processing what she'd said. Learning. It was one of the things Spenser loved and respected most about Amanda—her willingness to be taught and to learn. Most of her other deputies didn't have that sort of desire to add to their base of procedural and investigative knowledge like Amanda. Most of them seemed content to clock in, clock out, and maybe do a little police work in between, which was fine. She needed foot soldiers and those willing to just follow orders. But she also needed leaders. That was Amanda.

Spenser moved to the tent and began carefully sifting through the debris, doing her best to avoid mucking up the blood or other evidence that lay on the floor. She noticed the cuts in the nylon tent were clean and precise. Whatever had been used to slice through them was incredibly sharp, most likely a box cutter or another razor-like implement of some sort. She laughed to herself, not doubting that Amanda and Lane would see claw marks, rather than those of a manmade tool.

Moving one of the sleeping bags aside carefully, she paused. "Amanda, do you have any evidence bags on you?"

"I do," she said. "What did you find?"

Spenser lifted a pair of wallets out of the debris and opened the first one. The photo on the ID depicted an attractive young woman with shoulder-length dishwater blonde hair, brown eyes, and sharp, angular features. She was listed at a petite five-one, one hundred and two pounds.

"Rachel Kehoe," Spenser said and handed the robin's egg blue wallet to Amanda.

As Amanda studied the woman's ID, Spenser picked up the second wallet. This one was black leather and was distinctly masculine. The driver's license was for twenty-four-year-old James Burnham. Five-eleven and a trim one-hundred-sixty-pounds, Burnham had chestnut-colored hair and light blue eyes. He was an unassuming and plain-looking guy without any distinguishing or memorable features. Physically speaking, Burnham was the sort of guy you'd forget five minutes after meeting him.

Spenser handed the wallet to Amanda then looked up at her. "I guess we've found the first piece of the puzzle."

"Looks like it."

"All right. Call Arbery to come out and process the scene," Spenser said. "We'll head back to the office and get to work."

"Okay. Let's get it."

CHAPTER FIVE

"How are you feeling?" Marley asked.

"Tired. A little sore, I guess."

"You overdid it yesterday."

"I didn't."

"Hiking out to Crystal Creek while you're still recovering from a brutal stab wound to your abdominal cavity is what we in the medical profession like to call overdoing it."

Spenser's lips twisted ruefully. "Touché. Brat. Did Ryker run and tell you everything?"

"Pretty much, yeah."

They sat together in Sunny Side Up laughing and having a little breakfast together before Spenser went into the office. Ryker had a meeting that morning and couldn't shadow her, so Marley took up the slack. Spenser was apparently not going to get any time alone any time soon. She loved them both dearly and knew they were simply worried about her, but Spenser didn't like being fussed over. She hated that about as much as she hated admitting she had limitations. This injury, though, underscored the fact that she did, and having Ryker and Marley doting over her the way they were only served to highlight it.

"Well, if it makes you feel any better about it all, I'm letting Amanda run point on this case," Spenser stated.

"Until you decide to jump in and take control, anyway."

"I'm sitting here having breakfast with you. That's about the opposite of taking control."

"Yeah, but I'm not an idiot. When you go to work, I'm not fool enough to think you're just going to sit in your office doing paperwork while all that is going on. I mean, that's what you said you were going to do yesterday, and you ended up hiking out to Crystal Creek," Marley countered. "You physically can't stop yourself. You can't sit on the sidelines. No, you have to be in the middle of the action. That's just who you are."

Spenser grimaced. She couldn't really argue with Marley since she wasn't wrong. She probably shouldn't have gone traipsing out into the woods, but she wasn't the sort of person who was comfortable sitting on her hands when there was work that needed to be done. Unlike some she'd worked with before, Spenser led from the front.

"So, the Okasha, huh?" Marley asked, breaking the awkward silence.

Spenser rolled her eyes. "Don't even get me started on that. Amanda and Lane are convinced it's running around out there abducting campers."

"Come on, in a universe as vast as ours, you won't even allow for the possibility that there's a mysterious creature out there in the woods?" Marley asked with a mischievous twinkle in her eye.

"Not even a little bit."

"This world is full of mysteries and things that can't be explained. Science is uncovering them all the time."

"This isn't one of those things."

"Then what is it? From what I hear that campsite was thoroughly trashed."

"Which could easily have been done by a human being or an animal."

"Could have been," Marley teased. "But then, it could have been the Okasha."

Spenser chuckled and shook her head. "You're a woman of science. How in the world can you even consider the idea there's a monster in the woods out there?"

"It's because I'm a woman of science that I'm open to the possibility of the unexplained," Marley said. "I know better than most that science can't explain everything in this world. I've seen plenty of things that defy anything close to rational or logical explanation."

"Well, once we've ruled out all terrestrial explanations, I guess we'll start looking for monsters in the woods. Until then, though, we're going to focus on human leads," Spenser said.

Marley smiled around a mouthful of her pancakes, clearly amused that she'd gotten under Spenser's skin. She always enjoyed teasing her and Spenser walked into it every single time. A rueful expression on her face, she took a bite of her steak and mushroom omelet then chased it with a swallow of coffee. As much as it galled her to not be the one in charge of the case and getting her hands dirty chasing it, there was some small bit of Spenser that enjoyed having a casual breakfast with her best friend while other people handled things. She supposed it was possible that like Amanda, she had plenty of room for growth.

"Do you guys have any leads yet?" Marley asked.

"We have the IDs of the two campers," Spenser said. "Amanda is working to confirm they're actually missing. We can't say for sure there's a crime yet until we're sure the two campers aren't where they're supposed to be."

"Seems unlikely, given the condition of the campsite."

"Agreed. But the last thing we need is to launch a search effort only to find they got drunk and they're safely at home," Spenser said. "We have evidence they were drinking and smoking weed, which means it's possible they wandered off and a bear trashed the campsite later on."

"Seems more likely the Okasha dragged them away if you ask me."

"I'm so glad you're a doctor and not a cop."

They finished up their breakfast with some casual conversation. It was nice. But then Spenser glanced at her watch. Even though she wasn't running point on the case, she was still anxious to get into the office to see where things were at. She might not be able to go kick in any doors right now, but she could still help steer and guide the course of the investigation.

"So, Ryker told me something else," Marley said.

"Did he now?"

"In fact, he did," she replied. "And funnily enough, it was something I should have probably been hearing from you."

Spenser's face colored, and she glanced down at the table. "I was honestly going to, but it all happened kind of spur of the moment and then I got caught up in all this stuff..."

"Uh huh," Marley said as she arched an eyebrow.

Spenser took a sip of her coffee and tried to put her thoughts into some semblance of order. Ever since she told Ryker she was ready to move in with him, her head had been crowded with ten thousand competing voices, each one louder than the one before it. She couldn't make sense of it all. Worse, she still wasn't exactly sure what she thought of it or what had compelled her to tell Ryker she was ready to move in with him.

"Listen, Mar, I'm sorry I didn't talk to you about it," Spenser said. "Honestly, I didn't even know I was going to do it until I did it."

"Spense, this is great news. This is a good thing."

"Is it?"

"Why wouldn't it be? It seems like the natural progression of your relationship," Marley said. "You and Ryker have been growing closer for months now. You guys are inseparable and it's not hard to see that you're both crazy about each other. This is a good thing. A really good thing."

"Yeah. It is..."

Spenser's voice trailed off and Marley stared at her curiously. "Why do you sound like you're not so sure it is then?"

"Because I'm not sure. I mean… yeah, it is a good thing. I care about Ryker. I care about him a lot and he cares about me," she replied. "I'm just… I guess I'm scared. It just seems like it's getting real and that's when people get hurt. I mean, I'm terrified of losing him. I can't go through something like that again. It would break me."

"That's natural, hon. After what you've been through, I'd be surprised if you weren't scared," she replied softly. "But don't forget that he's gone through the same thing and is feeling all the same things you are right now. The fact that you two have this shared history sucks, but it means that you understand what each other has gone through. That's a positive, Spense. It means you can lean on each other. It means you can relate to each other in ways very few others can. You two are lucky you found one another."

"It's a pretty grim connection to share."

Marley looked at her over the rim of her coffee mug, her icy blue eyes penetrating deep into Spenser's soul. She had never been able to hide things from Marley. The woman had a frustrating knack for ferreting out information Spenser didn't want to give. She was subtle, but as persistent as any trained and seasoned interrogator Spenser had ever dealt with. It was undoubtedly a byproduct of having to deal with patients who would rather hide their maladies than be honest with their doctor. And the gleam in her eye told Spenser the woman had caught a scent and wasn't going to stop until she'd gotten what she wanted from her.

"What's really going on here?"

"What do you mean?"

"What I mean is that, on paper, you and Ryker are perfect for each other. It's obvious just how much you care about one another. But you seem hesitant to give yourself fully to what the rest of us can see. Why? What's really happening with you?"

Spenser hesitated and looked into her mostly empty coffee cup, thought and emotion inside her head colliding so hard, it left her paralyzed.

"Spense?"

"I just… Ryker makes me happy. Happier than I've been in a really long time."

"And you deserve to be happy, hon."

"Do I really?"

"Of course, you do."

Spenser swallowed hard and spun the butter knife on the table as she tried to rein in the emotions churning in her belly. She knew exactly why she was having the reaction she was having. She was just having a difficult time giving voice to it simply because of how insecure-slash-crazy she was going to sound. But, if she couldn't allow herself to be vulnerable with her best friend, then who could she do that with?

"Spense, what is it?" Marley prompted.

She blew out a loud breath. "Sometimes, I'm not so sure I deserve to be happy, okay? And most of the time, I'm not sure I deserve to have somebody be as good to me as Ryker has been."

Marley gaped at her like she'd lost her mind and was silent for a long moment. She took a sip of her water and gently set the glass back down before raising her gaze again.

"That's about the most asinine thing I've ever heard you say," she finally said. "And given how long we've known each other and the sheer number of asinine things I've heard you say, that's really saying something."

Spenser's lips flickered with amusement, but she appreciated the fact that Marley always knew how to lighten a mood and get a laugh out of her.

"You're such an idiot," Spenser said.

"Yeah, but I made you smile, so I win."

"I guess you did."

Marley leaned forward, her gaze intense. "Listen to me, Spenser. You deserve to be happy. And you absolutely deserve somebody to be as wonderful to you as Ryker is. Why on earth would you ever believe otherwise?"

"I'm not sure," Spenser replied quietly. "I guess there's still that small part of me that's afraid of moving on with my life. Afraid that I'm somehow betraying Trevor."

Marley's expression softened, and she took Spenser's hand. "Hon, trust me when I tell you that Trevor would have wanted you to move on. More than anything, he would have wanted to see you happy. The last thing he ever would have wanted was for you to spend your life miserable and alone."

Marley and Trevor had been close back in med school. She was the one who'd introduced her to Trevor and knew him about as well as she did, so Spenser didn't take what she was saying lightly. It didn't make it any easier for Spenser to quiet that voice yammering away in the back of her brain, though. It kept whispering in her ear, telling her she was being unfaithful. Disloyal. It kept telling her she didn't deserve to be happy. That she didn't deserve Ryker, and that she was only going to get him killed. The voice in the back of her mind kept telling her she was destined to be alone and that she should just accept her fate rather than keep fighting it.

"Trevor would have wanted you to find happiness again, Spense."

"My brain knows you're right. But try telling that to my heart."

Marley offered her a sympathetic gaze. "It's probably natural to have all these feelings the first time you get involved after... well... after. But you deserve to be happy. You deserve to have a wonderful life," she told her. "Life is short. Much too short to spend it alone and unhappy. We only get so many chances to find that happiness and fulfillment. Ryker is good to you. He makes you happy. You're being given a second chance. So, take it. Take it with both hands and don't let go. You need to learn to accept that you deserve it. Because you do."

Spenser held her hand in return. She appreciated Marley's effort to assuage her guilt and fears about her relationship with Ryker and where it was all going. She wanted to be able to lose herself in her feelings for him. Wanted to be able to accept that she was worthy of his affection. But at the moment, his affection and care felt like a sweater that was five sizes too big for her. Spenser wanted to believe it was going to fit one day, but she wasn't there just yet.

"Thanks, Mar," she said softly.

"Anytime, hon. Anytime."

CHAPTER SIX

"ALL RIGHT, WHERE ARE WE AT, BOYS AND GIRLS?" Spenser asked.

Jacob and Amanda looked up as she gimped her way into the conference room and closed the door behind her. Leaning on her borrowed cane, Spenser made it to her seat and dropped heavily into it. Jacob stared at her for a moment with a mischievous gleam in his eye.

"What?" Spenser asked.

"What? Nothing."

"Spit it out."

"I was just going to say those flames on your cane were a good call," Jacob said. "Makes you look faster. Sleeker."

Spenser fixed him with a sour expression. "You're going to see just how fast this cane is when you find it in your backside."

"No need to create a hostile working environment, boss," he said with a chuckle. "It's good to have you back. Having my sister in charge has been unbearable. It's giving me horrible flashbacks to when our parents would go out and leave her in charge."

Spenser grimaced. "You're older than she is. How did that work?"

"That sentence kind of tells you all you need to know, doesn't it?" Amanda asked.

"Touché," Spenser replied with a smirk.

Jacob's lips twitched and a slow chortle floated from his mouth. "But seriously, I'm glad to see you're on the mend, Sheriff. It's good to have you back in the office."

"Thank you. It's good to be back," she replied. "Now, what can you tell me about Rachel Kehoe and James Burnham?"

"Well, they are both definitely missing," Amanda said. "Both attend Southern Cascades and neither showed up for classes today."

Spenser sat back in her chair and frowned. It wasn't unexpected news and bolstered her concerns. While there were still a thousand explanations that could explain what happened out at the campsite, it definitely wasn't a good sign.

"I'm already mustering a search team," Amanda said. "We've got volunteers coming in to help us search the woods out at Mossy Flats. I was just about to head out there to organize it."

"That's good. Smart."

"And you are not going out there to search the woods with us. Not while you're still all banged up," Amanda stated firmly.

Spenser opened her mouth to object, but Amanda held up a finger, cutting her off before she could speak. The younger woman wore a stern expression as she shook her head.

"I'm aware that sitting on the sidelines is difficult for you, Sheriff. But in your current condition, you'd be more of a liability out in the field than an asset," she stated. "You wanted me to take on more of a leadership role so that's what I'm doing. We need able bodies out there searching and can't afford to assign somebody to walk you through those woods. We need to move quickly."

Spenser frowned but nodded. Deep down, she was impressed with her undersheriff taking control of the situation and making the tough decisions. She was proud of Amanda. More so because she was right.

"Okay," Spenser agreed. "What can I do to help?"

Amanda looked like a thousand-pound weight had been lifted off her shoulders. Knowing how difficult Spenser could be to deal with sometimes—especially when she'd gotten her mind set on something—Amanda had obviously been dreading having that conversation with her. It couldn't have been easy for Amanda. But she'd done it anyway, which impressed Spenser all the more.

"The Kehoe family is over in Westerton and the Burnhams live in Millbrand," Amanda replied. "I thought you could start by interviewing them? Some background might be helpful."

"That's good, Amanda. I'd be happy to," Spenser lauded her.

"Thanks, Sheriff," Amanda said, her cheeks flushing. "I should get out there and start coordinating the search."

"All right. Keep me in the loop."

"Will do."

Still beaming with pride, Amanda slid a pad of paper over to her then hustled out of the conference room, leaving Spenser alone with Jacob. She tried to maintain that chipper demeanor, mostly to cover that she suddenly felt adrift. Not being the one in charge, not being the one out there organizing the volunteers and leading the search party was strange, and she wasn't quite sure what to do with herself. Spenser shifted in her seat and drummed her fingers on the table.

"You don't like not being the one calling the shots," Jacob noted.

"I'm just not used to it. That's all. But I'm learning to delegate. I need to learn to delegate and let others do the heavy lifting now and then. I'm good with it," she said, sounding as if she was trying to convince herself.

She sat back in her seat, her gaze drifting all around the conference room. Spenser glanced at the pad of paper in front of her, reading then rereading Amanda's notes then pushed it away with a frustrated breath bursting from her mouth, drawing an amused smirk from Jacob.

"Okay, yeah, I hate it. I absolutely hate it," she said.

"Well, it's not as if you don't have things to do yourself," he offered brightly. "Amanda left you with plenty of work to keep you occupied."

"Yeah, yeah, yeah," she muttered. "I'm just used to being the one in the field."

"Life is all about change, boss. Learning to adapt to new roles and new situations," he said. "Look at me. I was on a train to nowhere good before you pulled me into the department and gave me a job. A good job. You've helped put me on track for a better life because I adapted to this new role. I feel like I'm actually making a positive difference in this world, and I never imagined I'd say this, not in my wildest dreams, but it's a nice change of pace."

"It helps that you're really good at what you do."

"Let's not undersell it, boss. I'm the best at what I do. It's okay for you to say it," he crowed, earning a laugh from Spenser. "But really, I wouldn't be half the person I am today if not for you. Your belief in me has made me better. More confident. You've made me see I can do better things with my life and make a real difference. You've shown me I can have a positive impact in this world. And I see you doing that for my sister. I've never seen Amanda so confident and happy. Not only that, she's never really believed she's as smart and capable as she is… not until you put your faith in her. Now, she's really started to believe in herself. And that's because of you."

Spenser shook her head. "That's because she is smart and capable."

"She is. But she never accepted that because when she started working here, nobody ever showed her she was. You did. You showed her it was okay to believe in herself. That she was smart enough and worthy enough to do this job. You've helped her grow, boss. You've helped both of us grow, not to mention Lane and some of the other deputies here, too."

Spenser traced a circle on the table with her fingertip, doing her best to fight off the unexpected wave of emotion that was swelling in her breast. She didn't consider herself an overly sentimental person, but Jacob's words struck a chord that resonated deep within her.

"What I'm saying is that, sure, you're not out there kicking in doors and busting heads right now, but that doesn't mean you're not influencing things. That you're not having an impact on me, Amanda, and everybody else in this department. And it's an impact that's going to last a lot longer and be more beneficial to everybody in this town than anything Howard Hinton ever did in the thousand years he was running things around here. You don't always need to be out front, leading the charge to make a difference. That's all I'm saying," Jacob said.

The corners of Spenser's mouth flickered upward, and she gave herself a moment to swallow the lump in her throat before speaking. She hadn't expected a speech like that from Jacob. But she also couldn't deny that it was something she didn't just appreciate hearing but needed to hear.

"Thank you, Jacob. That means a lot," she finally said, her voice thick.

"Just telling you the truth."

"I appreciate it. More than you even realize," Spenser told him.

Jacob sat back in his seat, seemingly content that his point had been made. Filled with a renewed vigor and sense of purpose, Spenser sat forward again and looked at the notes Amanda had left for her to review.

Spenser cleared her throat. "Okay, let's get to work then. What can you tell me about our pair of possibly missing students?"

"Thought you'd never ask," he said.

Jacob tapped out some commands on his keyboard and the monitor at the front of the room came to life, showing the DMV photo of the woman whose ID Spenser had found in the tent.

"Rachel Kehoe, twenty-two years old. She was born and raised in Westerton, which is an affluent bedroom community about half an hour northeast of us. She still lives with her parents and her younger sister, Veronica. By all accounts I've found, they're the perfect All-American family," Jacob said. "Rachel is a psych major at Southern Cascades and according to a quick jaunt through her socials, she has been seeing our second possible victim, James Burnham, for a little over a year."

Spenser jotted down a few notes on the pad Amanda had left for her, questions already forming in her mind.

"Okay, what about the other one?" she asked.

"James Burnham, twenty-four years old, is a senior majoring in chemistry at SCU. He's got an apartment near the school," he replied. "His parents are still together, he's got one younger brother, and they're all every bit as wholesome as the Cleaver family," Jacob reported. "Their family runs a ranch over in Pineworth that's been in the Burnham family for three generations."

"Okay, that's a good start," Spenser said. "Do either of them have a record?"

"Nope. They're both clean as a whistle. I've perused their socials and they both seem like good, wholesome, well-adjusted people who are very much in love. Not a red flag for either of them that I could find. Frankly, I found it kind of disturbing. Nobody should be that clean."

Spenser chuckled. "Believe it or not, some people are."

"They should obviously not be trusted."

"Well, if it makes you feel any better, I found weed out at the campsite I assume belongs to them, so they aren't one hundred percent squeaky clean."

Jacob shrugged. "That's marginally better, I suppose."

Spenser looked at the pad again and a grin flickered across her lips when she saw the word "Okasha" with a question mark behind it in Amanda's scrawling script. With everything going on and her instant rejection of all things paranormal, Spenser realized she didn't really know anything about the mythical monster.

"Tell me about the Okasha," she said.

"I thought you didn't believe."

"I don't," she replied. "But I'm curious."

"Okasha is the Snohomish word for the creature, which is also known as the Sweetwater Devil, basically the Sweetwater Falls version of Bigfoot. You find a different myth for basically the same creature in different regions of the country—the world, really. In Florida, you have the Skunk Ape. In Missouri, it's Momo. In Ohio, it's the Grassman and on, and on," he said. "Anyway, the

Okasha, like all the rest, is a large, bipedal creature covered in dark fur, blah, blah, blah. It's the usual description of Bigfoot you get. Some of the stories claim it's got red, glowing eyes, massive claws, fangs, and has a taste for human flesh."

"Do you believe in it?"

He shrugged. "Not really. I think it's a story that's been perpetuated through the ages as a means of controlling the behavior of young people. Don't go into the woods at night or the Okasha is going to get you. Don't do this or the Okasha is going to carry you off. I mean, what do kids do in the woods at night? They drink, smoke, and have sex. Some mythical monster lurking in the woods that likes to eat people seems like a pretty convenient story to curb that sort of behavior, doesn't it?"

"Of course. Most modern myths and urban legends, if you really look at them, are all aimed at controlling the behavior of one group or another—usually young people," Spenser agreed.

"No doubt. That being said, there are things in this world that can't be explained by science or rational means," he added. "So, is it possible there's some unknown creature out there in the woods? Yeah, it's possible. Did it carry these two kids off? No idea. But I'm open minded enough to not instantly rule it out."

Spenser smirked. "You believe in UFOs, too, don't you?"

He guffawed. "Of course, I do. Because they're real. And the government knows it. They're hiding alien bodies and tech out at the Air Force base in Colorado Springs, not Area 51 out in Nevada like most people have been duped into believing. Anybody who knows anything knows they shut down Area 51 and moved everything to Colorado Springs a long time ago."

"Is that so?"

"That is so. And if you're interested, I've got loads of research—"

"I'm sorry to interrupt, Sheriff."

Alice stood in the doorway of the conference room and Spenser grinned, thankful Jacob had been cut off before he could don his tin foil hat and really get rolling.

"Oh, thank God," Spenser said, drawing a small smile from Jacob. "No interruption at all, Alice. What is it?"

"Well, Veronica Kehoe is here to speak with you?" Alice replied. "She's the missing girl's younger sister."

"She's here?" Spenser asked. "With the parents?"

"No. She's alone," Alice responded.

Spenser took a beat to shift gears. She hadn't expected the girl's family to show up out of the blue like that. But she wasn't about to turn her away.

"Right, right. Great. Thank you," Spenser said as she quickly tried to put together a list of questions in her mind. "If you could put her in one of the interview rooms and get her some water or something, I'd appreciate it. Tell her I'll be along here in just a moment."

"Of course," Alice replied then turned and headed off to do as she'd been asked.

"Okay," Spenser said, getting to her feet. "Time to do some work."

She headed for the door then paused and turned back to him. "Thank you for the chat, Jacob. I really appreciate it."

"Anytime, boss," he replied. "And if you're interested later, I can show you all the research on the UFOs out at—"

"Bye, Jacob."

CHAPTER SEVEN

SPENSER STEPPED INTO THE INTERVIEW ROOM AND CLOSED the door behind her. The young woman sitting at the table shifted in her chair and wrung her hands together. No more than five-three with a petite yet curvy figure, she was twenty years old but with the bubble gum pink streak in her champagne-blond hair and her boho vibe, she appeared younger. Spenser set the file in her hand on the table in front of her then took a seat across from the girl who started to gnaw on her already raw thumb. She leaned her cane against the table and sat forward.

"Thanks for coming in so quicky, Ms. Kehoe," Spenser started.

"Just call me Veronica … or Roni. Most of my friends do."

"Okay, Roni. Thanks for coming in," Spenser said. "Are your parents—"

"They're out with the search party in the woods," she responded. "They asked me to come down and talk to you."

"Okay. Well, thank you for coming in."

"Do you have any idea where my sister is or what happened to her?"

"We're still working on that," Spenser said.

"Then what are you doing here? Why aren't you out there looking for her?"

"There's currently a search party underway. They're combing the woods around the campsite where her ID was found," Spenser said then motioned to her cane. "I'm not able to be part of that right now, so I'm getting some background information."

The girl glanced at Spenser's cane as if seeing it for the first time. "Oh. Right. Sorry."

"It's all right," Spenser said. "When was the last time you heard from your sister?"

"Um… the day before she and James went out to go camping, so I guess it was last Thursday," she said. "They were supposed to stay Friday and Saturday night then come home at some point on Sunday."

"Was that something they did often? Go camping?"

She nodded. "Yeah. That was kind of their thing."

The girl's eyes reddened and shimmered as they welled with tears. Spenser handed her the box of tissues that sat on the table and the girl took one with a grateful nod then dabbed her tears away. She sniffed loudly and cleared her throat, taking a moment to gather herself.

"Are you okay?" Spenser asked.

"Yeah. I'm good."

"Okay. Good," Spenser said gently. "And how was your relationship with your sister?"

"It was good. She's my best friend."

"And her relationship with your folks?"

"It was fine. Everybody's happy."

"So, no arguments lately or…"

Roni gave her a withering glare. "We argued like sisters do sometimes. And she butted heads with our parents occasionally. We're like any family, but we are very close. Like I said, she's my best friend and my parents dote on her. On both of us," she said, her tone hard and cold. "And before you ask, I was at work most of the weekend and with my boyfriend when I wasn't. We went to a show on Friday night and a museum on Saturday. I can provide you with receipts if you want. But if you really think I did something to my sister, you're way off the mark, Sheriff."

Spenser studied her for a moment. She had a temper, that much seemed obvious. But Spenser didn't get the sort of vibe off the girl that she was capable of harming anybody. She seemed genuinely upset that her sister was missing. More than that, she seemed authentically fearful that something bad had happened to her. Still, Spenser had to do her due diligence, so checking her alibi would be simple enough. She did have questions she wanted to ask the parents, but that would have to wait. She had to deal with what was on her plate right now, and currently, that was Rachel's little sister.

"I apologize, but it's my job to ask these kinds of questions," Spenser said.

She sighed heavily. "I understand. I'm sorry, I just..."

"There's no need for you to apologize. I'm sure this situation is upsetting for you," she replied. "How about Rachel's relationship with James? Any issues there?"

Roni shook her head. "No, they were totally in love. I mean, they squabbled sometimes, but what couple doesn't? They were in love, Sheriff. They were talking about getting married once they got out of school. There's no way he would have done anything to her. Besides, it makes no sense. I mean, isn't he missing, too?"

In most cases, crimes against a person are carried out by somebody close to them. And the overwhelming majority of crimes against women are perpetrated by a boyfriend or husband. If something bad happened to Rachel Kehoe, statistically speaking, it was likely done by James Burnham. And if he had done something to her, there was a chance he'd have gone on the run. Many men who hurt or killed their loved one fled afterward.

Some killed themselves. It was a tale as old as time itself and Spenser had seen it happen more times than she could count.

"Yes, he's missing and I'm not saying for sure that he did anything. But like I said, we're still trying to piece together what happened, Roni. Right now, we're looking at everything and can't afford to rule anything out," Spenser told her.

"You're wasting your time looking into James or their relationship. He's the gentlest guy like, ever. Personally, I wouldn't mind seeing him get an edge. He's a little too passive for my liking. But that's not him. He's not that guy, Sheriff."

"Okay, fair enough. Then, can you tell me if either Rachel or James was having a problem with anybody? Were they being hassled or stalked? Anything like that?"

She shook her head. "No. Not that I'm aware of."

"Rachel never mentioned anything strange going on to you? Strange calls or anybody following her around?"

"No, nothing like that."

Spenser scanned the pages in the file. "You and your sister still live at home?"

"Yeah. Like I said, our family is close and our parents like having us at home," she said. "Rachel's eventually going to move out, but she's saving on rent while she's in school."

"Okay, good. We're going to need to come by and check it out—"

"Why would you need to do that?"

"We'll need to look through Rachel's room. If she's truly missing, there might be some clue as to who might have taken her."

"What do you mean, if she's truly missing? She hasn't come home, and from what I understand, her campsite was trashed. Of course she's missing."

"That's the way it looks right now, Roni. But like I said, we can't rule anything out at this point," Spenser said. "I noticed that she and James had some marijuana out at the campsite—"

"Which is legal in this state."

"I'm aware. What I was going to say, though, is there's a possibility that while under the influence, something happened and they… left the campsite."

"Left? Are you telling me you think they trashed their campsite and just… left?"

"It's possible. As I keep saying, nothing is off the table right now. This is the way investigations work. We have to look at the macro before we can hone in on the micro. Understand?"

Roni sat back and sighed as she folded her arms over her chest. Her expression darkened. She was getting defensive and her tone bordered on hostile. She obviously didn't like the fact that Spenser seemed to be going after her sister.

"Veronica, was your sister into any drugs other than weed?" Spenser asked.

"No, she doesn't do any other drugs," she said. "And she barely smokes weed. It's just once in a while with James. My sister isn't a loadie."

"Okay, but what about James? Does he do anything other than smoke weed?"

"I don't think so," she said slowly. "But I really can't say what he gets up to when he's not at the house. I've never seen him do anything other than blaze with my sister."

Spenser jotted a few things down to remind herself to check on later—James' potential drug use chief among them. If he had any sort of habit, Spenser wanted to know. She wanted to check into the possibility that what happened out at the campsite was some sort of drug deal gone terribly wrong, retaliation for a drug debt, or related to drugs in some fashion. It was just something else they were throwing against the wall. If it stuck, it gave them an avenue to pursue. If it didn't, so be it. They'd move on to something else.

"Roni, did Rachel owe money to anybody? Any sort of outstanding debts?"

"No. She didn't owe anybody anything. Our parents taught us early on that you don't borrow money. They taught us that if we don't have the money, you work for it. They always told us that borrowing is a sign of weakness and can only get you into trouble."

"That's pretty good advice."

She looked at Spenser with a wry curl to her lips. "That's not great advice when you're thirteen years old and you want that cute new pair of shoes."

"That's fair," Spenser said with a chuckle.

Spenser looked at the papers in her file, giving herself a moment to search her mind for any other questions. But she came up empty. They simply had too little to focus in on one thing just yet.

"Okay, Roni, what I'd like is for you to go home while we do our jobs. It's possible that Rachel turns up there," Spenser said. "If she contacts you, please do me a favor and call me right away."

She nodded. "Yeah. Okay."

"Great. Thank you for coming in and answering my questions. It was very helpful."

The girl stood up on obviously unsteady legs. She braced herself on the table and took a moment to gather herself. Her eyes shone with tears again and she grabbed another tissue, quickly dabbing her face as they began to roll down her cheeks.

"You're going to find her, aren't you, Sheriff?" she asked, her voice trembling as hard as her hand. "You're going to bring her home. Right?"

"We're going to do everything we can to bring her home, Roni. I promise you."

Veronica's expression tightened, but she seemed to recognize that was about the best Spenser could do, and gave her a small, sad nod. Spenser wanted to reassure the girl and tell her that everything was going to be okay. But she wasn't willing to make promises she might not be able to keep. She wasn't going to give her false hope. For all Spenser knew at that moment, Amanda and her volunteers had found Rachel's body out in the woods already. Or might soon.

Either way, Spenser wasn't going to broker in platitudes and maybes. She only worked in facts. And the fact of the matter at that moment was they had no idea where Rachel Kehoe and James Burnham were or what happened to them.

"Go on home. Get some rest and try to keep your head up," Spenser said. "I'll give you a call the moment we find anything."

CHAPTER EIGHT

"I know how difficult this is for you, but I'm proud of you," Ryker said.

"Yeah, yeah," Spenser muttered under her breath.

Ryker laughed lightly as he poured her another glass of wine. Spenser had come home from the office to find a wonderful dinner already on the table—steaks with pan-seared scallops and roasted asparagus. It was incredible. Stuffed and content, Spenser picked up her glass of wine and sat back in her chair. Soft music played from the other room and the dogs were sitting at attention next to the table, hopeful for a treat. Ryker obliged and tossed them both a piece of steak.

"You realize you're teaching my girl bad manners," she said.

"Like you don't spoil these two."

"I do. But I don't usually indulge them with table treats. They're going to get used to it and make dinnertime unbearable," she teased.

Ryker looked over at the dogs who licked their chops as they wagged their tails, looking at him with wide eyes, desperate for another treat.

"Sorry, guys. Mom has spoken," he apologized.

The dogs looked from Ryker to her and whined, as if they understood that she was the reason they weren't getting the goodies.

Spenser giggled. "Oh sure, make me the bad guy."

"Hey, it's your rule."

"You are awful. Just awful."

"Yeah, but you kind of like it."

Her eyes glittered in the dim light. "Yeah. I guess I do."

They sipped their wine in silence for a couple of minutes. The dogs let out dissatisfied chuffs as they settled down onto the floor, upset they weren't getting any more table treats but hopeful they still might. She loved their optimism. The entire scene was so peaceful and domestic that it filled her with warmth and contentment. It seemed right. It seemed like the way things should be and she loved it. And because she loved it, part of Spenser was freaking out, telling her to not get too used to it because love and life were fleeting things. That voice in the back of her mind reminded her darkly that it could all be gone in the blink of an eye.

As those whispers of dread threatened to overwhelm her, Marley and Jacob's voices echoed through the other side of her mind, both of them telling her that life was all about adjusting to new roles and new situations. That she deserved to be happy. She wanted to embrace that. She wanted to give herself over to it fully. But there was still a part of her that wouldn't let her. That told her she was unworthy.

"I'm going to have all your things moved up from the cabin tomorrow," Ryker said. "If you're still okay with that?"

Spenser hesitated and looked down into her glass of wine, fear flowing through her veins faster than a river after a rainstorm. Ryker set his glass down and looked at her curiously.

"Spenser?"

She took a swallow of wine, trying to fortify herself. One thing she had learned was that all relationships, be they with friends or lovers, required communication and trust. If she wanted things to work with Ryker, and she really did, she was going to have to learn to talk openly and honestly with him and trust that he would be receptive. Trust that he would understand and appreciate that she was sharing with him.

"I'm scared, Ryker," she finally said. "I mean… moving in together is a big step forward and I guess now that I've had a little time to really think about it… I'm just getting worried."

He frowned. "Are you not ready to take that step yet?"

"I am. At least, I'm pretty sure I am. I… I'm honestly not sure what I'm thinking right now."

He sat back in his seat and couldn't hide his disappointment, which sent a dagger of guilt straight through Spenser's heart. There was such a tangle of emotion twisting around inside of her that it mucked up and confused everything. She was having trouble forming a coherent thought, let alone giving voice to it.

"Are you having second thoughts?" he asked, his tone as disappointed as his expression.

Spenser pursed her lips and silently scolded herself for not being able to get her words out in an intelligent way. That inability to speak had hurt Ryker, and she hated herself for that.

"I mean, it's not you I'm having second thoughts about," she replied softly. "I'm having second thoughts about me."

"What do you mean?"

She popped half a scallop into her mouth and chewed, giving herself a couple of beats to gather her wits. When she was reasonably coherent, Spenser raised her gaze to Ryker and told him about her conversation with Marley. She shared her thoughts and her fears. She told him all about the doubts she still carried about herself. Spenser talked for almost half an hour, saying far more than she had intended to say, and when she was done, she slumped back in her seat. She felt suddenly wrung out and took a drink of her wine.

Not really used to giving long, emotional speeches, Spenser was emotionally exhausted from the effort. But she was inwardly satisfied that she'd said what she needed to say. Coherently and concisely. The problem wasn't Ryker. It was her. And Spenser was sure she'd managed to convey that to him. Ryker took a drink of his wine and was silent for a moment as he absorbed everything she'd just spewed all over him. It was a lot.

"I'm well aware I sound like a lunatic," she said. "And I wouldn't blame you if you ran for the hills. If I were you, I might."

He chuckled softly. "If you think that's enough to make me run, you don't know me very well. I've been in far scarier situations."

"Bombs and bullets don't compare to a woman's emotional baggage."

"True. Emotional baggage is like walking through a minefield while blindfolded. But it's just a different kind of danger. That's all," he said with a mischievous gleam in his eyes.

They shared a quiet smile and relief washed over Spenser as she realized that rather than getting upset, Ryker seemed to understand her feelings. It was yet another way he continued to prove how much he cared about her and just how good he was to her. It was enough to stack more logs on that bonfire of unworthiness burning in her heart.

"Everything you're feeling right now? I feel it, too," Ryker said. "I'm scared. I oftentimes don't feel worthy of your affection. I'm terrified that, one day, you're going to come to your senses and realize that I'm not."

"That's just silly."

"Why is it silly for me but perfectly normal for you?"

"Because… you're good to me, Ryker. Like really good to me."

"And you're just as good to me."

"That's not true. I've never built you a dog park. I've never even cooked dinner for you."

His eyes flickered with amusement. "I've had your cooking before. Trust me when I say you not cooking for me is a kindness."

Spenser gasped then groaned loudly as she threw her napkin at him. Ryker caught it and grinned at her. There was just such an ease between them that Spenser wanted to believe that everything would work out. That everything was truly as right as it seemed. But the fear that stained her heart and soul the night Trevor was murdered continued to bleed into and taint everything.

"What is it really, Spenser? What's really holding you back?"

"Honestly?"

"I hope you know me well enough by now that you know I'd rather you give me a hard but honest truth than a soft and pretty lie," he replied.

"I do know that."

"Is it me? Are you having second thoughts about us? Is that what's holding you back?" he asked. "If that's what this is about, you can tell me. I want you to tell me."

"No to all of that."

"Then what is it?"

Spenser sighed and tried to shut out the images of Trevor being shot that seemed to be playing on an endless loop through her mind. It seemed as if every time she got close to touching those emotions inside of her and even considered opening that door inside of her, she was reminded of that terrible night all over again. It was almost like an unconscious self-defense mechanism. It was like her brain began acting of its own accord to protect her if she even thought about letting herself give her heart to somebody again.

Spenser knew the root of her issues. The problem was she wasn't sure what to do about it. Maybe actually speaking it out loud and sharing it with Ryker would help. Or maybe it would only make things more complicated. The last thing a current boyfriend, if that's what Ryker was, wanted to hear about was an ex. And the fact that her ex had been brutally murdered seemed to make the situation even more tangled and complex.

"Spenser?"

"I… I'm afraid I'm going to lose you, Ryker," she blurted out before she could stop herself. "I couldn't stop something bad from happening to Trevor and I'm terrified it's going to happen with you, too. That will absolutely break me."

His expression softened, and he looked at her with an even deeper understanding. Reaching across the table, Ryker took her hand and gave it a gentle squeeze.

"Ever since Bryce was murdered, I've been afraid to let myself get close to anybody. My fiancée's murder made me shut myself off from the world," he said. "But you've helped change me. You opened up those doors inside me I had locked and sealed up a long time ago. I've been where you are. You and I have walked the same path."

"You give me too much credit."

"But I don't," he said. "I've done the work—continue to do the work—sure. But it wasn't until you came into my life that I even accepted there was work to be done. Or perhaps more accurately, it wasn't until you came into my life that I found myself wanting to do that work. You made me want to be a better man. And no, that's not giving you too much credit."

Spenser's lips curled gently. When she first got to Sweetwater Falls, Ryker had a reputation as the town's resident Boo Radley. Some people cruelly referred to him as a cave troll. Ryker was notoriously antisocial and misanthropic, only coming into town when it was absolutely necessary and refusing to speak with anybody he didn't have to. She normally didn't give any credence to rumors and gossip, but when she first met him, Spenser thought his reputation was well earned. They had initially gotten along about as well as cats and dogs.

Over the ensuing months, though, as they'd gotten to know each other, she'd come to see him for the amazing man he truly was. He had done a lot of work on himself and had grown as a person in ways that still astonished her. Ways that she herself had not grown. Although she had worked on herself, in a lot of ways, Spenser was still locked in the tragedies of her past. Tragedies that, if she didn't figure out how to move past them, would not only continue to plague her but could end up defining her.

"I just… you deserve somebody who's more mentally and emotionally healthy and stable than I am, Ryker," Spenser said quietly. "I'm still pretty screwed up and the last thing I want to do is force you to have to deal with me."

"I'm not sure if you know this about me, but I don't do things I don't want to do. Ever. Nobody ever forces me to do something I don't want to do."

"Yeah, but this is different."

"It's really not," he said. "Look, we've both suffered horrible tragedies in our lives. We're both screwed up people. We've got scars. But we can also relate to each other in ways we don't relate to other people. You and me, we just get each other. That's not something you're going to find in a lot of people out there."

"We do get each other. But you've grown in ways I haven't. I still haven't fully been able to leave the past in the past—"

"Neither have I. And we never will. Not fully. And if you assume we can, you're fooling yourself, Spenser. Our pasts, the good and the bad, helped shape us. We'll never be able to leave them behind and close the doors on them forever. You're going to mourn your husband for the rest of your life. As I will mourn my fiancé. But that doesn't mean we can't build something new and something just as special together," he said. "That's what I want. With you. I want us to build something new together because I care about you, your scars, imperfections, and all. And underneath all the fear that's choking you, I'm sure you care about me the same way. The question now is, what do you want? Are you going to be able to embrace your past while moving forward? Or are you going to remain stuck in place and never move forward?"

"I want to move forward. And I want to move forward with you…"

"But?" he pressed.

"But I'm scared."

He squeezed her hand gently and as his dark eyes burned deeply into hers, the full weight of his emotion pressed down on her. Seeing just how much he cared about her warmed Spenser's heart. At the same time, though, it was overwhelming. It was almost suffocating in its intensity.

"Being scared is okay. It's natural. I'm terrified. If something happened to you, I told you already, I wouldn't be able to handle it," he said. "But learning to love again carries an inherent risk. Not just of disappointment, but the risk of losing that person. It's just how life works, Spenser. Are you satisfied living like I did? Shut off from the world? Or do you want more?"

Spenser gazed deep into his eyes as her heart stuttered drunkenly in her chest. He truly was better to her than she deserved. She did want to build something new with him. She did care about him very deeply. And she did want more. She wanted him. Just looking into his eyes as the realization sank in deeper, filled her belly with butterflies. At the same time, though, it filled him with a powerful dose of anxiety that sent a dark quiver through her heart.

Spenser wanted to be happy. And she wanted to be happy building a life with Ryker. What she wasn't sure about was whether she could overcome her fear to move forward with him. Some moments she was sure she could. Some moments she wanted to more than anything. At other moments, her fear crippled her and left her completely paralyzed.

And that was the problem.

CHAPTER NINE

SPENSER SLUMPED BACK IN HER CHAIR AND STARED AT THE page of notes she'd scribbled on the pad that sat on the table in front of her without actually seeing it. Her mind was somewhere else entirely. Nothing with Ryker had been settled last night, and it was bothering her. He was understanding and even supportive, which only made her feel even more terrible that she seemed to be waffling about their relationship. She cared about him. A lot. And he'd been clear about how much he cared for her. Spenser hated that she was making him even question her feelings for him. She was an absolute mess.

Marley was right. On paper, they made sense. On paper, they were great together. And on paper, their relationship seemed to be one that would be joyous and fulfilling. But relationships weren't had on paper. Relationships were emotional, messy things that often didn't make sense, and they could be completely illogical. Having a relationship in real life with a real, living, breathing person was something else entirely.

"Hey, are you okay?"

Spenser looked up to see Amanda walking into the conference room, looking at her with a concerned expression on her face. The younger woman appeared exhausted as she dropped into her usual chair at the table.

"Yeah. I'm good," she replied.

"You sure? Seems like something's bothering you."

With everything going on, the last thing Spenser wanted to do was muck things up with her personal drama. Her personal drama had no place in this conference room.

"No, I'm good," she said. "How did the search go yesterday?"

"Not good. We searched until we lost the light last night," Amanda replied then glanced at her watch. "We're scheduled to get back to it in an hour."

"No joy, huh?"

"None," she said, her voice tight with frustration. "Other than the drag marks in the dirt leading away from the camp, there's no trace of them. It's like they vanished into thin air."

"Well, that's not possible. I'm sure you're going to find something today."

"I hope so. To be honest, I'm starting to get a little worried. I don't need to tell you the longer we go without finding any trace of them—"

"The more likely it is that something bad happened. Yeah, I get that," Spenser finished.

The mood in the room grew heavier with the reality of the situation settling down over them. Though they tried to remain optimistic, it had already been a couple of days without contact from either Rachel or James, making it likely that something terrible had already befallen the couple.

"Veronica Kehoe, Rachel's sister, came in yesterday," Spenser said.

"She came in?"

Spenser nodded. "She's worried about her sister. Said her parents were with the search party yesterday and asked her to come talk to us."

"Can confirm. Her parents were there," she replied. "What did she have to say?"

"Nothing useful, unfortunately," Spenser replied. "Rachel had no enemies, no stalkers, nothing like that. According to Veronica, her sister is as squeaky clean as she seems."

"Do you believe her?"

"I do. I didn't get any weird hits off her. She seemed really rattled by her sister going missing. It seemed genuine," Spenser said.

"What about her folks?"

"I'm going to try to chat with them today if they're not out helping with the search," Spenser said. "If nothing else, I want to get a peek through Rachel's room and see what I can find. There might be something in there that might help."

Amanda nodded. "That's good."

"Did you happen to see the Burnhams at the search yesterday?"

She opened her notebook and quickly scanned the volunteer sign-in list. "Nope. It doesn't look like they were there."

"I didn't hear from them either," Spenser said. "I'll stop by and talk to them today, too."

"It's odd they weren't there, right?"

"Not necessarily. James is a twenty-four-year-old man who doesn't live at home," Spenser said with a shrug. "And they live a town over, so it's possible they're not even aware he's missing yet."

"Fair point. Okay, that's good. Thank you, Sheriff."

"No need to thank me for doing my job."

"I'm thanking you for not making this weird and awkward for me," Amanda said. "It's really weird having to sideline you. But I'm doing it for your own good—"

Spenser cut her off with a laugh. "You don't need to thank me for that, Amanda. Actually, I'm really proud of you for asserting yourself and taking charge of the investigation the way you have. I'm my own worst enemy and I'm a liability in the field right now.

So, I appreciate you stepping in and not letting me do something stupid. You're doing great."

"Thank you, Sheriff."

"Sheriff Song. Undersheriff Young."

Spenser turned to see Noah Arbery, her lead forensics tech standing in the doorway of the conference room. Five-five and nattily dressed in Dockers and a dark blue sweater vest, Arbery was thin, his movements quick and birdlike, and his demeanor was a little prissy. However, there was no denying that he was excellent at his job. It was why she fought with the city council so hard for the funding to bring him on full time. His skills made it easy to overlook his eccentricities.

"Dr. Arbery," Spenser said. "How are you today?"

"I'm fine, thank you," he replied curtly.

"What can we do for you, Doctor?" Amanda asked.

"I just wanted to inform you that we have finished analyzing the crime scene and unfortunately, there isn't much to go on. We have taken samples of the blood, of course, and will submit it for DNA testing to confirm it belongs to our two missing campers, but that will take some time. It seems safe to say, however, that it will belong to them," he said.

"Probably so," Spenser agreed. "Did you find anything else out there?"

"Very little. We did find their cellphones and also a few scraps of burlap, though I cannot say they have anything to do with what happened at the campsite. I cannot even accurately say how long they were out there."

"Burlap?" Amanda asked.

"Yes, burlap. Thin, rectangular strips to be precise," he said. "But again, they are dirty and look very aged and were half-buried in a pile of leaves. I almost missed them. There is no telling how long they were out there. They are aged and weathered, so it is possible they have been out there for years. There is unfortunately no way we can verify that. I wish I had something more to offer."

"I do, too. But things don't always break our way," Spenser said. "Thank you, Dr. Arbery."

"I'll get back to you if I am able to find anything else."

"Thank you," Spenser said.

Arbery turned and walked briskly out of the conference room, quietly closing the door behind him. Spenser leaned back in her seat and blew out a frustrated breath. She'd hoped Arbery and his team would be able to find something out there, but like she'd said, things didn't always break their way. It was a hard and irritating fact of life and police work.

"All right, I guess I need to get out to Mossy Flats," Amanda said.

"Good luck out there today. Keep me in the loop."

"Will do," she replied but didn't sound like she was expecting a win today.

Amanda got to her feet and headed out of the conference room, leaving Spenser alone with her thoughts. It wasn't the most auspicious start to the day, but then, very few were in her line of work. She would just roll with it like she always did. And just like she always did, she would keep banging away at the problem until she was able to solve it.

If only she could do the same thing with the problems in her personal life.

CHAPTER TEN

BURNHAM DAIRY FARM SAT ON THE FAR WESTERN EDGE of Pineworth and had been a fixture in town for generations. While Amanda and the volunteers were scouring the woods for a second day, Spenser made her way out to Pineworth to have a chat with the Burnhams. She drove down the long, paved road that ran between massive fenced-in fields that were dotted with hundreds of cows, all of them out grazing the day away.

The road led her to a large farmhouse style home, although mansion was probably the more accurate description of the mammoth house that sat in front of her. She parked in the circular driveway that fronted the staggered, multi-level structure that was predominantly white clapboard and red brick. The house was thoroughly modern in design, but with its high-peaked roofs and multiple brick chimneys, it still managed to maintain some of its farmhouse charm.

The front door opened even before Spenser had gotten to the top of the set of stairs that led to the wide, covered porch. A large man stepped onto the porch and paused, looking her up and down through icy blue eyes set in a leathery, russet-colored complexion. The sleeves of his blue flannel shirt were rolled up over his forearms, thick with corded muscle, and his wide shoulders and large, calloused hands were those of a man who'd spent his life working the farm.

"William Burnham?" Spenser asked.

"Will," he replied in a deep, gruff, slow drawl. "What can I do for you?"

"Spenser Song. I'm the sheriff over in Sweetwater Falls."

"Uh huh."

"I'm here about your son, James."

Irritation flashed across his face. "He do somethin'?"

"Can we talk inside?" Spenser prompted.

"Will, honey, who's at the door?" a woman's voice called from inside the house.

He paused for a moment then gave Spenser a nod. "Come on in."

Spenser stepped into the foyer and looked around as Burnham closed the door behind her. A woman walked down a hallway toward the door and looked worriedly from the large man to Spenser then back again. Five inches shorter than Spenser's five-nine frame, she was wide through the bust and hips and had dirty blonde hair pulled into a tight braid that fell to the middle of her back. She wore blue jeans, doeskin boots, and a dark denim shirt with the sleeves rolled up to her elbows. She looked like she worked the farm right alongside her husband.

"Hi, I'm Lilian Burnham," she said, the worry in her tone matching her expression.

"Lil, this is Sheriff Song from Sweetwater Falls."

"I see," she said. "And what's this about?"

"I'm here about your James."

She wrung her hands together, the worry on her face deepening. "Well, why don't you come to the kitchen? I was just putting some lunch out."

Will walked down the hallway, brushing past his wife without a word. He clearly wasn't happy about something, which told Spenser there was a story there, to be sure. Lilian gave her an apologetic smile then motioned for Spenser to follow her. They walked down the hallway that opened up to a kitchen on the left and a sunken living room on the right. A large, plush, u-shaped sofa surrounded a long coffee table and sat across from a movie theater-sized television screen. It seemed to be a comfortable place where the family hung out.

To the left, Will Burnham sat in a tall chair at the large island in the center of the country-style kitchen. Lilian bustled around to the other side of the island where she was putting together sandwiches for her and her husband. White shaker cabinets lined the walls and there was plenty of counter space all around. All the appliances were sleek and modern, and through a door on the far side of the kitchen, Spenser spied a formal dining room that looked to be elegantly done in light wood and, from what she could see, had a rustic flair.

"Sheriff, may I get you something to eat or drink?" Lilian asked.

"No, I'm fine. But thank you," Spenser replied. "I understand you're both busy folks, so I'll try to not take up too much of your time today."

"You said you're here about James?" Lilian prompted.

"I am. When was the last time you spoke with him?"

"Oh, it's been a couple of weeks," she replied. "He and Rachel were here for dinner a couple of weeks ago, but we haven't talked to him since then. He's very busy with school and all."

"What is this about, Sheriff? What kind of trouble he get in?" Will asked gruffly.

"Why do you ask if he's in trouble, Mr. Burnham?"

"I don't figure a sheriff is going to turn up on our doorstep asking after our son if it was for somethin' good," he replied.

"Fair enough," Spenser said. "To be blunt, your son is currently missing—"

"Missing?" Lilian gasped.

Will's face hardened. "If he's missing, why are you standin' in our kitchen rather than bein' out there lookin' for him?"

"Will," Lilian admonished him.

Spenser gestured to the cane in her hand. "As you can see, I'm not really suited to be out there traipsing through the woods. But my team has been running a search through the woods for the last two days now. I assure you that they are working very hard to find your son, Mr. Burnham. My role is to gather background information that could prove useful."

"What happened, Sheriff?" Will asked.

"As best as we can tell, James and his girlfriend were camping in Mossy Flats over the weekend. A pair of hunters found their campsite abandoned and torn apart," Spenser said. "A subsequent search of the site turned up IDs belonging to your son and his girlfriend. We've confirmed with Rachel's family that they have not heard from her and neither have been in classes these last couple of days."

Lilian covered her mouth with a trembling hand. "What happened to them, Sheriff?"

"We aren't sure yet. We did find marijuana at the scene, so it's possible they had a bad reaction, or perhaps their pot was laced with something that triggered something and sent them both running—"

"Were they abducted, Sheriff?" Will asked.

"That's a possibility as well, yes."

Lilian gasped and looked away as her face turned bright crimson. Tears rolled down her warm, tawny cheeks, but Will stared at her stone faced. She couldn't tell if he was distraught or pissed off. The man was impossible to get a read on.

"Can either of you tell me if James was having trouble with anybody? Did he owe money or just have a bad interaction with somebody that you're aware of?" Spenser asked.

"No. Not, not that I'm aware of," Lilian answered. "Will?"

The man shook his head. "He never mentioned having trouble with anybody to me. And we taught him to never borrow money. If he needed it, he would have come to us."

Given how stone faced and frosty Will Burnham was, Spenser had to wonder how comfortable James would be coming to him for money. There was something there, perhaps about their relationship, that piqued her curiosity.

"Mr. Burnham, how was your relationship with your son?" Spenser asked.

He shrugged his broad shoulders. "Fine."

"Did you two ever argue or—"

"We butted heads now and then, yeah. Same as any other father and son out there."

"They're more alike than they care to admit," Lilian chimed in. "And because of that, they sometimes get on like oil and water."

Will grumbled under his breath but didn't refute his wife's characterization of their relationship. It was a revealing look behind the curtain, but Spenser was sure there was more there she wasn't seeing yet. There seemed to be a tension that ran deeper than normal family drama. Lilian looked at her and seemed to sense that Spenser had more questions because she nodded to herself, almost as if she had to decide whether to share or not.

"James was supposed to take over the farm once Will retired—"

"Lil, we don't need to air out our family laundry," he cut her off.

"The sheriff is looking for our missing son," she said, her voice as tight as her expression. "I'd rather she not waste time looking in the wrong places—namely, at you—by withholding any information. We've got nothing to hide, Will."

He turned away and muttered darkly to himself, still clearly upset that his wife was, as the kids today said, spilling the tea. But she rightly explained to him that by coming clean now, it would save time and keep Spenser from spinning her wheels chasing shadows. Every moment that passed without finding their son didn't bode well for a positive outcome. Lilian clearly understood that, which Spenser appreciated.

"James didn't want to follow in his father's footsteps and take over the farm. He wanted to follow his passion," Lilian said. "That, as I'm sure you can imagine, has led to some hard feelings within the family."

Spenser took a beat to digest the information. It was reasonable. It made sense. For a son to reject his father and chart his own course, it had to rub a proud man like Will the wrong way. The Burnham farm had existed for generations, passed down from father to son, and James had turned his back on all those years of tradition. That was a plausible explanation for the tension Spenser had picked up on.

"Our son Adam will be taking over the farm and is very excited about it. And James, he says that with the education he's getting, will be able to lend some expertise to the operations as we become more… modernized," Lilian went on. "It's not as if James wants nothing to do with the farm, he just doesn't want to be responsible for the day-to-day operations. But you understand how hard-headed, stubborn fathers can be when it comes to their first-born sons."

Will scowled, his face dark and tight. The truth of his wife's words hitting the mark was easy for Spenser to see. Although she still had some questions, she was growing more comfortable putting the idea that Will Burnham might have had something to do with his son's disappearance on the back burner.

"So, James never mentioned anybody he'd fought with recently to you? Nothing like that?" Spenser asked.

Will shook his head and for the first time, Spenser saw a hint of worry on his face. "No. But, he probably wouldn't. My son keeps his own counsel most of the time."

"Okay. And was there anybody from his past, perhaps, who might have wanted to hurt your son?"

Lilian put a hand to her chest and drew in a long, shaking breath, as if the thought of somebody hurting her son was almost too much to bear.

"Like I said, my son pretty much kept to himself. He didn't associate with bad people. And other than Rachel, he didn't socialize much at all," Will said. "He was serious about his education and put all his energy and focus into that. I can't imagine he crossed anybody out there so badly that they'd want to hurt him. He didn't ruffle feathers or cause trouble. That just wasn't my son."

It seemed to line up with Veronica's description of the young man. Quiet. Kept to himself and didn't seem to go out of his way to rock the boat. On the surface, it was hard for Spenser to imagine him upsetting somebody so much, they'd take him. However, people had two sides to them. There might be facets of James that neither she nor his parents had seen, and it was within those hidden aspects where the trouble most often occurred. Of course, it was just as possible that Rachel was the focus of the crime and James was just collateral damage. She just didn't have enough information to determine that yet.

"I don't suppose James has a room here?" Spenser asked.

Lilian shook her head. "No. He hasn't lived here in quite a while. We rent an apartment for him closer to the school."

"Great. Can I have your permission to search the apartment? There might be something that can help explain what's happened there."

"Of course," Lilian said. "Do whatever you need to do to find our son, Sheriff."

Spenser took a beat and ran through her mental checklist, making sure she'd crossed off all the items on it. Satisfied she had, she nodded to herself as she got to her feet.

"That's all I have for the moment," Spenser said. "But I'll be sure to keep you in the loop as the investigation unfolds."

"Sheriff, find my boy," Will said, his voice thick with emotion. "Please, find him."

"I'm going to do my very best, Mr. Burnham. You have my word."

CHAPTER ELEVEN

DAY TWO OF THE SEARCH ENDED THE SAME WAY THAT DAY one had. Amanda and the volunteers had found nothing. And as they began day three, with an immense amount of forest still out there to cover, they were all starting to lose hope. Spenser had done what she could to lift Amanda's spirits and give her some motivation, if not a shred of hope to hold on to, then sent her off to begin the search anew. And while that was happening, Spenser used the key the Burnhams had given her to get in and search their son's apartment.

She stood in the living room of the small, one-bedroom apartment. The place was immaculate. It was probably unfair stereotyping, but the apartment was far cleaner than she had expected from a twenty-four-year-old man. Everything had a place, and everything was in its place. Spenser had to admit that he kept a nicer house than she did, much to her enduring shame.

"In my defense, though, I have a giant dog," Spenser said to the empty room.

Starting in the bedroom, Spenser sifted through his drawers, finding nothing interesting, then moved on to the closet. She didn't find much more in there. The bed was neatly made, the room was freshly vacuumed, and she couldn't see a speck of dust anywhere. The most interesting thing about the bedroom was that James sorted his clothing by color. It was a level of almost obsessive organization that reminded Spenser of serial killers.

Moving from the bedroom to the kitchen, Spenser dug through the cabinets and drawers, finding nothing more than the same level of cleanliness and organization. Finished in the kitchen, Spenser walked into the living room and paused. The silence was heavy. There was a physical weight to it pressing down on her that made her skin break out in goosebumps. It was as if the room itself was holding its breath. It was eerie.

"Pull yourself together," Spenser muttered to herself.

A couch sat against the wall beneath the one large window in the room and across from it, a large, flat-screen television was mounted on the wall. On a long table below that there was the current PlayStation gaming system with an assortment of games—mostly of the first-person shooter variety. As was standard in James' apartment, the cords were neatly wound and clipped, the games and accessories all lined up just so.

Spenser sat down at the desk in the corner of the room and after checking the drawers and not finding anything useful there, moved on to checking the books and textbooks that sat on top of it. Again, nothing. She opened up the laptop, and when it woke up, she was surprised to see that it wasn't password protected. But then, perhaps because he lived alone, he didn't need to lock everything down so tightly.

She perused the online files and folders and couldn't find anything that would point her to any problems James was having. After that, she called up his search history and didn't clock anything particularly interesting. His internet searches were mundane. Boring. He didn't even visit porn sites, which was shocking for a guy his age. Everything she'd found indicated that what Veronica Kehoe, as well as his parents had told her, was true, and he really did focus and pour all his energy into Rachel and his studies.

Spenser unplugged the laptop, closed it, then slipped it into a plastic evidence bag. She'd take it back to the office and let Jacob have a crack at it. She was admittedly something of a technological Neanderthal, so he might be able to find something she couldn't. If there were any hidden files, secret websites, or anything like that, she was confident he'd be able to ferret them out. She was troubled to find that she was sharing a brain with Jacob and assumed that James was a little too squeaky clean. He didn't seem to have any skeletons in his closet. Perhaps she'd grown cynical and jaded, but she didn't quite trust it. Everybody had skeletons.

"Excuse me? Who are you?"

Spenser turned to see a young woman standing in the doorway. An inch taller than Spenser, with long dark hair, dark eyes, and an olive-colored complexion, she was a beautiful woman. She looked like she could be a model. Spenser looked down at herself and realized she wasn't in uniform. In blue jeans, a black, long-sleeved button-down, and black Doc Marten boots, she could see why the woman was questioning her presence. She did have her star on her belt, though, but it was covered by her shirt, so she unclipped it and held it up for the woman to see.

"Sheriff Spenser Song," she replied. "And you are?"

"Julie Lewan. I live next door," she said. "What's going on? Where is James?"

"When was the last time you spoke with him?"

"Uhh… Friday morning," she said. "He and Rachel were heading out to go camping. Has something happened to him?"

"And you're friends with him?"

"Yeah. With him and Rachel. We all hang out sometimes," she replied. "What's going on here, Sheriff? Where is James?"

She was getting frustrated with Spenser for not answering her questions, but Spenser couldn't let the girl control the interview. She needed to get whatever answers she could get. And if anybody was going to be able to give her honest answers, it would more likely be a friend than his family.

"Julie, can you tell me if James has ever mentioned anybody he was having problems with? Anybody he might have argued with?"

"No. He wasn't having trouble with anybody. He kept to himself for the most part and didn't go out looking for trouble. Sheriff—"

"Did he owe anybody money that you're aware of?"

"No. But I doubt he'd talk to me about that," she said. "I mean, we're friends but we're not super close or anything."

"How about drugs, Julie? Was James involved with drugs?"

"No. I mean …"

The woman's voice trailed off as an almost panicked expression crossed her face. She clearly didn't want to say too much and risk getting James into any sort of trouble.

"Relax, I couldn't care less about any drug use. That's not why I'm here," Spenser told her. "I'm just trying to find out if he was involved with anybody in the drug trade who might be capable of doing something to him."

Her eyes widened, and her pale complexion seemed to grow even paler. "Oh my God. Something happened to him, didn't it? What happened, Sheriff? Is he okay? Is he alive? Is he—"

Spenser sighed and held a hand up, cutting off the barrage of questions from the woman. Julie frowned but fell silent.

"I'll answer your questions as much as I can," Spenser said. "But I need you to answer my questions first. All right?"

She pursed her lips, an onslaught of questions sitting on the tip of her tongue, but then nodded, albeit slowly and grudgingly.

"Now, like I said, I'm not interested in any potential drug use," Spenser said. "I just want to know if James was involved with anybody who might be willing to do him harm."

Julie shook her head. "All he did was smoke weed now and again. I never saw him doing anything harder than that. He has a good head on his shoulders, Sheriff. He's got plans. And he's not going to screw his life up getting into hard drugs."

"So, you never saw anybody shady or questionable coming or going from his apartment?"

"No. Never. Like I said, he didn't do that kind of stuff or associate with people who did."

"And you're certain of that?"

"One hundred percent," she responded. "I don't hang out with people who are into that kind of lifestyle either. That's not my scene."

"Some people are good at hiding that sort of thing."

"Not from me. I grew up around people who were into that hard stuff, Sheriff. I can spot all the warning signs. And trust me, James was not involved with that."

"Okay. That's good."

"Now, can you tell me what happened to him?"

"All we know right now is that he is missing. Their campsite was trashed, and there's been no sign of them," Spenser said. "My deputies and a team of volunteers have been combing the woods for the last few days, but they haven't found James or Rachel just yet."

Her eyes shimmered with tears, and an expression of absolute horror crossed her face. "What? How did this happen?"

"We're not sure yet. We're still trying to find them and figure out what happened."

"That can't be real. There's got to be an explanation."

"That's what we're hoping to find. But, so far, all we're finding are more questions."

Julie covered her mouth with a trembling hand and let her gaze fall to the floor as she seemed to be trying to hold back an avalanche of emotion. Spenser's phone rang, so she slipped it out of her pocket and saw it was Amanda. She quickly connected the call and pressed the phone to her ear, taking a couple of steps away from Julie.

"What do you have, Amanda?"

"Problems. I need you out here at Flick's Sporting Goods like now."

In the background, Spenser could hear what sounded like dozens of raised and angry voices, filling her veins with a fiery adrenaline.

"What's going on?" she asked.

"Please, just get out here."

"I'll be there in ten."

CHAPTER TWELVE

ONE OF THE MANY GOOD THINGS ABOUT LIVING IN A town as relatively small as Sweetwater Falls was that you could get anywhere you needed to be in a matter of minutes. After leaving James' apartment, Spenser was pulling into the parking lot of Flick's Sporting Goods and Hunting Supplies in eight minutes flat. And what she saw as she hobbled out of the Bronco sent her heart shooting into her throat as her belly churned.

A group of fifteen to twenty men were gathered in the parking lot, all of them angry, shouting, and armed with more weapons than an Army brigade, looking as if they were about to go to war. All that was missing to complete the picture they were painting were torches and pitchforks. She had no idea what was going on yet, but she was instinctively sure it wasn't good. That much anger combined with that many weapons was a recipe for disaster. Amanda stood in front of them, her face red, talking to the assembled mob, doing her best to calm them down. Unfortunately for her and everybody else, it wasn't having much of an effect.

"What in the hell is going on here?" she demanded as she stepped up beside Amanda.

"I can't calm them down, Sheriff. I've been trying, but they won't listen to me."

"Where did they all come from?"

"These are some of the volunteers," she replied. "We didn't find anything out there again today, and they got frustrated."

"Frustrated?" Spenser said dubiously. "That's one word for it."

Spenser turned to the crowd of red-faced, angry men and took a step forward. The man in the center of the mob, getting everybody fired up, was unsurprisingly Hurley Weaver. Sixty-two years old, the man was five-eight and heavyset with iron-gray hair, dark eyes that seemed permanently squinted, a jowly face, a sallow complexion, and a red bulbous nose completing his look. Hurley was a man known to have a bad temper. That temper only seemed amplified when he drank... something he did often. He was in the Whistle Stop so often, he had his own stool at the bar.

He didn't seem especially tanked at the moment, but he also didn't appear to be in full control of his faculties. In addition to being the town drunk, he was also known as something of a rabble-rouser. He was bored with his life and simply enjoyed pushing people's buttons and causing trouble wherever he went. Chaos was his love language, and he seemed to thrive on the drama. Hurley was one of the more unpleasant residents of town Spenser ever had to deal with, and she wasn't particularly surprised to see him in the middle of all this.

Spenser raised her arms. "Settle down. Everybody, settle down and shut up!"

Slowly, the crowd subsided, and they grew quiet, though they looked no less hostile. Hurley had done a fantastic job of riling them up. There was no more potent brew than alcohol and trumped-up outrage.

"Hurley, what in the hell are you doing?" Spenser growled.

"I'm doin' what you all shoulda been doin' from day one. We're goin' out to kill the thing."

"What are you talking about?"

He looked at Spenser like she was a simpleton who didn't understand the most basic things.

"The Okasha," he said like he was speaking to a child. "We're goin' out there to end that thing once and for all."

Spenser glanced at Amanda, who merely shrugged. Shaking her head, she pinched the bridge of her nose, the first stirrings of what might be a nasty headache coming on. After taking a beat, she raised her gaze to the assembled mob again.

"Are you serious, Hurley?" she asked.

"As a friggin' heart attack, Sheriff."

"Fellas, listen to me," Spenser called. "There is no such thing as the Okasha. It's a story. A myth. There is nothing out in those woods."

"Then what took them kids?" Hurley shot back. "Tell us that, Sheriff. What snatched them and wrecked their campsite?"

"We're still working on that—"

"Then you can't say it wasn't the Okasha!" Hurley howled.

"I can say it wasn't because the Okasha doesn't exist," Spenser countered. "It's a children's story. Are you really going to go hunt a children's story? How ridiculous are you people?"

Not wanting to incite the crowd further, Spenser bit off the string of expletives that sat on the tip of her tongue. She needed to bring the temperature down, not throw gasoline on the fire. That was only serving to get them to dig in harder and rile them up further.

"Okay, listen to me," Spenser said. "We are doing everything we can to find our two missing campers. But I can assure you they were likely taken by a very real, very human person and not some mythical creature."

"A very real, very human person you all can't seem to find, never mind a trace of them kids," Hurley spat. "Lemme tell you somethin', Sheriff. I been around a while and very real, very human people don't just kidnap two people then disappear into thin air."

Spenser's blood pressure was rising, and her heart was pounding in her ears. She was clenching her fists so hard, she was half-afraid her nails were going to puncture her palms. Spenser held her breath for a silent five count then let it out slowly, trying to find some sense of calm. She tried to find some bit of understanding. It didn't work. She reminded herself that these people were scared, and from her years of experience, she knew that scared people seldom thought or acted rationally. They let their fear consume them. They let their emotions overwhelm them and drive anything logical or rational out of their brains.

"Listen, I understand you aren't familiar with the way investigations work," she said. "But they take time. They take patience—"

"And while you're taking time and bein' patient, that monster is out there killin' people! That thing is slaughtering kids—"

"Okay, first of all, the missing campers aren't children. They're both in their twenties. Young, but not children, so let's tone down the rhetoric," Spenser corrected. "Second, we can't say for certain that they were actually taken. There is still the possibility they left of their own accord. We can't say yet because we're still searching for evidence."

"I heard their tent was soaked in blood, Sheriff!" a man in the crowd yelled.

"That's inaccurate. Whoever is spreading that rumor is spreading absolute crap. So, again, let's stop listening to rumors and tone down the panicked rhetoric. It's not doing anybody any good, gentlemen," Spenser said. "As I told you, we are doing everything we can to find them. Many of you have been out in the woods with Undersheriff Young—"

"And we ain't turned up a damn thing in days," Hurley growled.

"And what, you think if you and your posse here go charging out into the woods with your guns at the ready, you're going to find them?" Spenser asked.

"Maybe," he replied. "And maybe we'll find and kill the thing that took them, too."

"Gentlemen, I've seen this sort of thing before. I've seen groups of people with this same kind of fervor before. You're scared, and you want answers. I get that," Spenser countered. "But let me tell you, when you storm out there with your emotions dialed up to eleven like they are, it's more likely that you're going to accidentally shoot somebody else than you are to find and shoot the Sweetwater Devil. Do any of you really want the blood of an innocent person on your hands?"

The group fell quiet, and for the first time since she arrived, she saw uncertainty on the faces of the men all around her. As if he sensed the mood of the mob shifting, Hurley looked around, his already red face turning an ugly shade of purple as he moved from merely angry to positively apoplectic. He wheeled around and glared at Spenser, clearly upset she was ruining his little hunting party. Hurley took a step closer to her, his lips curled back over his teeth. Amanda stepped between them, one hand on the butt of her weapon, the other on Hurley's chest, a dark and surprisingly intimidating look on her face.

"You don't walk up on Sheriff Song like that, Hurley. Back up," she cautioned.

Hurley stepped back and stared at Amanda with a completely flabbergasted expression on his face. Spenser understood. She'd never seen that menacing and protective side of the younger woman before either, and she rather enjoyed it. He snorted and shook his head, doing his best to recover his swagger.

"You can't stop us from goin' out into the woods, Sheriff," Hurley snapped.

"You're right. I can't," Spenser said. "But I just want you all to remember what I said here today. And if anything bad happens, which I guarantee you it will, I am going to arrest you. And I will speak with the DA when they charge you and push for you to get the maximum sentence possible because I've warned you not to go out there and chase this urban legend. You're only going to make things worse and make it harder for us to do our jobs and bring the two missing campers home."

A low murmur rippled through the mob as they all looked at each other with uncertainty on their faces. The specter of something going wrong and going to prison for the rest of their lives seemed to be looming heavy over all of them. Slowly, by ones and in pairs, the mob began to dissipate. The wind taken out of their sails, the men Hurley had whipped into a frenzy shuffled back to their cars. Hurley screamed at them to come back and join him in the hunt. Nobody did.

What troubled Spenser the most about this whole episode wasn't that a mob had assembled to go look for the campers. Emotions ran high in cases like this, and she couldn't blame people for wanting to protect their own. No, what bothered her the most was that these men were all willing to risk hurting an innocent person, or worse, because they were chasing something that didn't exist. They were more than willing to throw aside logic and reason in a vain effort to hunt down a children's story. It was crazy. More than that, it was disturbing.

"I hope you're happy," Hurley, now standing alone, growled.

"I am," Spenser shot back. "Nothing good was going to come of you and your mob traipsing through the woods. Nothing."

"You can't say that."

"I can say that," Spenser countered. "Undersheriff Young has been leading an organized search of those woods for three days now and hasn't turned up a thing. Why do you assume you and your boozed-up, gun-toting buddies would find them when nobody else has?"

He opened his mouth to reply but closed it again when he didn't seem able to come up with an intelligent response. Not surprising.

"Yeah, well, I'm still goin' out there," he said.

"Good. Go. Just remember what I said. If something bad happens, I promise you that I will push for the maximum sentence. I'm not blowing smoke, Hurley."

It seemed like the man wanted to continue arguing and stirring up drama, since that was pretty much his only reason for existence anymore, but he didn't have an audience anymore, which left him a little deflated. Spenser's phone rang, and she turned her back on the man as she pulled the phone out of her pocket. She frowned, curious, when she saw the call was coming from Magnolia General—Marley's hospital. Spenser connected the call and pressed the phone to her ear.

"Sheriff Song," she answered.

"Spense, it's Mar."

"What's up?"

"You're going to want to get down here right away," she said.

"What's going on?"

"Just… you're going to want to see this."

Spenser glanced at Amanda, then watched as Hurley walked back to his car, muttering to himself as he went. She was satisfied the situation had been defused.

"On my way," she said.

CHAPTER THIRTEEN

"You want to come with me," Marley said the moment Spenser walked through the door of the emergency room.

"Mar, what's happening?"

"Just come with me."

Her cane tapping a determined and steady rhythm on the tiled floor, Spenser let Marley lead her through the department and to the intensive care unit. A large, bulky man wearing a hospital security uniform stood outside the door of a private room and eyed them as they approached. He seemed to relax when he saw Marley and gave her a curt nod before opening the door for them. Spenser followed her inside, and the guard closed the door behind them. When Spenser saw the figure in the bed before her, she gasped.

The battery of machines the young man in the bed was hooked to beeped and chimed softly. Even in the dim lighting of the room, Spenser saw that his face was swollen, an array of cuts crisscrossed his cheeks and forehead, and his skin was stained with terrible, lumpy purple-black bruises. The young man was nearly unrecognizable, but Spenser was able to identify him well enough.

"James Burnham," she whispered.

"Yes," Marley replied with a nod.

"Have his parents been informed yet?"

"I called them about an hour ago," she said. "They said they'll be in soon."

"Okay, good. How did he get here?"

"Richard Feller found him in a ditch out on Taylor Road," she replied. "Richard said he assumed he was dead until James moaned, so he got him here as fast as he could. Good thing he did, too. Given his wounds and all the blood he'd already lost, I'm not sure how much longer he would have lasted out there."

"Was he conscious?"

Marley shook her head. "No. He's been out since he was brought in. The poor guy looks like he was put through a meat grinder."

Spenser stepped closer to the bed and looked down at him. Marley wasn't exaggerating. He really did look like he'd been put through a meat grinder. Somebody had definitely tried to kill him. It was strange, though, that whoever that person was didn't make sure they finished the job. It told Spenser she was looking for somebody who was sloppy. That suggested the person was inexperienced and may have been too rushed to finish James off. That further suggested to her that this had nothing to do with James at all. That left her with the unsettling realization that Rachel Kehoe had been the target of this attack all along. This whole thing was about her.

"What can you tell me about Richard Feller?" Spenser asked.

"I don't know him all that well, to be honest. But he's a handyman around town, and people seem to like him well enough, I suppose. I've never heard anybody speaking poorly of him."

"Is he capable of doing something like this?"

Marley shook her head. "I'm not sure. Like I said, I don't know him well, but it doesn't make sense to me that he would have done this. I mean, if he had, why bring him in? Especially if James could identify him?"

She was right. If James could ID the man, it didn't really stand to reason that Feller would bring him into the hospital alive. But it also wouldn't be unprecedented. Especially if it was Feller's first time doing this sort of thing. It was possible that guilt could have overtaken him, prompting the man to bring James in to help save him. As unlikely as that was, Spenser had seen that sort of thing before. Guilt was a powerful drug.

"I don't think he's your guy, Spense," Marley said. "Feller is crotchety, but he seems like a quiet, mild-mannered kind of guy. I just don't see this kind of savagery in him."

"It sounds like a cliché, but a lot of times, it's the person you'd least suspect."

"It does sound cliché."

"Clichés become clichés for a reason."

The corner of Marley's mouth flickered upward. "I suppose so."

"Feller might really be nothing more than a good Samaritan, but I'm still going to need to have a conversation with him," Spenser said. "What are James' injuries?"

Marley flipped through his chart. "Good God, where do I start? He's got multiple deep lacerations and multiple stab wounds. It's a miracle the attacker didn't hit anything vital. James has a broken arm, several broken ribs, a collapsed lung, a badly sprained ankle," she read. "He was severely beaten with what appears to be a blunt instrument of some kind… somebody really worked this kid over and left him for dead in that ditch, Spense."

"But he's going to make it?"

"He's stable for now," she responded. "But these things can go south quickly, so I don't want to make any predictions. We're in wait-and-see mode."

Spenser listened to the soft beeps and sighs of the plethora of machines Burnham was connected to. The machines that were tracking the life he was barely clinging to. He was pale and looked so fragile and Spenser was sad for him. She was sympathetic to all victims of vicious crimes, but something about younger casualties struck a deeper chord within her. It seemed such a waste of life. James had plans. Ambitions. He shouldn't be lying in that bed, clinging to life by his fingertips. It was such a terrible and senseless waste.

Marley walked to the side of the bed and raised the blanket, revealing a long, white bandage on James' side. She gingerly peeled back the bandage and showed Spenser a gash that was at least six inches long and, although it had been stitched up, the edges of the wound were still red, angry, and weeping small crimson drops. After giving Spenser a look, she gently replaced the bandage and pulled the blanket over him again.

"What does that look like to you?" Marley asked.

Spenser looked at her, not understanding the question. "It looks like a cut. A bad cut, probably made by what appears to be a long, sharp blade."

A sour expression touched Marley's face. "You don't think it looks like it could have been made by like… a claw?"

Spenser pulled a face. "Mar, please tell me you're kidding."

"I'm just curious," she said. "I mean, everybody's been talking about the Sweetwater Devil taking these two people and now James shows up absolutely shredded. It's just a little… odd. That's all I'm saying."

"This town is losing its collective mind," Spenser muttered. "Mar, that gash was most likely made by something with a long, sharp blade. A machete or a sword, perhaps."

"Because there are a lot of people running around with swords in the woods?"

"It wouldn't be the weirdest thing we've seen," Spenser responded. "But if it wasn't a sword, then it was likely a dagger or some other type of long blade. I highly doubt that the gash was made by a claw. Please don't give in to this hysteria. This was not done by some mythical creature nobody has ever seen that's running around in the woods, Mar. Also, you said it appears James was beaten savagely with a blunt instrument. When was the last time you heard of Bigfoot wailing on somebody with a Louisville Slugger?"

Marley's cheeks flushed as she seemed to find herself boxed in by Spenser's logic. In the bed, James stirred, drawing their attention. He groaned, wracked with pain, and his eyes fluttered. Spenser stepped back as Marley flew into action, taking James' vitals and checking his responses. His face contorted as pain ravaged him and he cried out, prompting Marley to call for a nurse to come in to assist.

James lay flat on his back, and his eyes flew open. His already pale face blanched as he gritted his teeth. He looked terrified. Haunted by what he'd seen. He was conscious, though just barely, and Spenser had the sense that this might be the only chance she had to get him to answer her questions.

"James, can you tell me who did this to you? Can you tell me what happened?"

"Spenser, this isn't the time," Marley scolded her.

"Can you tell me what happened?"

Marley scowled at her. "You need to go. Now."

One of Marley's nurses bustled into the room and set to work as a low keening groan drifted from James' mouth, and the look of horror on his face intensified. He swallowed hard and shook his head, and when he spoke, it surprised them both. His voice was raspy and weak. And it was low, little more than a whisper.

"It was the Okasha. The Okasha took Rachel."

His voice trailed off, and he slumped back against his pillows, lapsing back into sleep as whatever burst of energy had taken hold of him faded. Marley turned to Spenser, the anger that had twisted her features a moment before now gone, replaced with eyes that were filled with both fear and wonder at James' declaration.

"You heard that, right?" Marley gasped. "You heard him say it was the Okasha."

Spenser ran a hand over her face and shook her head. Talk about throwing gasoline onto the bonfire. That was sure to get the tongues around town wagging, and that was likely going to lead to more scenes like the one she'd just come from, with the likes of Hurley Weaver whipping people into a terrified frenzy. There would be bands of armed men roaming the woods, and it was only a matter of time before somebody screwed up and touched off an accidental bloodbath.

Unless they solved this case and managed to do it quickly, proving it was a human being who'd done this, things were going to go off the rails. Unless they found who'd attacked James and taken Rachel, things were going to get bad. Really bad. This was going to be a mess.

CHAPTER FOURTEEN

After a night of tossing and turning, her mind filled with troubled dreams, a sense of dread wrapped itself around her as Spenser's eyes fluttered open. She stared at the sky beyond the window. Thick white clouds that looked like cotton candy cluttered the azure field and she could see the trees swaying in a gentle breeze. It was too nice of a day to deal with the nonsense she was going to have to deal with once she got to the office today.

"How are you doing?"

Ryker's voice shattered the stillness of the morning. Startled, she rolled over and found him gazing at her, his dark eyes warm and inviting.

"How did you know I was awake?" she asked.

"Your breathing changed."

"It's kind of creepy that you notice something like that."

"I notice all sorts of things."

"Yeah? Like what?"

"Well, the way you were thrashing around in your sleep told me you were having bad dreams last night and didn't get a lot of rest," he said.

"That's pretty good."

Spenser took a quick mental inventory and realized she was better that morning than she had since being stabbed by Alex Ricci. She wasn't pain-free by any means, and she wasn't ready to get out there and run marathons or kick in doors yet, but she was better. The pain that had been a constant roar in her body had been muted. It was more of a dull throb than anything, and moving around no longer seemed like an exercise in medieval torture.

The lessening of her pain made her want to turn somersaults of joy. She didn't, though, knowing that would likely set off another explosion of agony. Instead, she snuggled closer to Ryker, laying her head on his chest, and listened to his strong, steady heartbeat as she traced a circle on his flat stomach with the tip of her finger. Ryker leaned down and gently kissed the top of her head. They lay in silence for a couple of minutes, just soaking in and enjoying the new level of domesticity that seemed to exist between them.

"So, what were you dreaming about?" he finally asked.

Spenser laughed softly to herself. "I'd rather not say."

"Come on. You can tell me."

She sighed. "I was dreaming about the Sweetwater Devil."

Ryker grinned brightly. "This case is really getting in your head, huh?"

"Don't they all?"

"They do. But that's why you're good at this job. You care."

"Yeah, well, caring isn't going to solve this. We need to figure it out quick and find Rachel, or we're going to find ourselves in a whole world of crap," she said. "And it also didn't help that James dropped that little nugget when he woke up. That story is going to spread like wildfire and whip everybody into a frenzy."

"People do love a good ghost story," he said.

"Unfortunately for us, yeah, they do."

"So, what's your game plan?"

Spenser shook her head. "I need to find my way around this eight-ball I'm behind. James isn't in any condition to answer questions, and I have no idea when he will be, so we still have absolutely nothing," she said. "I talked to Amanda last night and told her to center today's search party out by the road where James was found. I'm hoping they can find a clue out there, but honestly, I'm not overly optimistic they will. Whoever is behind this is either incredibly lucky or incredibly good."

"Might be a bit of both."

"Right. He's definitely a bit of both."

"Okay, so what are you going to do?"

"I'm going to talk to some of Rachel's friends and her family. Somebody is going to know something, even if they don't realize it right now."

Ryker slipped his arm around her and pulled her closer to him. Spenser reveled in the warmth of his skin as she melted against his toned, taut body. She'd spent plenty of nights in Ryker's bed, but in the back of her head, it was always kind of… temporary. She was still living in the cabin and could always retreat there if she needed to. Now, since they had started talking about moving their relationship forward and making this a permanent thing, it had imbued them with a closeness and intimacy that surprised her. It was something she liked. A lot.

"And you're sure this was about her?" he asked.

"I am. James was left for dead, and the attacker kept Rachel. That tells me she was the target all along, and he was simply collateral damage. James was in the way; he needed to be disposed of."

"It's a reasonable but grim conclusion to draw."

Spenser smiled as she snuggled even closer to him, drawing on his strength and warmth. She enjoyed being able to talk things over with Ryker. He often helped her untangle the knots that frequently cropped up in the middle of her brain during a case. It helped her to bounce things off him just to get her thoughts out. It helped even more that Ryker tended to be logical and unemotional about these things in ways that she and Amanda weren't. Spenser's emotional investment in cases and the victims was a plus and helped her in many ways, but it could sometimes cloud her mind and leave her with blind spots. It helped to have somebody like Ryker to talk things out with. And she appreciated that he was always willing to listen and lend his perspective.

Ryker looked down at her with a mischievous gleam in his eye. "I'm going to guess that Amanda is going to be all in on the Okasha theory?"

"I'm sure she is. But for my sake, she's playing it straight right now."

"And you're sure it wasn't the Okasha?"

Spenser rolled her eyes. "Like I told Marley, unless Bigfoot learned to use a baseball bat or a lead pipe, I doubt James' injuries were caused by anything other than a human being. The cuts on his body were likely made by a long blade. And for me, at least—not that I'm giving it any serious consideration—it doesn't track that a creature that feeds on human flesh would leave an uneaten body behind."

Ryker shrugged. "The consumption of human flesh is a relatively new story that wasn't in the original legends about the Okasha. That last bit was added by white teenagers who were sitting around the campfire telling scary stories."

Spenser looked at him for a moment before remembering that Okasha was a Snohomish word, and as a member of the tribe, Ryker might have a unique insight into the lore. She wanted to kick herself for not putting that all together until just now.

"Why did you not remind me that you'd heard the original stories?" Spenser groaned.

He chuckled. "I was confident you'd get there. I don't like to be too heavy-handed and prefer to just let you do things your way. You always come around to the right answers… eventually."

Spenser punched him playfully in the stomach and laughed along with him. He was teasing her, but she appreciated that he gave her the space to operate her way and didn't seem to need to come swinging in to save her with the answers. She appreciated that he let her come to things on her own. It was a trait not all men had.

"So, tell me about the original legend. The real legend," she said.

"Back in the day, the Okasha was known as a protector spirit. It did not tolerate injustice."

"So, it was a good spirit."

"It was neither good nor evil. Those are concepts people have put on it. The Okasha was simply known as a being that would protect those who needed it," he replied. "This modern version of the myth is about as far from the original stories as you can get. It's become this evil, monstrous bogeyman people have created."

Spenser eyed him for a long moment as she absorbed his words. "Do you believe in it?"

"I respect tradition," he said after a long moment. "In its original form, it was a story meant to keep people from taking advantage of those who might be weaker or less fortunate. It was a means of keeping people from doing terrible things to others."

"And now it's a monster that lurks in the dark and eats people."

Amusement flickered across his face. "That is not the story you will hear among the Snohomish people."

"It's a story we shouldn't be hearing among anybody."

"People need their bogeymen."

"I suppose they do."

They lay in silence for a couple of minutes. It was a nice way to spend the morning. But she couldn't lie there all day. There was work to be done.

"How about we go take a shower, and after that, I'll make you some breakfast," Ryker said.

"That would be really nice," she replied. "Thank you."

He kissed her forehead. "It's my pleasure. I like having you here with me."

"I like being here," she said, and she meant it.

CHAPTER FIFTEEN

After her relatively leisurely morning with Ryker, Spenser had phoned the Kehoes to make sure they would be at home. Amanda had mentioned that Denise and Brock Kehoe, Rachel's parents, had been exhausted and left yesterday's search early, so Spenser had set up a time to speak with them. She pulled the Bronco to a stop at the curb and took a moment to study the modest ranch-style house in the nice, solidly middle-class neighborhood.

The Kehoe home was light gray with white trim and had a two-car garage offset to the right of the single-story structure. A white rail fence enclosed a neatly trimmed yard, and a stone walk led from the sidewalk to the portico that stood over the front door.

The low-peaked roof was slate gray, which accented the rest of the house, which was clean and well-kept. The entire neighborhood was quiet. It seemed to be a nice place to raise a family and not the sort of area you'd expect to find the sort of tragedy the Kehoes were dealing with. As Spenser was all too aware, though, tragedy didn't discriminate. It could and would strike anywhere.

Still leaning on her cane, though not nearly as much as before, Spenser slung her messenger bag over her shoulder, then made her way up the walk and knocked on the front door. A moment later, it opened, revealing a short, petite woman with red, rheumy eyes. Grief and fear marred her features. Her cheeks were flushed, and she looked drawn and unnaturally pale. Dressed in a light blue shirt and blue jeans, she wrapped her arms around her midsection almost protectively. The woman stared at her, although she didn't seem to actually be seeing her. She seemed far away.

"Mrs. Kehoe?"

"Yes," she answered, sounding as far away as she appeared to be.

"Mrs. Kehoe, I'm Sheriff Song. I was hoping I could speak to you for a couple of minutes?"

"Did you find her?" she asked, her voice flat and monotone.

She clenched her jaw and held onto the door for support. She seemed to be bracing herself to receive the news she had been dreading ever since she learned that Rachel was missing.

"No, not yet. But they're still searching today," Spenser said. "I'm here because I need to ask you some questions, if that's all right?"

Her shoulders sagged as if with relief. But her gaze was so empty, it was like the woman was staring straight through her. She nodded and turned away, leaving her at the door as she walked deeper into the house. It was a bit awkward, but Spenser walked into the house, closed the door, and followed the woman's shuffling footsteps. She led Spenser into a large kitchen that was modern and efficient. Plates and glasses cluttered the counters, mixed in with fast food wrappers and bags. It looked like it hadn't been cleaned for a while. Probably since they found out their daughter had gone missing, if Spenser had to guess.

Brock Kehoe sat at a table in the small breakfast nook, a coffee mug cupped in his hands, staring into his coffee. He barely looked up as Spenser limped her way in. His wife sat down across from him, cupping her own mug in her hands and adopted the same slumped, defeated posture as her husband. Spenser could practically smell the grief in the air. It was as if they had already given up all hope of finding their daughter alive. They looked like a couple devoid of hope.

"Mr. and Mrs. Kehoe—may I call you Brock and Denise?"

They both nodded but remained silent. The quiet and awkward tension in the air grew thicker, and Spenser vowed to herself that she would get out of there as quickly as possible, both for their sake and for hers. Brock finally looked up and at least seemed minimally engaged. It wasn't much, but it was something.

"Thank you. I'm Sheriff Song, but please, call me Spenser," she said. "First of all, let me just tell you how sorry I am for what you're going through right now. I promise you that we are doing everything in our power to bring Rachel home."

"Why are you here, Sheriff?" Brock asked. "Didn't Veronica already answer your questions?"

"We also spoke with Undersheriff Young already."

"Yes, I spoke with Veronica, and Undersheriff Young told me she'd talked to you," Spenser said. "I just have a few follow-up questions. Is it okay if I take a few minutes of your time?"

Brock made a gesture that could have meant anything, then returned his gaze to the dark brew in his mug. Spenser chose to interpret it as him giving his assent.

"Brock, Denise, did Rachel ever mention having trouble with anybody? Did she ever talk about getting strange phone calls? Anybody harassing her? Anything like that?"

Denise shook her head. "No. She never mentioned anything like that to us."

"Me either," Brock added.

That jibed with what Veronica had said when Spenser had asked the same question. She was still certain that Rachel was the target of the attack. She had been the target of somebody's obsession. Spenser had some experience with stalkers and cases dealing with dark fixations. She was familiar with the hallmarks and what to look for, and she was certain that what happened out in the woods wasn't a spontaneous act. This was something that had developed slowly, over time.

Rachel had crossed paths with somebody at some point and unbeknownst to her, they had developed an affinity for her. It was likely an interaction that was so inconsequential that Rachel probably wouldn't even remember it. But to that person, it was everything. It was the origin of their focus on her and, over time, that focus turned into an obsession. Eventually, that fixation on Rachel had grown darker. It had festered and, at some point, had turned malignant. And that had all happened, very likely, without Rachel ever knowing it was happening.

The man behind Rachel's abduction—and Spenser was comfortable saying it was a man for a variety of reasons—had harbored and nurtured that dark fixation on her until it became unbearable. Until it was too much for him, and he had to have her. Had to possess her. Rachel's stalker had followed her out into the woods, had attacked their campsite, and after leaving James for dead, had absconded with her.

That was the theory Spenser had been developing. And though she still needed concrete proof to back it up, she was positive it was sound. She'd seen enough of these cases that Spenser was sure she was on the right track. Finding James, but not Rachel, was the key that had unlocked her theory. It was the piece of the puzzle that brought it all into focus and tied it all together for her.

"Can you two tell me who Rachel's closest friends are?" Spenser asked as she removed a small notepad and pen from her pocket. "Can you just give me a few names?"

"Holly Mendoza and Madison Kirk are her two closest friends," Denise said. "They've been a trio since they were little girls—"

Her words were cut off by a choked sob as she buried her face in her hands. Brock frowned. He seemed to want to comfort his wife but wasn't sure how, especially when he was being choked by his own fear and grief. He settled for reaching across the table and taking one of her hands. Denise seized it, clutching her husband's hand like it was a life preserver, and she was lost at sea. In some ways, Spenser supposed the woman was.

"Would you two mind if I had a look around Rachel's room? I'd like to get a sense of her and see if there's anything that might prove helpful to the investigation," Spenser said.

"If it will help, yes. Take whatever you need from her room," Denise said.

"Please. Find our daughter, Sheriff," Brock added.

"We're doing everything we can," Spenser replied.

Brock nodded and though he seemed to be trying to hold on to the ragged scraps of hope, he seemed almost resigned to a less-than-favorable outcome. It was heartbreaking to see.

"Rachel's room is at the end of the hall. It's the third door on the right," he said, then turned back to his coffee.

"Thank you," Spenser said.

She adjusted the bag on her shoulder, then turned and walked out of the kitchen, finding her way to the hall that led to the bedrooms. Rachel's door was already open. The room was dim and had a quiet, stale air. The walls were light pink, and one wall was almost covered in photos of Rachel with her friends on their various adventures. Her bedding was black and pink and neatly made, although it was slightly rumpled. It was as if somebody had laid on her bed after it had been made. It was a poignant detail that, like watching Brock fighting to hold back his tears, tore viciously at Spenser's heartstrings.

The blinds were drawn over the large window that sat in the far wall of the room, so Spenser walked over and opened them, flooding the room with natural light and giving her a view of the backyard. The tall, towering trees of the forest behind the house pressed close to the back fence. Stacks of lumber and plywood sat next to sawhorses, power equipment, and the skeletal framework of a small building going up in the backyard. It also appeared that a room was being added to the main house. It appeared the Kehoes were in the middle of making a few minor alterations to their house. It was all silent and still now, though, the work having been abandoned and the moment frozen in time.

Spenser took a little time to sift through Rachel's closet and drawers, not sure what she was looking for exactly, but confident she'd know it when she found it. A quick perusal of the girl's diaries didn't turn up much. She didn't journal every day, but on those days she did, she mostly expressed angst over everyday things girls her age stressed about—school, boys, and the like. Overall, though, the girl was upbeat, optimistic, and was excited about her future. She was eager to do some good things in the world once she got her degree and started working in her chosen field. Spenser could hear the smile in the girl's words and immediately liked her.

She didn't find much of evidentiary value, though. Nothing indicating that she was afraid that somebody was stalking her. She'd already contacted Rachel's cell service provider and was trying to gain access to her text messages, but so far, they were stonewalling and refusing to play ball with her. Anticipating they would be troublesome, she'd filed for a warrant to get the text records, but that hadn't yielded any fruit yet either. It was a big gap in her investigation, and Spenser figured if there was something to be found, it would likely be there, in her phone.

Spenser was just about to leave when her gaze fell upon the laptop sitting on Rachel's desk. She opened it, waking it up, and saw that it was password protected. She looked through the drawers at the desk, hoping Rachel had written her password down somewhere, but she came up empty. Spenser gave brief consideration to asking the Kehoes if they had the password, but figured the odds of Rachel sharing that information with her parents weren't very good. In fact, the odds of Spenser sprouting wings and flying to the moon were probably better.

Closing the laptop, she quickly bagged it, then slipped it into her messenger bag. She settled the strap over her shoulder again, then went and thanked the Kehoes for their patience and did what she could to offer them some bit of hope to hold on to. They didn't seem particularly receptive to it, so she said her goodbyes and hustled back to the Bronco.

She had an idea and needed to get back to the office.

CHAPTER SIXTEEN

Spenser had gotten Jacob set up with Rachel's computer, instructing him to break through her security and scrub it for anything and everything that might be remotely relevant to the current investigation. She'd shared her stalker theory with him and asked him to find anything that might suggest she was on the right track. It was a challenge that he embraced by vowing to find anything that might be on her computer. There was only one person who was as good as Jacob with all things tech-related, but he was working for her good friend Paxton up in Seattle. She was confident that if there was something to find, Jacob would find it.

While she was at the office, she called and checked in with Amanda. The search was ongoing, but they still weren't finding a thing. She had concentrated the volunteers around where James Burnham had been found and ran a grid search from there. Amanda speculated that he'd been pushed out of a vehicle and left in the ditch where he'd been discovered. There was no trail through the woods, and the dogs hadn't picked up a scent either. It seemed clear to her that James hadn't come through the woods on foot.

Amanda promised they would keep looking, but also said that energy was starting to flag. She noted that they had fewer volunteers than she'd had the day before and expressed her fear that the turnout tomorrow was going to be even worse. She said people were quickly losing hope they'd find Rachel alive. And given how many days they'd been crawling through the woods without finding anything, Spenser couldn't really blame them. Hope was a fleeting and fragile thing. Spenser thanked her and made sure to tell the younger woman she was doing a great job. Amanda thanked her but was uncomfortable and sounded as if she didn't deserve the praise.

With that all done, Spenser drove out to Hogtown, a section of Sweetwater Falls that had once been heavily dominated by meat farms and slaughterhouses. There were still a few meat farms, but the slaughterhouses were all gone, and those who raised the pigs and cows for slaughter sent them out to have the work done. For the most part, though, Hogtown, still filled with farmhouse-type homes, had been settled by families who were looking to live in a more "rural" rather than suburban tract-home-type setting.

Spenser drove down the long dirt road that led to a small, two-story, white clapboard farmhouse that sat at the end of it. The house was a little worn and aged. It could have used a fresh coat of paint and some other repairs. The husks of a few rusted-out cars sat in a small field to the left of the house amidst a host of other… junk. The field of debris that sat beside the house looked like something out of an episode of *Hoarders*.

As she climbed out of the Bronco, the front door of the house opened, and a man stepped out and stood on the porch with an unfriendly scowl on his face. Dressed in faded blue jeans, a ratty black t-shirt, and scuffed, worn work boots, the man put his hands on his hips and worked the toothpick that sat in the corner of his mouth, and stared at her with dark, menacing eyes. He was a few inches taller than her, heavy-set, an ample midsection, tawny wrinkled skin, and a mop of tangled, wavy black hair.

"What can I do for you, Sheriff?" he asked.

She had expected his voice to be gruff and gravelly but was surprised to hear it was higher and nasally. It didn't match his appearance at all.

"Richard Feller?" she asked.

"That's right."

Leaning on her cane, Spenser limped to the bottom of the three-step staircase that led to the porch. His eyes narrowed as he watched her. He was twitchy and nervous, giving Spenser the idea that he was armed. She didn't see a weapon, but assumed he had one tucked into his pants at the small of his back. She moved slowly and made sure to keep her own hands well away from her weapon. She didn't want this situation to go sideways.

"Mind if I come up?" she asked.

"Got a warrant?"

"I don't."

"Then I mind."

"I just want to have a conversation with you, Mr. Feller."

"You can have a conversation just as easy from down there as you can up here," he said. "I don't see no need for you to come up here."

He obviously didn't like it and didn't trust the police. That was nothing new. But the tension in the air between them was heavy. Suffocating. And with his hands on his hips, he was more than halfway to pulling the weapon she was growing more certain he had tucked into his belt behind him. She needed to defuse the tension. Needed to make him see she wasn't a threat to him. With her cane in one hand, she raised the other to show him her palm, keeping it far away from her Glock.

"That's fine. I can stay down here, Mr. Feller," she said. "Let's just talk."

"You here about the boy I found?"

"I am."

"I don't know what else to tell you that I ain't already said."

"Well, can you tell me how you came to be out there to find him in the first place?"

He spat a big, brown glob of tobacco on the wood planks of his porch. Not wanting to offend him, Spenser did her best to hide her distaste. She'd always found chewing tobacco to be absolutely repulsive. It was just gross.

"I was out lookin' for aluminum and spare metals. I do that every day," he said. "You can check with anybody. I got a usual route I follow every day. I pass down Taylor Road every day and I saw him half-in-half-out of that ditch. I figured he was dead, but turned out he wasn't."

"Had you ever seen him before?"

"Nah. I ain't seen him before in my life."

"And how about Rachel Kehoe? Have you ever met her?"

"Who?"

"Rachel Kehoe."

He pursed his lips and looked off, seeming to ponder it for a moment before shaking his head.

"Nope. Ain't heard that name before."

"So, it was just dumb luck that you found James?"

He scoffed and hocked another brown glob onto his porch. "Can't really say it's luck of any kind. It just happened," he said. "Course, now that I got the cops bangin' down my door, I wish I'd never found him."

"Why is that, Mr. Feller?"

"Because I like to be left alone. I don't like people comin' out here botherin' me. Especially cops," he growled.

"Do you have a specific problem with cops?"

"Had a specific problem with the fella who had the job before you—him and his cronies."

"Well, I'm not him," Spenser said. "And I'm doing my best to clean up the department. I'm sorry if you've had bad experiences in the past, but I hope you'll give this new department—my department—a chance."

"Yeah, well, a cop's a cop to me. Too many bad experiences with you people to be comfortable around you. No offense."

"None taken," Spenser replied evenly. "So, you said you hadn't met either James Burnham or Rachel Kehoe before?"

"That's what I said. A couple of times now."

"Mr. Feller, would you mind if I had a look around your property?"

A smirk creased his lips. "You got a warrant, Sheriff?"

"I do not."

"Then I mind."

"You're not hiding a young woman in your house or anywhere on your property, are you?"

His expression turned sour. "No. I'm not. Like I said, I never laid eyes on the kid until I pulled him out of that ditch yesterday, and I ain't sure who the hell this Rachel girl is."

Spenser watched and listened to him closely, searching for the slightest hint of deception. But she didn't see any in his face nor hear it in his voice. His distrust and dislike of the police aside, she wasn't getting a bad hit off him. He also didn't seem to be in particularly good shape, nor did he seem very athletic—two things Spenser was profiling their guy to be. Their kidnapper would have to be somewhat physically imposing to keep both James and Rachel in line while traversing the terrain he'd marched them through. That didn't seem to be Richard Feller. He said he'd never met James and Rachel, and she didn't get a hint of deception. Every instinct she had told her he was telling the truth.

"Okay, Mr. Feller. I appreciate your time."

"Uh-huh," he said and spat another glob of tobacco on the porch.

Spenser turned and headed to the Bronco. The back of her neck was itchy, and she knew the man's eyes were on her the entire way. As she drove away, Spenser glanced in her rearview and saw him still standing on the porch, watching her go. He was odd, a bit creepy, and certainly didn't care for her, but that didn't make him a killer. Spenser didn't think much of him as a person, but he didn't seem to fit the profile of the man she was sure had taken Rachel, so she was comfortable putting him on the back burner.

CHAPTER SEVENTEEN

"Holly Mendoza?"

"Yes?"

"Sheriff Spenser Song," she said. "Can I speak to you for a minute?"

"Uhh, sure. Yeah. Of course."

She opened the door and stepped aside, letting Spenser into her apartment. It was small but looked comfortable. An oversized, stuffed sofa sat against the far wall beneath a pair of windows, and across from it a large, flatscreen television sat atop a narrow credenza. The oval-shaped coffee table that sat in front of the couch was cluttered with textbooks, papers, and a laptop.

"Homework?" Spenser asked.

"Yeah, I'm working on a paper for my comparative literature class."

"What are you majoring in?"

"English," she responded. "I'm planning on teaching when I'm done."

Spenser nodded. "That's good. That's a good career choice."

"I'm excited and know I'll enjoy it."

The young woman wrapped her arms around her midsection. She was several inches shorter than Spenser, with black hair that reached her waist, warm, tawny skin, and eyes the color of onyx. Holly was petite but with a compact, athletic, and powerful frame that made Spenser think she might have been a gymnast at some point. Holly hugged herself tighter as her eyes watered and her cheeks turned red. She was struggling to hold back the tears.

"A—are you here about Rachel?" she asked.

"I am."

"Do you have any idea where she is or what happened to her?"

"We're still working on that. I just wanted to ask you some questions."

She frowned. "Me? I'm not sure what I can do to help. I don't really know anything."

"You might know more than you realize."

She gnawed on her lower lip. "Umm. Okay?"

"Great. Mind if I have a seat?"

"I'm sorry. Of course. Yes. Please. Have a seat."

Holly perched on the edge of her sofa, leaving Spenser to move the stack of books off the folding chair. She set them down on the coffee table, and then took a seat. Holly wrung her hands together, cleared her throat, and licked her lips. Her eyes darted left, right, and everywhere around the room, but she couldn't seem to bring herself to meet Spenser's gaze.

"Have you spoken with Rachel's family?" she finally asked.

"I have."

"They're probably better able to answer your questions than I am."

"They were able to answer some," Spenser said. "But I've been doing this job long enough to know that people sometimes tell their friends things they don't share with their parents. And Rachel's mom said you were her best friend?"

She nodded. "It's me, Rachel, and Maddy—Madison. We all grew up together and have been best friends since like, kindergarten. We're all supposed to be the Maids of Honor at each other's weddings whenever we get married."

The memory brought a fresh wave of tears and a choked sob bursting from Holly's mouth. Her hand trembled as she wiped the tears away, and Spenser gave her a couple of beats to collect herself. She sat up and cleared her throat again, then gave Spenser a small nod.

"Are you okay?" Spenser asked.

"I'm okay. Just… is… is she dead, Sheriff?"

"We have no reason to assume that, Holly. Right now, we're still operating under the belief that she's alive and that we're going to bring her home."

She swallowed hard and nodded. "Okay. I heard they found James?"

"They did. He's in the hospital right now."

"How is he?"

"He's stable, and the last I heard, he was awake. I haven't been told much more than that, though."

She frowned. "James is a really good guy. We were all really glad when she got together with him. He treats her really well. He treats her like she deserves to be treated."

"Right now, the best thing you can do is keep him in your prayers."

"I will."

"Holly, did she ever mention having trouble with anybody?"

"Trouble?"

"Did she mention anything about anybody following her? Making her uncomfortable? Anything like that?"

She turned inward for a moment, then shook her head. "No, she didn't mention anything like that to me. But she had an ex who was kind of problematic."

Spenser's ears perked up at the mention of a problematic ex. As Ryker was fond of reminding her, it's always the significant other. Or, in this case, the ex-significant other. But a bad break-up could definitely lead somebody to do something unthinkable. That was a storyline so common it was bordering on cliché.

"How was he problematic?" Spenser asked.

"They had a bad break-up. But that was, like, a long time ago. But he just wouldn't let it go. Kept trying to get her back—even after she got together with James," she said.

"Why did she break things off with him?"

"Rachel just wasn't into him anymore. She said he drank too much, smoked too much weed, and didn't have any motivation to do anything with his life," Holly said. "Rachel is a go-getter. She's got plans and life goals. And she wants somebody who can match that energy."

"What is his name?"

"Lee Nash," she said. "He's a bartender over at the Pour House."

Spenser jotted that down in her small notebook. "So, you said it was a bad break-up, and he was being problematic. He didn't take the break-up well then?"

"God, not at all."

"What did he do?"

"Endless calls and texts," she said. "Rachel eventually had to block his number and block him on all her socials."

"I take it that wasn't the end of it?"

"Unfortunately, no. He showed up to Overtime a few times. Rach and I both work there, but we're usually on opposite schedules, so I didn't see it happen," she replied. "Anyway, I heard he got to be such a pest that our boss, Adam, banned Lee from ever coming in again. Said he'd call the police if he ever saw him hanging around again."

"What was he doing?" Spenser asked.

"Just hanging around bothering Rach, mostly from what I heard. He'd get loud and beg her to take him back, and when she ignored him, he'd scream at her. He was disrupting and upsetting the rest of our customers. Adam tried to be cool with him at first, but Lee burned through any goodwill pretty quickly after that."

"Holly, is Lee a violent person? You said he screamed at her, but did he ever show any other violent tendencies?"

She grimaced as she pondered about the question for a moment. "Honestly, I couldn't say. I never saw him be violent, and Rach never mentioned anything about him hitting her or anything. But I guess anybody can be, right?"

Spenser nodded. "That's true. Anybody can be."

They were both silent for a moment, the air between them suddenly growing heavier. It was obvious how much Holly cared about Rachel, and it seemed like she was having a really hard time dealing with her friend being missing. It seemed like she was barely holding it together. Spenser guessed that Marley had gone through that same complex web of emotions when she was in the hospital after Alex Ricci's attack. With that understanding, her heart went out to the girl.

"Holly, was there anybody else that Rachel might have had some trouble with? Anybody who might have been upset with her?"

She shook her head. "No, she didn't have problems with anybody, really. Everybody loves Rach."

"Okay, let's look at it from the other direction," Spenser said as the question occurred to her. "Is there anybody that might have been paying a little too much attention to her? Anybody who might have been making her uncomfortable that way?"

"I mean, some of the guys down at Overtime flirt with her. Some of them flirt with her pretty hard, but nobody really takes it all that seriously. It's all just part of the game we play. Flirting usually ups our tips."

"And there isn't anybody who might not realize it's a game that comes to mind?"

"No, nobody comes to mind. Like I said, some of the guys flirt pretty hard, but they're all harmless. Nobody seemed to take it too seriously. She never mentioned having problems with anybody down there to me, but you might want to talk to Adam."

"I'll do that."

Spenser flipped her notebook closed and tapped her pen on it. She racked her brain for a moment but didn't have any more questions for the girl, so she got to her feet. Holly jumped up, her face lined with anxiety as she wrung her hands together.

"Okay, that's all I have for you right now. Thank you very much for giving me your time today, Holly. I appreciate your help."

"I'm not sure I helped all that much, but you're welcome."

"I'll touch base if anything comes up."

"Thank you, Sheriff. I really appreciate all you're doing."

"We're doing our best. I promise you that."

She was trying to look hopeful, but Spenser could see the cracks in the façade. She gave Holly an encouraging smile and a gentle squeeze on the shoulder, then walked out of the apartment. She'd gotten one good lead out of Holly, which was more than she'd been expecting to get, so her interview with the younger woman wasn't a complete waste of time.

It wasn't much, but it was a place to start.

CHAPTER EIGHTEEN

Spenser pulled to a stop at the curb in front of the Nashes' quaint, ranch-style home. Lee Nash was in the driveway of his parents' home. He was six-feet-tall, tan, lean, and wearing nothing but board shorts as he washed his car—a red 1965 fastback Mustang. Spenser wasn't much of a gearhead, but she certainly appreciated a pretty car when she saw one, and she'd always had an affinity for vintage muscle cars.

She climbed out of the Bronco and headed up the driveway. The Stones' classic hit, 'Sympathy for the Devil,' was blasting as the young man leaned over the hood of his car, a cigarette dangling precariously from the corner of his mouth, diligently wiping away the streaks and smudges on the windshield. It seemed obvious that he cared a lot for the car and took good care of it.

"Beautiful car," Spenser said.

Lee stood up and plucked the cigarette from his mouth, his posture stiffening and his eyes flashing with worry as he watched Spenser approach. He reached over and turned down the music, not bothering to try to hide the small pipe and bag of weed on the table beside the radio. He watched her as he drew another drag from his cigarette, breathing out a thick plume of smoke that rose into the air like the fluffy white clouds that dotted the sky overhead.

Lee had the stereotypical surfer look that said he'd rather be smoking weed and riding waves than doing anything useful with his life. He looked like a slacker. And she'd seen plenty of that type in her life. Spenser could see why, as Holly had said, his energy didn't match Rachel's.

"You restore her?" Spenser asked, motioning to the car.

"I rebuilt the engine. But I got the body like this."

"It's a good-looking car."

"Thanks," he replied.

"You're a bartender down at the Pour House, right?"

He nodded. "Yeah. That's right."

"What else do you do, Lee?"

He shrugged. "Work at the bar. Spend a lot of time working on my car, I guess."

"You don't go to school or anything?"

"Nope."

"Are you considering going back to school?" she asked. "What kind of plans are you making for the future?"

He snorted. "What is this, career counseling or something?"

"No. Just trying to get a better sense of you."

"Why?"

"Why not? I like to get to understand the people in town," she told him. "I'm just curious what your future plans might be."

He shrugged. "Haven't really considered it. Something'll come up."

"You ever been out to Mossy Flats?"

"Sure. Everybody has."

"Recently?"

Lee dropped the rag in his hand into the bucket, then took another drag on his cigarette. He was trying to play it cool and low-key, but he couldn't quite mask the hint of worry that tinged the curiosity in his eyes. He was wondering why she was there. Spenser let the silence between them linger for a long moment, giving the tension a little more time to simmer in his gut.

"What's with all the questions? Why are you really here, Sheriff?" he finally asked. "I'm starting to see that this isn't just a social kind of thing. Seems like you've got an agenda."

"You're perceptive."

"So? What do you want?"

"I wanted to talk to you about Rachel Kehoe."

Although he didn't look surprised, Lee frowned and took another drag off his cigarette, taking a beat to gather his thoughts. Spenser let him.

"What about her?" he asked after a huge sigh.

"I assume you've heard that she's missing."

"Of course, I have. Nothing happens in this town without everybody hearing about it," he said. "I'm sure you've figured that out by now."

Spenser nodded. "I have."

"Well, I didn't have anything to do with what happened, if that's what you're really trying to ask. So, you wasted a trip out here."

"Maybe. I still need to ask you a few questions, though."

He sighed again, then took another drag of his cigarette and exhaled as he dropped the butt to the ground and crushed it beneath his flip-flop.

"Don't you need a warrant or something?" he asked.

"To have a conversation with you? No, I don't."

"So, I'm, like, not under arrest or anything?"

"No, I'm not here to arrest you, Lee."

"Do I need a lawyer?"

Spenser grimaced. "Not unless you want one. That's your right. But like I told you, I'm only here to have a conversation with you. I just have a few questions and hope you can help clear a few things up for me. After that, I'm out of here."

He stared skeptically at Spenser for a long moment, as if deciding whether or not she was trying to trick him. Lee shook another cigarette out of his pack and lit it, taking a deep drag as he eyed her through the cloud of smoke. He extended the pack toward her.

"Smoke?" he offered.

"No. But thank you."

"Sure."

"So, will you answer a few questions for me?"

"Fine," he finally said. "What can I tell you?"

"Well, I understand that your break-up with Rachel was a little difficult on you."

"Yeah. I guess so."

"Why is that?"

He squinted at her with disdain. "You ever have somebody you cared about break up with you for no reason, Sheriff?"

"Who hasn't? It's just part of life."

"Well, then, you've been there. It's hard. It can mess with your mind and stuff," he replied. "We were together for about a year, but I really loved her. She was the one for me. Wanted her to be anyway. So yeah, I took it hard when she broke things off."

"Fair enough," she replied. "But not all of us would show up to that person's workplace and cause a scene. Can you tell me about that?"

He drew deeply on his cigarette as a myriad of emotions scrolled across his face. He very clearly still had big feelings about the break-up.

"Look, I did some stupid stuff. I was still hurting and probably had too much to drink, and yeah, I showed up to her work and made an idiot out of myself. I was stupid. But as far as I know, there's no law against being stupid."

"There's not. But there are lines you can't cross—"

"Rachel's manager made it clear what would happen if I showed up there again," he cut her off. "I haven't been back to the restaurant since, and I haven't tried to contact her again since that night. Message received, okay?"

"So, you never tried to contact her after her boss threatened to get the police involved if you showed up to Overtime again?"

"Not once."

"And if I checked her call and text logs—"

"She blocked me, Sheriff. On everything. I couldn't have contacted her if I'd wanted to."

"There are ways around that. Burner phones—"

"Look, I assume you're going to check her phone, if you haven't already. But I don't have a burner. If anybody was calling or texting her or whatever, it wasn't me."

"So, you just walked away?"

"Yeah. I walked away. I cared about her and had to try, but I finally got the message. I wasn't going to get her back. And I wasn't trying to go to jail over it. I guess it was a wake-up call," he told her.

Spenser scrutinized him closely, trying to determine whether he was being honest with her or not. She was having a hard time getting a read on him, though. On the surface, he ticked off some of the boxes on the profile she had in her head—he was hung up on Rachel, was relatively fit, and was intimately familiar with the area—but not all of them. Lee had the motivation, the means, and possibly the opportunity to wreck her campsite and snatch her. But she wasn't sure he had. Not because she necessarily bought into his great awakening but because it would have been a lot of work. And when he said he didn't want to go to jail over it, it rang true.

The trouble she was having with him was whether he was obsessed with her enough to do it. Spenser was all in on her stalker theory. Being that heartbroken and hung up on somebody so long after a break-up was one thing. But the sort of obsession required to hunt, stalk, then grab somebody—and beat that somebody's boyfriend to a pulp—was a level of fixation Spenser wasn't sure he possessed. He wanted Rachel, but only on his terms. At his core, Lee Nash was a slacker. He wanted to smoke, drink, and play with his car. His personality, as she'd seen it thus far, told her that abducting Rachel and nearly killing James might have been too much work for the guy.

There were also two facts that she couldn't escape. The first was that she couldn't see any sort of defensive wounds on Lee's shirtless body. She would have expected to see scratches or bruises on Lee since James wouldn't have taken a beating like that without fighting back. The second was that if Lee had been the one who'd taken her, why wasn't he with her? The level of obsession Rachel's abductor possessed meant he wasn't going to let her out of his sight. He'd be with her and wouldn't leave her side. He certainly wouldn't be casually washing his car.

No, the more she talked to Lee and studied him up close, the more certain she was that he didn't do it. He was a slacker and hung up on a girl who'd dropped him a long time ago, but she wasn't sure he was more than that. She'd do her due diligence on him, but she was fairly sure he wasn't anything more than a nuisance with a broken heart.

"Can you tell me where you were over the weekend?" Spenser asked.

"I'm telling you, I had nothing to do with this."

"I just need to check off all my boxes. Please."

He sighed, irritation flashing across his face. "I worked Friday night, and on Saturday, I was with a buddy up in Seattle for a car show."

"And your friend's name?"

"Connor Addison."

Spenser pulled out her notebook and jotted down a few notes. "And Sunday?"

"I worked the afternoon shift at the bar."

It would all be simple enough to verify. But Spenser already had a feeling it was all going to check out. His words rang true. She tucked her pen and notebook back into her pocket as Lee exhaled noisily, blowing a thick plume of smoke into the air. His patience seemed to be at an end.

"All right, Lee. Thanks for talking to me today," Spenser said.

"Sure."

"Stay out of trouble," she said, then turned and headed for the Bronco.

CHAPTER NINETEEN

DONE IN A LOT OF DIM LIGHTING, DISTRESSED WOOD, AND red brick, the current incarnation of the Pour House was that of a grimy dive bar. The bar had been a fixture in town for decades. Every few years or so, it would slough off its skin and become something new, catering to an entirely new clientele. Right now, it was like flowers to a honeybee for the hipster crowd who filled the place at night. By day, though, the Pour House was still a grimy place for the disconsolate, downtrodden, and depressed to drown their sorrows.

When she walked into the bar, the stench of cigarettes and desperation lingered in the air. A trio of barflies sat a couple of stools apart, hunched over the bar, staring into their glasses, lit cigarettes dangling from their fingertips. They all turned to Spenser as she walked through the room, none of them seeming to care they were breaking city and state ordinances that banned smoking in public establishments. Of course, the men sitting at the bar were drinking in the middle of the day, telling Spenser they didn't seem to care about much of anything.

"What can I do for you, Sheriff?"

Five-ten with a stocky build, Tad Doolan had been the owner and operator of the Pour House for the last twenty years. And like his establishment, he had changed with the times and shifting demographics of his clientele. His long brown hair was fashioned in a man-bun, and he had the thick, oiled beard favored by the hipsters who filled the place after work hours. It was kind of ridiculous, but Doolan knew his clientele well and catered to them. She had to admit it was smart business tactics.

"Afternoon, Tad," Spenser replied. "I need to speak with you."

"Sure."

He motioned her down to the end of the bar, well away from the trio of day drinkers. He leaned on the bar and fixed Spenser with a steady, curious gaze. She hadn't had cause to deal with Tad often, but on those few occasions when they've interacted, she's always found him to be pleasant. He was smart, witty, and was always ready with a joke and a laugh. But more importantly, he seemed honest and the kind of person who strove to do the right thing.

"What's up, Sheriff?"

"I needed to ask you about one of your employees."

"Great. Who's in trouble this time?"

"Nobody's in trouble," Spenser said. "I just need to verify a few things."

"Okay, so who is it?"

"Lee Nash."

A grimace colored the man's expression. "Does this have anything to do with the missing girl?"

"What makes you ask that?"

"It wasn't exactly a secret that he was hung up on her," Tad said. "Talked about her all the time. I tried to tell him he needed to move on, but he was just stuck on her. The more she rejected him, the more he wanted her."

"Did he talk about her recently?"

"Oh yeah. That girl owned Lee's soul," he said with a rueful chuckle.

"I see," she replied. "Tad, can you tell me what hours Lee worked this past weekend?"

He opened his mouth to respond, then closed it again as what she was getting at finally seemed to sink in. Tad cleared his throat as a serious expression stole over his face.

"Listen, Lee is an odd kid, no question about that. But he's not a bad kid," he said. "He's got some issues, but he's worked for me for a couple of years now, and I have a pretty good sense of him. Trust me when I say he's not the sort to hurt anybody. He's all bluster."

Spenser tapped her finger against the polished wood bar. "Would it surprise you if I said he showed up at Rachel's workplace and created a scene? Several times, in fact."

"No, that wouldn't surprise me. Like I said, he's an odd kid and has some issues with letting go of that girl. But there's a world of difference between being an idiot and harassing a girl like that and killing somebody."

"I never said Rachel had been killed."

He pulled a face. "She's been missing, what, almost a week now? I'm not a cop but even I know things aren't generally good for somebody who's been missing in the woods that long. It'll be a miracle if that girl turns up alive."

He wasn't wrong, but Spenser wasn't about to throw gasoline on the fire, so she didn't confirm that she'd had the same grim musings. It would serve no purpose other than to throw more grist into the churning wheels of the rumor mill.

"And in your opinion, Lee isn't capable of hurting her?"

Tad shook his head. "Nah. He's hung up on her, but he's not a violent guy. He's just heartbroken. That's all."

"Plenty of heartbroken guys end up being murderers," Spenser pointed out.

"I'm sure they do. But Lee is a mellow dude. And if you want my honest take, the guy is too timid to do anything like that. I mean, he's full of bluster and swagger, but deep down, he's a scared kid who's never even been in a fight. In fact, I've seen him actively avoid fights in here more times than I can count. I can't see somebody who runs from confrontation working up the nut to go on a violent murder spree. It just doesn't track for me, Sheriff."

"I appreciate your perspective, Tad. I do," Spenser replied. "But can you tell me what hours he worked over this weekend?"

"Yeah, sure. He was here from six in the evening 'til two in the morning on Friday night. Then, on Sunday, he came in at eleven to open the bar and then worked until eight that night. He didn't work on Saturday but said he had tickets to some car show up in Seattle."

It tracked with what Lee had told her. Spenser was cynical, though. It could have all been a carefully laid alibi. Her conversation with Tad strengthened her belief that her read on Lee Nash was the right one, but she would be sure to check it all out anyway. She would also be sure to check all the relevant phone lines just to be sure Lee hadn't placed a call to Tad before she arrived and asked his boss to cover for him. Tad didn't seem the sort who would provide Lee cover like that, but she wasn't going to leave any stone unturned.

"I'm telling you, Sheriff, the kid is a knucklehead, but he's not the kind of guy who would take somebody's life. I'm telling you, he doesn't have it in him," Tad said.

"Do you have timecards that can back up that Lee was here at those times?"

"Yeah, of course," he said. "He's on the internal security cameras, too, if you want the footage from those."

"I'd appreciate it if you could send me that footage."

"Sheriff—"

"I understand your concerns, and I'm not trying to pin anything on him. If anything, I'm trying to rule him out as having had anything to do with what happened, Tad."

Some of the tension seemed to ebb from his shoulders. Her words seemed to have reassured him, if only a little. For whatever reason, it was apparent that Tad was fond of Lee and was doing what he could to protect him.

"I'll make sure to get that over to you today," he said.

Spenser pulled one of her business cards out of her pocket and laid it on the bar. "That would be great. You can email to the address listed here."

Tad picked the card up and nodded. "I'll be sure to do that."

"Great. Thanks for your time. And I appreciate you answering my questions."

"Of course. And I hope you figure out who really did this," he said.

"We will," Spenser replied. "We're absolutely going to find him."

As she walked out of the bar and back to the Bronco, though, a creeping sense of doubt ensnared her heart and mind. She'd started the day with two potential suspects—Lee Nash and Richard Feller—and came away all but certain neither had done it. Spenser found herself back at square one, which was bad enough. But she had no clear path forward, which was even worse.

CHAPTER TWENTY

"I GOT THE FOOTAGE AND TIMECARD REPORTS FROM THE bar," Jacob said as Spenser dropped into her chair at the table in the conference room. "Time stamps show that Lee Nash was indeed at work when he told you he was."

"I kind of figured that would be the case."

"I've also got him on video at the car show and corresponding debit card purchases," Jacob added. "I also spoke to that Connor Addison, who confirmed it all."

"All right. I guess we can cross the ex-boyfriend off the list."

"Unless he has an evil twin?"

Spenser chuckled. "If only the answer was that simple."

"If what answer was that simple?"

Amanda walked into the conference room and dropped heavily into her seat. Her complexion was pale, her face was drawn, and the dark half-moons beneath her eyes stood out. She was tired. Wrung out. But more than that, she seemed disappointed. Frustrated. And the ragged ends of her nails and raw, bloody nail beds spoke to her level of stress.

"You okay?" Spenser asked.

She waved off the question with a grumble. "What were you two talking about when I walked in? If what answer was that simple?"

"I said it'd be a lot simpler if Lee Nash had an evil twin," Jacob answered.

"Does he?" Amanda asked.

"Yes," Jacob said with faux solemnity. "He's seven feet tall, fiery hair, has red glowing eyes, and a taste for human blood—"

"Shut up," Amanda snapped. "I'm really not in the mood."

Spenser exchanged a glance with Jacob, who was shocked by his sister's outburst. It was rare to ever see Amanda in a dark mood; it was even rarer for her to snap like that.

"What's going on with you, Amanda?" Spenser asked.

She brushed the hair off her face and blew out a frustrated breath. "I'm suspending the search for Rachel."

"Why is that?" Spenser asked.

"The volunteers—the few we have left anyway—are exhausted," she said. "We've been out there for days and haven't found a single thing. The woods are just too vast for us to feasibly keep looking. I mean, we could search for weeks and still not find anything."

"That's reasonable."

"She's still out there somewhere, and it's like we're abandoning her."

"We're not abandoning her. We just need to shift our focus and put our attention into other avenues," Spenser said.

"I feel like we are."

"You're exhausted yourself," Spenser responded. "Like you said, you've been out there for days and running on next to no sleep. I want you to go home and get some rest."

"I'm fine, Sheriff. I can—"

"That wasn't a request, Amanda. I want you to go home and get some sleep. You'll be of more use to me and, more importantly, to Rachel if you've got all your wits about you."

"Sheriff, honest, I'm fine."

"This isn't a discussion," Spenser said. "You're worn out. I need you fresh. So, I'm banning you from the office for the next twelve hours. Go home. Get some rest."

She sighed and slumped back in her chair, disappointment and frustration on her face. But then she sat forward again.

"Can you at least update me on where we are before I go?" she asked.

"Sure. So far, we've been able to rule out Rachel's ex-boyfriend," Spenser replied.

"Did you talk to the guy who found James? What was his name?"

"Richard Feller. Yeah, I spoke with him."

"And?"

"I'm all but certain he's not our guy either. He doesn't fit the profile and says he's never met Rachel before. As far as I can tell, he's telling the truth," Spenser answered. "Jacob is checking everything just to make sure there are no connections between them we haven't seen yet, but I'm already assuming that's going to be a dead end."

Amanda frowned. "Do we have any other suspects?"

"Not at the moment," Spenser answered honestly.

"Hold up for a second," Jacob said.

"What do you have?" Spenser asked.

"I finally got through the security on her laptop and accessed her cloud. I found some messages she sent through an app on her computer and also her call and text logs."

"And?"

"Give me just one second. I'm sifting through it all on the fly here."

A bolt of adrenaline-fueled hope blossomed in Spenser's chest. She mentally crossed her fingers, silently praying there was something of value hidden in Rachel's cloud. As the minutes ticked by, Spenser's shoulders grew taut, the bands of tension that had wrapped themselves around her squeezing tighter. So tight, it was almost as if she couldn't breathe.

Hunched over his laptop, Jacob's fingers flew over the keys with the tip of his tongue poking out from the corner of his mouth. He was locked in on what he was doing. The reflection from the screen of his laptop gave his face a ghostly glow that somehow added to the intense concentration etched into his features.

"Okay, I found some messages from around eight months ago between Rachel and somebody named Madison Kirk—"

"That's one of her best friends," Spenser confirmed.

"Right, okay. Anyway, in these messages, she mentions that she was being watched. No specifics, but she said she just has a creepy feeling," he said.

He tapped another key, and the monitor on the wall across from Spenser lit up as he posted the first email he'd found. Spenser's eyes scanned the text on the screen. Rachel's initial comments about being watched were flippant, almost as if she was aware that she sounded paranoid and ridiculous—something Madison's snarky replies seemed to reinforce. But in reading between the lines, Rachel sounded genuinely worried.

Jacob flipped through a few more emails that made passing mention of being watched, but if Rachel was really afraid that somebody had eyes on her, she didn't explicitly say so. That fear was there, though, between the girl's words. When she did mention it again, it was in an almost joking manner. Perhaps it was because Madison had seemed so dismissive that it made Rachel hold her fear in check. But the fact that she'd mentioned it again, several times, told Spenser she was, in a way, calling for help. Or at least, some acknowledgment that her fear was valid. But she didn't get that.

"Check this one out," Jacob said.

Another message, this one from just a few weeks ago, appeared on the screen. Spenser took a minute to read Rachel's words to her friend Madison, and as she did, a cold chill slithered down her spine.

"Mads, are you almost here? That guy I told you about is hanging around outside," Spenser read. "I'll be waiting inside. Call me when you get here."

Madison had texted back a few minutes later, telling her to relax and that she'd be there in just a few minutes. Silence descended over the conference room as they all absorbed Rachel's messages and their meaning.

"Uh, you're going to want to see this," Jacob said, a note of alarm in his voice.

"What is it?" Spenser asked.

The screen flashed, and another message appeared, which Amanda quickly read. "You looked beautiful today. I saw you, but you didn't see me, and that is the way it will stay for a while. When the time is right, we will be together."

"That's from just a week ago. And there are a few like that," Jacob said.

"Who sent it?" Spenser asked.

He shook his head. "As near as I can tell, it's an unassociated burner. No name on it."

"Wonderful."

"The stalking had been going on for months," Amanda said. "You were right, Sheriff. This is an obsession that developed over time."

Spenser gave her a smirk. "So, you're done with the Sweetwater Devil theory?"

Amanda snickered. "I reserve my right to believe in all things paranormal. But in this case, yeah, this looks like it has an earthlier origin."

"Okay, so, we need to figure out where this obsession began. Where did Rachel cross paths with this man, and what was the nature of the interaction?" Spenser mused. "It probably meant little to her at the time, but it meant everything to our offender."

"I'm not even sure where to start," Amanda said.

Spenser frowned. "We've somehow got to figure out where she was, who she saw, and what she did eight months ago."

"I'm good and all but building a time machine is a little outside my wheelhouse, I'm afraid to say," Jacob chirped.

Spenser sat back in her chair and rubbed her thumb along her lower lip, working the knot that had formed in the center of her brain.

"She talked to Madison about it but didn't get anywhere. Didn't get that validation and permission to be scared she seemed to be looking for," she said.

"Permission to be scared?" Amanda asked.

Spenser nodded. "She wanted Madison to tell her it was okay to be scared. That she wasn't being paranoid. Something like that. Madison never gave her that and for the most part, she stopped talking to her about being watched."

"She mentioned it in this other email," Amanda pointed out.

"She did. But it was tentative, and it was just a line. It seems like she was putting it out there again to see if she would get the validation she was looking for," Spenser answered.

"Okay," Amanda said slowly. "But what is your point?"

"My point is that she likely talked to somebody else—somebody who might have given her what she was looking for," Spenser replied.

Amanda looked up in thought. "Her other best friend? What's her name again?"

"Holly Mendoza," Spenser answered. "Maybe so."

"Okay, I'll run over and talk to Holly—"

Spenser cut her off with a sharp look. "No. You are going home to get some sleep… as I ordered you to do. I will go talk to Holly. Period and end of story. If I see you back here before tomorrow morning, I'm going to suspend you since that might be the only way I can force you to get some rest. Am I clear?"

Amanda sighed, her face dark with frustration. "Crystal."

"Good. Go home, and I will see you in the morning—and not before then," Spenser said, her voice firm and brooking no argument.

"Yes, ma'am," she said, her tone dark and tight.

"Jacob, keep digging. We need to find anything we can," she said. "I'll check back in with you later. I've got some people to talk to."

CHAPTER TWENTY-ONE

"MADISON KIRK?"

The girl's blue eyes widened as she looked at Spenser, and her full, red lips quivered. "Yes?"

"I'm Sheriff Song. I'd like to talk to you for a minute, if that's all right?"

"What's this about? Have you found Rachel? Are you here about her?"

"In a way, yes. May I come in and ask you a few questions?"

"Umm. Yeah. Okay."

She held the door open and allowed Spenser inside as she took the air pods out of her ears. Twenty-one years old, Madison Kirk was Spenser's height with white-blond hair pulled back into a braid, a perfect porcelain complexion, and a curvy, athletic frame that was accentuated by the tight black yoga pants and matching SCU sports bra she was wearing. Beads of sweat dotted her brow, her face was flushed, and she had a towel around her long, swan-like neck. Spenser had obviously caught her after a workout.

Spenser followed the girl down a short hallway. Madison moved with a dancer's grace, making Spenser feel like an absolute stumbling clod in comparison. They stepped through a rounded archway and into a kitchen that, like the rest of the house, was stark white and minimalistic, save for the modern appliances, which were all chrome. The whole house seemed antiseptic and sterile. It definitely wasn't Spenser's style, but to each their own. Madison walked around the center island, perhaps unconsciously keeping some distance between them.

"Are your folks home?" Spenser asked.

"No, they're at work."

"Have any siblings?"

"A little sister and brother, but they're both on vacation."

"And you? Why aren't you on vacation?"

She sighed and looked away. "I've got summer courses. I'm trying to graduate early."

"Ambitious."

She shrugged. "I guess."

Madison walked over to the large refrigerator and opened the doors, taking a moment before plucking a bottle of water out of the rack.

"Get you some water, Sheriff?"

"No, I'm fine. But thank you."

She closed the doors and opened the bottle as she walked back to the center island. The girl took a long swallow of water then set the bottle down and used the towel around her neck to dab her lips and wipe her forehead. As Spenser waited, she slipped her notebook and pen out of her pocket and flipped to a clean page.

"So, what is this about?"

"You and Rachel are close," Spenser started.

"We've known each other since we were practically babies," she said. "I love her like she's my own sister."

"It's good to have friends like that."

Madison's face flushed, and she held a trembling hand to her mouth. She fell silent for a moment as she gathered herself. She finally raised eyes which were growing red and watery, and seemed to be fighting back her tears.

"Do you have any idea where she is or what happened to her?" she asked, her voice trembling.

"We're working on that," she responded. "I just need to talk to you about some texts you and Rachel exchanged some months back."

She cocked her head, and a strange expression crossed her face, obviously disturbed that she had read her supposedly private exchanges with her friend.

"We text a lot," she said.

"We all do," Spenser replied. "But I want to talk specifically about some messages you two sent back and forth about when Rachel mentioned that somebody was watching her?"

Madison looked away and seemed to be trying to remember. After a few moments of reflection, she seemed to recall the conversation and nodded.

"Yeah, I remember that. I remember that I didn't give it a lot of credence at the time," she said slowly. "Rachel is paranoid, and she's always jumping at shadows. She's always looking over her shoulder like somebody's out to get her."

"As a woman in the world today, it's not a bad idea to always keep your eyes open."

"I don't disagree. But like I tell Rachel all the time, you can't live your life in fear, or you're not really living. Bad things happen sometimes, and you can either choose to let them define you and make you live in fear for the rest of your life, or you can choose to overcome them, take control of yourself, and live the way you want to live."

Spenser nodded. The girl had a good head on her shoulders. Her words brought to mind how she was reacting to moving in with Ryker and the fear it inspired within her, how it threatened to paralyze her. Worse, how it was threatening to make her run away from something good. Something pure. Something she never dared think she'd have in her life again.

"Like I tell her, you can be smart and aware of your surroundings without assuming there's somebody in every shadow you pass," Madison finished.

"So, nothing about her telling you she was being watched seemed different to you this time?"

She shook her head. "No. It's not the first time she talked about somebody watching her. It happened so often. It just kind of got to be a joke between us."

"Holly is the third of your group, right? I hear you all are like the Three Musketeers?"

"We are."

"From what I understand, which admittedly may not be much, Holly never mentioned Rachel talking to her about any of this."

Madison grinned ruefully. "Hols is a sweetheart, but she can be a little hardcore. She's got no filter and if you're being an idiot, she's not afraid to tell you that. Rachel didn't tell her because she didn't want to be told she was being stupid and to grow up. She doesn't mean it in, like, a mean way or anything. But she just kind of tells the hard truths whether we want to hear them or not. Rach talked to me about stuff like that because I'm usually nicer about it."

A wry laugh floated from Madison's mouth as she considered her words, but it quickly faded away as a look of horror replaced it as realization stole over her.

"Sheriff, did I—"

"No, Madison, this isn't your fault. You couldn't have known."

"But if I'd taken it more seriously."

"Like you said, she jumped at shadows. There is no way you could have known what was going to happen," Spenser tried to reassure her. "The only person to blame is the person who took her. Period. So, try not to beat yourself up."

"I just… oh my God."

The tears spilled from the corners of her eyes and raced down her face. Madison used the towel to wipe them away, then buried her face in it, hiding herself from Spenser, her shoulders shaking as she sobbed. Spenser gave her a few minutes to settle down.

"I'm sorry," Madison said, her quavering voice raspy.

"It's okay. There's nothing for you to be sorry about," Spenser replied.

She wiped her face with the towel again, then drew in a long, shaky breath and held it for a few seconds before letting it out again. Spenser gave her a couple of beats to compose herself. The guilt seemed to be overwhelming her.

"Madison, I'm assuming Rachel spoke to you about somebody watching her outside of your text exchanges?"

She nodded. "Yeah. She did."

"And what did she tell you?"

She shrugged. "I mean, it was a while ago. I don't really recall everything."

"That's okay. Just tell me what you remember."

The girl chewed on the end of her towel for a minute as she looked away, trying to dredge up those memories.

"I mean… she was just saying things like she was being watched. Like everywhere. At home, school, work… she wasn't specific about anything. It's not like she saw the guy. She just told me that somebody was watching her and mentioned that things from her room went missing a couple of times—"

"Wait, she said things from her room went missing?"

"Yeah, things like little pieces of jewelry. Oh, and a couple of pairs of her panties," she said. "But you have to understand Rach. She's kind of absent-minded sometimes. She's always losing things. I can't tell you the number of times she's lost her sunglasses or her phone only to find it in her bag later. Her telling me things went missing is as common as her telling me something's creeping her out. It sounds terrible—even more so now—but it kind of got to be like the boy who cried wolf. I'd just tease her and try to take her mind off it."

Misplacing her glasses or phone was one thing. Pairs of panties going missing was something else entirely. That spoke to another level of obsession. Knowing Rachel's stalker had been in the Kehoe house—in her room—and had taken personal trophies added a whole new layer of danger to this whole situation. It made things even more urgent than they already were.

"Actually, she and her boss Adam are pretty tight," Madison said thoughtfully. "Like, a month ago or so, I remember she said there was some guy in the restaurant that was creeping her out. She told me she made Adam walk her out to her car. Nothing came of it, but I remember she was kind of freaked out about it. He might be able to tell you something that can help."

"And do you recall anything happening after that?"

The girl shook her head. "No, I don't remember her mentioning anything. I'm sure she would have told me if it had."

Spenser tucked her small notebook into her pocket and was just about to wrap things up when something Madison had said earlier flashed in her brain like a neon sign. She silently kicked herself for not seizing on it earlier. For letting her thoughts about Ryker and that whole situation cloud her mind and get in the way of her doing her job.

"Madison, earlier you said something like, bad things may happen—did something bad happen to Rachel?" she asked. "Did this bad thing that happened cause her to become paranoid and start jumping at shadows?"

The girl's eyes widened as she realized she may have said too much. She gnawed on her bottom lip and looked away, obviously reluctant to answer the question. Her hesitation to reply told Spenser something had indeed happened. Something that had left Rachel traumatized and fearful.

"Madison?"

She ran a hand across her face. "I'm the only person she told about it, and she made me swear that I would never tell another soul."

"I'm sure she'd understand. Especially if it helps us find her."

"Trust me, it won't. She would kill me if I told you."

"Madison, knowing what happened to her might be really important to her disappearance."

The girl shifted on her feet and looked positively tormented. She was caught between wanting to help her friend but also wanting to keep her word to her. She finally sighed and seemed to deflate, her decision made.

"When we were sophomores in high school, we were at a party, and she was attacked by a senior named Billy Keene. He tried to rape her," Madison finally admitted. "One of his friends,

Doug Pillar, walked in on them and pulled him off before he could, then got Rach out of there."

"Billy Keene?"

She nodded. "I say it has nothing to do with what's going on now because Billy died in a car accident a year later. He was drunk and slammed into a tree," she said, then muttered, "Good riddance to bad rubbish."

"What about this, Doug—"

"Was killed along with Billy," she responded. "But that's when Rach started to jump at shadows. That's when she got paranoid. It took her forever to trust people again, but she was never really the same after that."

"That seems to explain things."

"Sheriff, you can't tell anybody. She never told her parents… not even Holly. She only told me because I was there at the party with her. You have to keep this to yourself."

Spenser considered it for a minute. She'd do her due diligence on Doug Pillar and Billy Keene, but if they truly were dead, then Madison was right, and she didn't see how it could be a factor in Rachel's disappearance. It didn't seem relevant to the case. About the only bearing it had was that it gave her some background on Rachel Kehoe, so she nodded.

"You have my word," Spenser said.

"Thank you, Sheriff."

"Okay, I seem to have what I need then. Thank you for your time, Madison."

As Spenser made her way out of Madison's home, the sound of the girl's soft crying chased her all the way to the door. It tore at her heart but filled her with even more determination to figure out what happened and find Rachel Kehoe.

She just hoped she'd be able to find her alive.

CHAPTER TWENTY-TWO

As Spenser pulled into the lot outside of Overtime Sports Bar & Grill, she received a text from Jacob, who confirmed that both Billy Keene and Doug Pillar were, in fact, dead. They'd been killed in a single-car accident a year after they'd graduated high school. Keene's blood alcohol content at the time of the crash was 1.2, far higher than the state's legal limit of .08.

"What a waste," she muttered.

As she found a parking spot, Spenser pondered the relationship between the girls. She thought about the fact that Rachel had shared things with Madison that she hadn't shared with Holly and probably vice versa. It made her consider the nature of her own relationships, and, until that moment, Spenser hadn't really realized there were things she didn't share with Marley and other things she didn't share with Ryker.

Like Rachel, Spenser didn't tell everybody everything. She could see that she kept some things to herself and sometimes tailored her messages to the audience. With that perspective, Spenser understood why Rachel might share with one friend but not the other. Because they'd all grown up together and were tighter than sisters, Rachel obviously knew who she could talk to about her fears and who she couldn't. She knew who would be more receptive, who'd be more dismissive. She would know who she could get what she needed from.

She climbed out of the Bronco and reached in to grab her cane, then paused. She was feeling good. Better than she had in forever, really. The pain that had been so intense it stole her breath after she'd left the hospital had dulled significantly. She was almost to the point where she could get around without wanting to cry, and she wasn't leaning on the cane nearly as much, which she considered real progress. But Marley and Ryker would have her butt if she pushed herself too hard and took a step backward, so she kept the cane but was optimistic she'd be able to ditch it in the next day or two.

Pulling the door open, she stepped into Overtime, and her senses were immediately assaulted by a barrage of sight and sound. The one word that came to mind as she looked around was chaos. It was like that chain restaurant TGI Fridays had made a baby with Dave & Buster's and birthed the most obnoxious sports bar in America. It looked like two different establishments slapped together under one name. On the left was the sports bar side of the place. A myriad of TV screens showed soccer games, sports highlight shows, and music videos. It was stuffed with small, round tables, and a collection of memorabilia from every sport imaginable. It also had so much neon, that it made Spenser wonder if she'd somehow teleported to Vegas.

On the right side of the building was the restaurant. It was a world away from fine dining, but the food on the tables of the half-filled place didn't look half bad. The lighting was soft, without a trace of neon to be found, but TV screens still hung all over the place, allowing people to have a meal without missing whatever game was on at the time. The restaurant side of the building was decorated with a collection of mismatched, vintage items, giving it an eclectic, bohemian motif.

A large U-shaped bar sat flush between the two sides and serviced both with seating all around it. Other than the aroma of frying food, the two sides of the building didn't seem to match each other in any discernable way, and yet, she had to admit that it still somehow… worked. Overtime was chaos. Pure and utter chaos. But there was an energy in the place that was infectious. If she were a sports fan, she might want to hang out there.

"Sheriff Song."

Spenser turned to find a man she'd never met before stepping over to her. Mid-thirties, about her height, the man had cappuccino-colored hair neatly cut and parted on the right, milk chocolate-colored eyes, and a slight build. He was dressed in a black button-down shirt with the sleeves rolled up to his elbows, black khakis, and black shoes. Without a hair out of place or a speck of lint on his uniform to be seen, the man was fastidious in appearance and prim in demeanor.

The silver, oval-shaped nametag hanging above the pocket on his left breast read, "Adam." He extended his hand, so Spenser took it. His grip was firm.

"This is fortuitous," she said. "You're just the man I came here to see."

"It's fortuitous indeed, then."

"Have we met before?"

"No, we haven't, but I'm familiar with who you are," he replied. "I keep up with things around town. I'm glad to see you back on your feet, Sheriff. It looks like you're on the mend."

"I am. And thank you."

"What can I do for you?"

"Can we have a word in private?"

His face darkened, and his expression sobered. "Is this about Rachel?"

"It is."

The emotion in his eyes was unmistakable. He cared for her. Adam took a moment to gather himself and then nodded.

"Give me just a minute," he said.

Spenser watched as Adam walked over to a young Hispanic woman and had a quiet word with her. Adam waved at Spenser to follow him, so she did. He led her through the kitchen and out a back door that led to the parking lot in the back. The door closed behind them, and Adam took a few steps away as he pulled a vape out of his pocket and took a hit. As a thin stream of smoke that smelled like cotton candy drifted from the corner of his mouth, he turned back to Spenser.

"Have you found her? Is she all right?"

"We haven't found her yet but are still working a number of leads. We will find her."

"Do you have any idea who took her?"

"We're still working on that."

He hit his vape again, unconvinced. "A lot of people around town say it was the Okasha… especially with how badly James Burnham was chewed up."

"Is that what you say?"

A wry chuckle drifted from his mouth as easily as his vape smoke. "No. Unlike some people in this town, I'm not an idiot. I'm just amazed that this sort of ridiculous hysteria takes root whenever something like this happens. It never fails. About five years ago, a kid went missing. People were absolutely sure it was the Okasha. Armed mobs were forming to go hunt the thing down. It was absolutely nuts."

"What happened?"

"Kid turned up a day later. Turned out, he was hiding out in the woods after getting into a fight with his brother."

Spenser grinned. "Well, I can assure you we are not looking for the Okasha."

Adam took another hit from his vape and nodded. "So, what are you looking for?"

"Right now, I'm looking for somebody who may have been stalking Rachel," she responded. "Somebody who'd been watching her. Following her around."

"Stalking her?"

"Yeah. We've developed some evidence that suggests Rachel might have had a stalker. She was afraid she was being watched.

That somebody was following her around," she said. "Did she mention anything about that to you?"

He opened his mouth to respond but then closed it again as if something had just occurred to him. Adam looked away, seeming to be struggling to remember what it was. Spenser gave him the time he needed to collect his thoughts, having a sense that whatever it was he was trying to recall could be important. It took a couple of minutes, but he finally raised his gaze.

"I honestly didn't think much of it at the time, but about a month ago, there was a guy in here who creeped out some of the wait staff. Rachel in particular," he said.

"Creeped them out. How so?"

"Just… I recall she said he was just staring at her. Made her uncomfortable."

"Do you know who he was?"

Adam shook his head. "As best I recall, it was a really busy night… there was a big game on or something, so we were packed. I didn't see the guy myself, but I got the sense that Rachel was familiar with him. I was just too busy at the time to question her about it."

"What makes you say she was familiar with him?"

"I… I don't really remember. There was something she said, but I can't quite recall what it was. I'm sorry."

A frustrated growl burst from his mouth as he realized he couldn't remember what might be a vital clue. Adam shook his head, looking absolutely sick to his stomach. He squatted down and drew deep on his vape, blowing out a long breath of smoke. Spenser could see that the emotion etched into his features was as strong and poignant as she'd seen on the faces of Holly and Madison. It was clear that Rachel had touched people's lives and that they loved her deeply.

"It's only now that you're here talking about a stalker that it even occurred to me," he said miserably.

He shook his head and ran a hand through his hair.

"You care about her," Spenser said.

"I do. Very much… but not in the way you're probably assuming," he added quickly. "She's like a little sister to me."

"Like a little sister?"

"Rachel introduced me to my boyfriend," he said, slamming that door in her mind.

"Oh. Right," she said.

Her cheeks flushed, and she was clobbered by a sense of stupidity for making stupid assumptions; Spenser took a second to recover and closed out any idea that Adam might be involved in what happened. Rachel was taken by somebody who wanted her. Who needed to claim her as his own. That obsession, combined with the offender's need to possess her, meant the abduction was sexual in nature, which seemed to preclude Adam. She mentally crossed him off the suspect list, which had been little more than a fleeting idea, anyway. But it was good to have one more investigative avenue shut down.

"Okay, so that night this all happened, what did you do?" Spenser asked.

"Like I said, I didn't have time to go and deal with it, and she didn't bring it up again, so I put it out of my mind," he said, sounding even more miserable than before. "But before she left for the night, I remember she was pretty rattled and asked me to walk her out to her car, so I did. And I swear I saw somebody out there in the parking lot, but I assumed it was a homeless guy. It didn't seem like a big deal, and I still had a lot to do before I could close up, so I watched her drive off, then went inside and went back to work."

His face reddened as he fought to hold his emotions in check. He sniffed back his tears, then cleared his throat and stood up a little straighter as he took another hit off his vape. Seeing how hard he was taking it was hard to watch.

"Did you happen to get a look at this guy?"

He shook his head. "No, I didn't. But some of the other wait staff did. I remember hearing them talking about it after I walked Rachel out."

"Do you remember who exactly?"

He looked away for a minute as he combed his memories. "Yeah, it was… it was Eric, Dominique, and Sage. Yeah, that sounds right."

Spenser jotted it down in her notebook, and a plan started to form in her head. She wasn't sure how effective it was going to be, but she was going to have to explore every avenue, regardless of how unlikely or how long the odds were.

"I need your help with something, Adam."

CHAPTER TWENTY-THREE

SPENSER SAT AT THE DESK IN HER OFFICE, TAPPING HER pen on the pad of paper in front of her. She stared off into nothing and continued to pick at the case in her mind. She had a pile of incomplete pieces and no idea how they fit together to make a coherent whole. Nothing was taking shape, and she had no idea what the final image even looked like. She had no idea where Rachel was or how to even find her. With a frustrated growl, Spenser launched her pen across the office. It hit the wall and bounced to the floor with a clatter.

"Wow. You could have put my eye out."

Ryker stood in the doorway with that adorable smile on his face that made him look like a little boy. The emotion in his gaze made her heart flutter. Her mind drifted back to what had gone through her head when Madison Kirk had talked about living in fear versus living freely earlier in the day. She didn't want to live in fear. She wanted to live free and to be happy. But she was so scared and couldn't seem to get out from beneath its dark shadow.

"What are you doing here?" she asked.

"Came to make sure you weren't overdoing it."

"As you can see, I'm not even doing it, let alone overdoing it."

"Good. I'm glad to see that," he replied. "How are you feeling?"

"I'm good."

He arched an eyebrow as he stepped into Spenser's office, dropped into the chair in front of her desk, and leaned back, holding her gaze steadily. Ryker's face was painted with skepticism. She rolled her eyes and gave him a little smile.

"Honest. I'm a lot better," she said. "In fact, I'm so much better. I can probably get off this cane in the next day or so."

"Is that so?"

Spenser stood quickly and bit back the quick flash of pain that shot through her abdomen. She bit the inside of her cheek until it subsided, which it did, far faster than it had just the day before. It was progress. Holding her arms out, Spenser turned in a circle.

"Did you want me to tap dance for you, too?" Spenser asked.

"If you're up to it, sure."

She grabbed a balled-up piece of paper on her desk and fired it at Ryker. It bounced off his chest, drawing a deep, booming laugh from him. Spenser sat back down again.

"So, are you just here to check up on me?" she asked.

"Partly," he replied. "I also figured since I was in the area, I might take you to dinner."

"I wish I could. But I've got a lot going on here."

"What's going on?"

"I've got some of the employees from Overtime coming in," she replied. "They're going to sit with Jacob for a composite sketch of our potential suspect."

"Jacob can sketch?"

"Right? Surprised me, too. But when I said I needed to get a sketch artist in, he said he could do it. He showed me some of his work, and yeah, he's pretty good."

"I had no idea he had such a hidden talent."

"Me either. I mean, he uses a computer program to help, but his freehand stuff is shockingly good," she said. "Hopefully, we can use the sketch to get an idea of who this guy is. If we can figure out who he is, we might be able to figure out where he took Rachel."

Ryker frowned, and his expression grew sober. "Do you really think she's still alive? I mean, it's been days since—"

"I'm going to believe she's alive until we find concrete proof that she isn't."

He nodded. "I understand that. I just want you to prepare yourself for this not having a happy ending. I don't want to see it hit you hard."

"If you're right, it's going to hit me hard whether I'm prepared or not. You, more than most people, know you can't prepare for a… bad outcome."

"No, I suppose you can't. But I can see you're taking this case to heart—"

"I take all my cases to heart."

"It seems like this one more than most."

Spenser sat back in her chair, a frown curling her lips. She supposed he wasn't wrong. She had a connection to this case that seemed stronger than most of her other cases. Spenser hadn't stopped to really analyze it too deeply, but she figured part of it was because Rachel was so young and still had so much life ahead of her. It probably wasn't fair or right, nor did it diminish the importance of all the cases she handled or how she handled them, but she seemed to take cases involving young people more to heart than others.

"Anyway, I should probably stick around and wait for the sketch," Spenser said.

Jacob stepped into the doorway of her office. "I just got off the phone with the witnesses. Two of the three are working tonight and won't be coming in until tomorrow morning. I'm going to sit with the one—Eric—tonight, but I want to wait to get the descriptions from the other two before I finalize the sketch."

"Damn," Spenser muttered. "I was hoping to have that tonight."

"Sorry, boss. It's not going to happen if we want the most accurate sketch we can get."

Spenser drummed her fingers on the desk, processing the information and trying to come up with a new plan of action. Jacob sighed dramatically.

"What I'm saying is, nothing is going to happen until tomorrow morning, so there's no reason for you not to go to dinner with this fine, handsome, upstanding gentleman who wants to take care of you," he said.

"Yeah. What he said," Ryker replied with a guffaw. "Jacob, you are a very smart, wise man."

"Yeah, I'm aware," Jacob replied.

Spenser smiled, trying to tamp it down. "Okay, okay. Point taken."

She got to her feet, packed a few things in her messenger bag, and then slung it over her shoulder. Ryker immediately took it from her and slung it over his own shoulder as she grabbed her borrowed cane from the corner where she'd stored it.

"Thank you for staying to do this, Jacob," Spenser said.

"Hey, it's my job."

"Thank you anyway."

"You're welcome," he replied. "Now, go on and have a nice dinner with this nice big hunk of man flesh."

Spenser's cheeks flushed, and she chuckled. "Call me right away if anything pops off."

"Of course."

"I mean it. Call me—not your sister."

"Hey, I remember that she's banished from the office until tomorrow morning," he replied. "I love my sister but I'm not taking a bullet from you for her."

Spenser turned to Ryker. "You're right. He's smart and wise."

"You're just now realizing that?" Jacob teased.

Spenser walked out with Ryker and once they got outside, she took his hand and gave it a squeeze, drawing a soft smile from him. They walked hand in hand to the parking lot but then Spenser paused with her keys in her hand.

"Why don't I drive? I'll bring you back to the office in the morning," he said.

"You sure you want to get up that early?"

"When do I ever not get up that early?"

"Good point."

"What are you in the mood for tonight?"

Spenser scrunched up her nose. "I'm actually kind of craving pizza."

"Pizza sounds good to me."

They climbed into Ryker's truck and pulled out of the lot. As they drove, Spenser's mind kept spinning around her conversation with Madison. She thought about the nature of her own fears, how she'd let it paralyze her, and how she'd let it put a strain on her relationship with Ryker. For his part, he'd been understanding and kind. But Spenser feared that if she kept up with this hot and cold, nail-biting, terrified of her own shadow routine, he would eventually grow tired of it and move on.

Some dark part in the back of her mind told her it might be better for him if he did. He didn't deserve to be jerked around like this. He deserved somebody who could give herself to him unabashedly and without reservation. Somebody who didn't let her fears overwhelm her. He deserved somebody who was capable of returning the emotional energy he was willing to give—the emotional energy he had been giving her. And though she held that same emotion in her heart and cared for him the way he cared for her, Spenser was still terrified of it.

Spenser wanted to be with him. But by the same token, she was afraid to be with him. And he didn't deserve that. He deserved somebody stronger. Somebody who wasn't such a train wreck. As much as he deserved somebody better than her, Spenser also didn't want to give him up. It was selfish. It was wrong. But she was a hot mess and couldn't manage to stop herself.

"Vinnie's okay?" he asked.

"You read my mind."

They climbed out of Ryker's truck, and she took his hand again as they walked into the restaurant together. Vinnie's Pizzeria was a small, locally owned shop that specialized in Spenser's favorite New York-style pizza. But they also made an impressive Chicago-style deep dish and a Detroit-style pan pizza. Very few places could master all the different styles, but Vinnie's managed to do them all justice. It was a popular place, with the high school set coming in after school or after big games. Vinnie's was rarely empty, as was the case as they walked in—the restaurant was three-quarters full, most of the crowd on the younger and louder side.

Vinnie's had a carefully crafted faux grimy look that marked some of the best pizza joints in New York, and the air was redolent with an aroma straight from heaven. Spenser's mouth was watering the minute they hit the door, where they were greeted by Vinnie himself, a mid-forties transplant from New York who was heavyset, had a thick mop of black hair, dark eyes, and a bushy mustache that made him look a lot like Super Mario, from that series of video games. He was a gregarious, good-natured man who had a smile and a kind word for everybody.

"Hey, Sheriff. Glad to see you back on your feet," he said in his distinctive east coast accent. "This fella takin' good care of you?"

"I'm trying to," Ryker replied.

"That's about all we can do, am I right?" Vinnie said with a booming laugh.

"Especially when you're trying to take care of somebody as stubborn as this one."

"I hear that," Vinnie said and clapped Ryker on the shoulder.

Spenser chuffed. "Standing right here. You guys know I can hear you, right?"

"Hey, don't get me wrong, Sheriff," Vinnie said. "I like that you do your own thing and don't let people walk all over you. It's very New York of you. Much respect."

They all shared a laugh as Spenser's stomach rumbled. She couldn't remember the last time she ate, and she now realized she was starving.

"You two look hungry. How about I find you a table?" Vinnie said.

"You read my mind."

"Follow me."

Vinnie led them to a table that was tucked in the corner near the front windows and gave them a view of the street outside. It was set apart from the main room where all the rowdy kids were running amok and tamped the noise down a bit. The table was covered with a red and white checkered vinyl cloth and held a jar for red pepper flakes, salt, and pepper, a chrome napkin holder, and a wicker basket chianti bottle that had been turned into a candle holder. It was high on the cheese factor but was somehow perfect. Once they were settled, he handed them paper menus and smiled widely at them both.

"I'll get somebody over here to take care of you," he said. "Good to see you both. Thanks for comin' in tonight."

"Wouldn't go anywhere else for pizza," she said.

"That's what I like to hear."

He bustled away and a moment later, a cute, perky girl no more than eighteen or nineteen flounced over, introducing herself as Eileen, and took their orders. Within two minutes, they had their wine, and a few minutes after that, they had their antipasto plate to tide them over until their pizza was ready. Ryker took a sip of his wine, eyeing her over the rim of the glass. His scrutiny set Spenser's stomach fluttering and brought a flush of heat to her cheeks.

"Why are you looking at me that way?" she asked.

"Because I can. Because I want to," he replied. "And because you're the most beautiful woman in the world."

She giggled like a schoolgirl as her face burned so hot that she expected to see columns of smoke rising from her ears. Ryker set his glass down softly, then picked up her hand and caressed her knuckles with his thumb.

"I want this to work, Spenser. I want you to be comfortable living with me," he said. "But I also wanted to tell you that if you're not ready yet, that's okay. I can wait. I don't want us to force anything or move before we're both ready."

Spenser's heart swelled so big that she was half-afraid it was going to burst in her chest. It was for reasons like that she was completely unworthy of him. His kindness, compassion, and most of all, his understanding of her quirks and her fears, made her feel lighter than air. It made her feel safe. And it made her feel secure. All of which gave her a sense of absolute terror that she not only didn't deserve it, but that she could lose it all in the blink of an eye.

But Madison and Jacob's words echoed through her mind. Fear and change. Fear of change. She could either remain a prisoner to her fears, shutting out the things that she wanted and made her happy, or she could break the shackles and take control of her life. She could choose to live.

"No," she said softly. "I'm ready."

"Are you sure?"

She nodded. "Yes. You make me happier than I have any right to be, and I want this. I want to build a life with you."

He raised her hand and placed a gentle kiss on her knuckles. Spenser's heart quivered with fear but was also infused with a joy she hadn't known in a very long time. Ryker leaned across the table and, gave her a chaste peck on the lips and smiled.

"You make me happy," he said.

"And you make me happy, too."

Movement in the corner of her eye drew Spenser's attention, and when she turned, the lightness in her heart turned dark and heavy. The smile slipped from her face, and she was suddenly consumed by a sense of dread mixed with grief. On the street just outside the pizzeria, Brock and Denise Kehoe shuffled along, passing out flyers emblazoned with the word "Missing" in bold, black letters above a photo of Rachel wearing a radiant smile.

Spenser met Denise's eyes through the glass, and her heart nearly stopped dead in her chest as guilt swallowed it whole. The woman's eyes were red, puffy, and encircled by dark shadows. She clearly hadn't slept in days and looked exhausted. Denise's face hardened, and she clenched her jaw, driving that dagger of guilt deeper into Spenser's chest. She could almost hear the woman's thoughts, sharp and accusing: "How could you be sitting there, having a nice meal and enjoying Ryker's company while my daughter's missing?"

After a few moments, Denise looked away. She and Brock shuffled on, handing out flyers to everybody they passed. Emotions swelled inside of Spenser so dark and thick, they threatened to choke her. Ryker took her hand again and gave it a firm squeeze.

"Are you okay?" he asked, his voice soft and gentle.

"Not really."

Spenser craned her neck and watched the couple continue on down the street, taping flyers to posts on the street and handing them out to the people they passed. Each one was like a hammer blow that drove her sense of culpability deeper.

"Actually, not at all," she said, her voice little more than a whisper.

CHAPTER TWENTY-FOUR

"IS THAT IT?" SPENSER ASKED.

"Uhh... yeah," Jacob responded.

She held up the page with the composite sketch Jacob had aggregated from the descriptions given by the employees who'd seen the man who had made them all so uncomfortable that night at Overtime.

"This could literally be just about any mid-thirties Caucasian man in town," Spenser said. "Hell, it could be almost any white guy in the entire Pacific Northwest."

Jacob shrugged. "I can only work with what I'm given. This is what they gave me."

"Wow," Spenser said.

There was literally nothing about the face in the sketch that stood out. Light brown or hazel-colored eyes, sandy blonde hair, six-foot-one to six-foot-two, with a lean build, and average in every single way. His features were symmetrical and ordinary. Regular-shaped eyes, a regular-shaped nose, and a regular-shaped brow. There was nothing distinctive about the man in the sketch. Nothing at all. It was the sort of face that was so plain that the man was probably invisible in a crowd.

Spenser was certain the employees who'd come in had done their best, but the aggregate of their memories was the sort of face that was so indistinct that Spenser had to wonder if it was real or just the jumbled, confused memories of people trying to recall something—anything—about a man they'd most likely forgotten five minutes after he left the restaurant.

"Sorry, boss," Jacob said.

"It's not your fault. Like you said, you can only work with what you're given. The sketch is really good. It's just really—"

"Plain. Indistinct. Ordinary. Vanilla."

"Right."

Amanda ambled into the conference room and plucked the page from Spenser's fingertips. "Wow. Should we put out an APB for generic white male? I'm sure that'll go pretty well for us."

Jacob pulled a face. "I remember Mom always telling us that if you don't have something nice to say, you should shut your cake hole."

"Yeah, Mom used to say a lot."

Spenser grinned. "Sounds like somebody got some rest."

"You were right about me needing some sleep. I'm good now," she said with a nod. "I'm fired up and ready to go, Sheriff. What's our next step?"

"As unhelpful as this sketch is, I want to get it into circulation," Spenser answered. "As generic as he looks, it's possible somebody might recognize this guy."

"I'm on it. I'll have flyers made up," Jacob offered.

"Good. Thank you," Spenser said. "Then give every deputy on duty a stack. I want them to start handing these things out."

"On it," he replied.

"I'll take one of the flyers by the Kehoe house and see if they have any idea who he might be," Spenser said.

"Where do you want me, Sheriff?"

"Take one of the flyers out to the Burnham house and see if they recognize him."

"Didn't you say this was about Rachel?"

"It is. But we still have no clue where his path crossed with hers. It might have been out at the Burnham place. Maybe he works on the farm out there," Spenser answered.

"Got it," she said. "That makes sense."

Spenser could see her tucking that away as another lesson learned in her deputy's ongoing education. She was trying to teach Amanda to take a three-hundred-and-sixty-degree view of a case and see all the angles rather than get locked into one narrow view. Yes, Spenser was certain this case centered around one man's obsession with Rachel. But where that obsession began was as important as anything else they might uncover. Finding that initial meeting could very well help the rest of the puzzle pieces fall into place.

Alice rushed into the room, looking as frazzled as Spenser had ever seen her. "Sheriff—"

"What is it, Alice? What's wrong?"

"You need to get out to Flick's. I'm afraid there's trouble brewing."

"Again?"

"I'm afraid so."

Spenser looked at Amanda. "Grab whoever's in the bullpen, and let's roll."

Climbing out of the Bronco, Spenser surveyed the situation in front of her. Another mob had gathered out in front of Flick's Sporting Goods again. And as he had the first time, Hurley Weaver was out in front, whipping the crowd into a frenzy. This time, though, he had a friend with him, working hard to fire everybody up.

"Rafe Johansen," Spenser muttered. "That's awesome."

Spenser glanced at the cane sitting on the front seat of the Bronco but left it where it was and closed the truck door. She couldn't afford to show the slightest hint of weakness. Small flares of pain burst in her abdomen as she walked across the parking lot, doing her best to keep from limping. Doing her best to project an image of strength. Three more squad cars roared into the parking lot behind her. Amanda, Deputy Bustos, and Deputy Summers jumped out of their cars and hustled over to catch up with her. Their bodies were taut, and the tension showed on their faces as they looked at the gun-toting mob in the parking lot.

"Settle down," Spenser muttered. "We're here to de-escalate the situation."

"It's a powder keg," Summers said.

"That's right. It is. And the smallest spark is going to set this thing off," Spenser replied. "Keep your hands away from your weapons and remain calm."

As she approached, Spenser caught Rafe's eye, and a grim, reptilian smile stretched across his thin lips. He glared at her with pure malevolence. His hatred for her began with her arrest of his son, which fueled his decision to run against her in the next election. But his campaign hit a big bump, and he clearly still hadn't gotten over being humiliated in front of the council. He still very obviously carried a burning grudge when she came out of his revenge fantasy unscathed while he left with a pile of eggs on his face.

But his setback obviously hadn't deterred him. If anything, it seemed to have made him even more determined to destroy her. Rafe was an opportunist, and he was clearly using Rachel's disappearance in an attempt to bolster his profile while trying to tarnish hers. Rafe turned back to the crowd. He and Hurley were busy whipping it into a frenzy.

"Here she is, folks," Rafe announced. "Sheriff Spenser Song, who, unless something has changed, continues to fail to protect our kids and this town. She owes us all an explanation and needs to answer some questions. What do you say?"

The crowd, about twice the size of the one Hurley had mustered a few days back, roared their approval, and dozens of angry eyes turned to her. She recognized many of the men in the crowd. Rafe had gone out of his way to draw the troublemakers, disaffected and perpetually angry, to his little rally. Now that he'd been discredited and embarrassed in front of the entire town, men like these were likely going to make up his voting base in the coming election.

As she surveyed the crowd, Spenser wondered how many of the men in front of her actually knew Rachel or the Kehoe family and how many of them were simply there because they wanted to vent their own anger. Or because they wanted to be part of something that might distract them from their own empty, meaningless existences. The crowd shouted questions over one another, creating a cacophony as loud as a jet engine.

"Have you even met Rachel Kehoe or her family?" Spenser asked.

"Of course. Would I be here trying to get justice for her if I didn't?"

"You'd stab your own mother to get ahead."

A cruel little grin spread across his lips that turned her stomach. He'd never met Rachel Kehoe. He wasn't there for her. As with everything else he'd ever done, Rafe Johansen was only there for his personal benefit. Spenser wasn't surprised.

"Still trying to breathe life into your corpse of a campaign, huh?" Spenser asked as she stepped up beside Rafe.

"By the looks of things out here, it seems like it's going to be a lot closer than you assume it's going to be," he replied.

"You really think there are enough gullible, angry men to push you over the top?"

"There are enough people unsatisfied with your performance in the job to do the trick," he replied smoothly. "Your failure to find Rachel Kehoe is just the latest example."

"So, keeping us divided and stoking fear and hate is the meat of your campaign, then?"

"I'll do whatever it takes to get you out of office."

Spenser turned to him. "You do realize your son committed a serious crime, right? I mean, you're pissed at me because I held your son to the same standards of the law I hold everybody else to. What makes him so special? What makes him deserving of special treatment? Do you think he's above the law because of his last name? Because he's a Johansen, he should be given some special consideration? Is that about right?"

Rafe's face darkened, and his lips curled back in a sneer. "My son is a good kid who made a stupid mistake. But rather than cut him a break, you ruined his life. No good college is going to take him after this. And any chance at a career? That's gone, too. Because of you."

"Because of his actions. Not mine."

Rafe growled and looked like he wanted to punch Spenser in the face. Part of her wanted him to try. Banged up or not, she was angry. He was pushing her buttons, and she had to resist the temptation to put her hands on him. As if he'd materialized out of nowhere, Ryker stepped between them and glowered at Rafe as he loomed over the man. Rafe took a quick step back and tried to bite back the expression of intimidation that flashed across his face.

"This isn't your concern, Ryker," he said. "This is between me and her."

"What do you mean? I'm here for you, Rafe," Ryker replied.

"For me?"

Ryker nodded. "Yeah. I'd hate to see you say or do something stupid and have this one beat you unconscious. I'm just looking out for you."

A sour expression crossed Rafe's face, and he took another step away, then turned to the crowd, holding up his hands for silence. It took a minute, but the shouting slowly tapered off. Spenser glanced at Ryker with earnest appreciation.

"Sheriff Song has failed all of us by not finding the monster who took Rachel Kehoe and left James Burnham for dead," Rafe called out, drawing an angry roar from the crowd. "We're going to go out and do what she couldn't—we're going to find this man who abducted one of our town's daughters and bring him to justice. We're going to do Sheriff Song's job for her!"

The men in the crowd cheered and looked ready to go into the woods and start shooting. Nothing good was going to come of it. Spenser rolled her eyes and shook her head, irritated that she had to have this conversation again… with many of the same men as the last time she'd had it. Spenser stepped forward and raised her arms, calling for quiet. That only seemed to rile them up even more as they hurled strings of sexist expletives at her. Off to the side, Rafe smiled, seemingly content that he'd done what he set out to do, which was turn the town against her.

Ryker stepped up beside her and glared at the men in the crowd, his eyes narrowed, his jaw clenched. Spenser had to admit, he cut an intimidating, even scary figure. The shouting tapered off once more as most of the men looked away, nobody seemingly able to meet Ryker's eyes. When the crowd was silent again, she turned to Ryker and gave him a silent thanks.

"Gentlemen, we've done this dance before. Just the other day, in fact," Spenser called out. "I can't stop you from going out into those woods with your guns. But I promise you that when something bad happens—and something bad will happen—I'm going to hold you accountable. I will prosecute you to the fullest extent of the law."

Jeers and shouts of outrage rained down on her, so Spenser let them have their moment. There was no use in trying to talk over them. That was a fight she wasn't going to win. Eventually, they settled down, though the hostility in the air was thicker than sludge.

"You can let carnival barkers like Hurley and Rafe here rile you up. You can take them at their word when they say I'm not doing my job. They're wrong and have absolutely no idea how to do this job, but hey, it's your right to follow them. And it's your right to go off into the woods on this idiot's errand they're sending you on," Spenser said. "But before you go, ask yourself this… when something goes wrong, and you accidentally shoot an innocent person—and mark my words, somebody in this audience will—are Hurley and Rafe going to be there by your side, helping you through it? Will they protect you? Will they even care? The answer to those questions is no. They're winding you up for their own purposes. You're pawns to them. That's all. But hey, do what you want, people. Just remember, when it all goes sideways on you, I will be there. They won't."

Spenser stepped back and cast a dark glare at Rafe before turning to her deputies. They all wore uneasy expressions.

"Let's go," Spenser said. "There's nothing we can do."

"They're all armed," Bustos said.

"Legally, they can be. If they want to go out in the woods and be morons because Rafe Johansen told them to, let them. We can't stop them. Let's get back to the office."

Without waiting for a reply, Spenser strode toward the Bronco. Ryker fell into step beside her. His truck was parked next to her. As they walked, Spenser saw a good portion of the crowd heading off into the woods on Johansen's fool's errand. Rafe himself was leaning against a post outside the store's doorway, his arms folded over his chest, a smirk on his face. What happened next didn't concern him. That smug look he wore said he'd accomplished what he'd set out to do in turning some of the town against her.

Spenser was certain that was going to be his game plan going forward—eroding small portions of her support until he had enough to undermine her completely. She wasn't sure he had the juice to do it. Not anymore. Not after his debacle down at City Hall and his failed attempt to assassinate her character. But he clearly wasn't going to stop trying. And that didn't mean he wasn't going to be able to notch footholds in voting groups here and there.

"Don't worry about him," Ryker said. "He's cooked. He just doesn't want to accept it."

She stopped at the Bronco and turned around, a slow, greasy sensation burbling in her gut. "I have a sick feeling that he's right."

"Right about what?"

"That this is going to be a hell of a lot closer than it should be," she said.

CHAPTER TWENTY-FIVE

Spenser knocked on the door of the Kehoe home and waited. And waited a little more. Two full minutes went by, and nobody answered the door. She knocked again and waited for another minute. When the Kehoes still didn't answer, an ominous sense of dread settled down over her. Surely, the man who'd taken Rachel wouldn't have come back for the rest of the family, would he? That didn't track with her theory of the crime.

Uneasiness gripped her tightly as Spenser walked around the house, peering in windows and trying doors. It was locked up tight, and she didn't see anything that raised any red flags. Moving over to the window that looked into the garage, Spenser peeked in and saw the family's car was gone and let out a small breath of relief. The car being gone, along with nothing looking amiss in the house, led her to conclude that perhaps they'd simply gone somewhere. Perhaps they needed to get away from the madness for a little while. She didn't blame them.

Spenser turned and looked toward the rear of the property. A six-foot high fence surrounded their backyard, but the tall pines of the forest loomed close to it; some of their bushy boughs even dipped over the border, a reminder that the more you tried to control Mother Nature, the less you were able to. As she stood there, Spenser heard footsteps approaching from behind. Casually sliding her hand to the butt of her Glock, she turned around. The tension in her shoulders and the adrenaline shot that had hit her veins ebbed immediately.

"Figured I'd find you out here," Amanda said.

"What are you doing here?"

"I finished up over at the Burnham place," she replied. "Spoiler alert, they didn't recognize Mr. Vanilla in our flyers."

"Can't say I'm surprised."

"What's going on here?"

"The Kehoes aren't home."

"That's kind of surprising. I'd have assumed they'd want to be close by just in case something in the case breaks."

Spenser shrugged. "Just because they're not here doesn't mean they're not close by. But even if they went to another state, I can't say I blame them for wanting to get away. Especially if they're convinced, Rachel isn't coming home alive."

Amanda was silent for a moment, then glanced at Spenser, with a strange, sad look on her face. "At this point, do you really think she is?"

"Like I keep telling everybody who asks the same thing… until we have proof that she's no longer alive, I'm going to keep working this case like she is."

"I understand and don't disagree, but she's been missing for days now. The likelihood that she's still alive out there somewhere—"

"Whether she's alive or not, whether she's been gone a day or a month, we're not taking our foot off the gas. We're going to keep working this the same way—as hard as we can. One way or the other, for the good or the ill, we're going to bring her home," Spenser said sharply.

Amanda's face flushed, and she shuffled her feet as she looked down. "I'm sorry, Sheriff. I didn't mean to imply we should lighten our approach or anything. I just … I can see how personally you're taking this, and I just want you to temper your expectations because I don't want to see this hit you hard if it doesn't break our way."

Spenser bit the inside of her cheek to keep from replying right away and saying something she might later regret. She was taking this case to heart. Like she'd told Ryker, she took all cases to heart. But something about seeing that sense of loss in the faces of Rachel's sister and parents, seeing just how lost and scared they were, struck a chord deep within her. Spenser wasn't sure why; she'd sat with the families of more than her share of victims of violent crimes in her day, but she couldn't get that haunted emptiness she'd seen in their eyes out of her head.

"I'm sorry I snapped at you. You're just watching out for me," Spenser said.

"It's okay. I'm sorry if you thought I was trying to undercut you. I wasn't—"

"I know you weren't trying to undercut me. And you don't have anything to apologize for," she replied softly. "I'm just not ready to give up on this girl. I'm clinging to the hope that she's still alive out there."

The odds weren't good. That was certain. But she hoped against all hope the man who took her was keeping her alive. Statistically speaking, once the object of a person's obsession was obtained, it was only a matter of time before the fantasy they'd conjured in their head would be shattered. And once that happened, more times than not, the offender would grow enraged and lash out at the one who'd destroyed their illusions. They would often kill that person before pivoting and finding somebody else to fixate on, starting the whole sordid, vicious cycle all over again. She just prayed that Rachel Kehoe would defy the odds.

Despite knowing all the probabilities and all the things she'd seen in her career, Spenser continued to cling to that faint flicker of hope in her heart. She wasn't ready to concede that Rachel was dead.

"What were you pondering so hard when I walked up?" Amanda asked.

"I'm not sure I was pondering anything, let alone pondering it hard."

"You had that look on your face."

Spenser grinned. "What look is that?"

"That look you get when you're starting to put things together."

"I definitely wasn't putting things together. I'm still completely in the dark."

"Are you, though? I usually only see you like that when you're onto something."

Spenser frowned. When Amanda had walked up, she'd had a tenuous grasp on the thread of something. She wasn't sure what it was, but when her concentration had been broken, it slipped through her fingers, no more substantial than a puff of smoke.

"What is it?" Amanda asked.

"I'm not sure. There's something… I just don't know what it is."

Closing her eyes, Spenser tried to clear her mind. Tried to focus. She listened to the sound of the wind rushing through the trees. Heard the creak of the branches and the dry, scratchy sound of them rubbing together in the breeze. A murder of crows, their caws shrill and piercing, echoed through the air as they noisily took flight.

As she absorbed the sound and sensations of the world around her, Spenser reached through the haze in her mind, trying to recapture that thread she'd lost. As she focused hard, her fingertips brushed it, sending a surge of adrenaline rushing through her veins. She reached for it again, and when she grasped it, it solidified in her mind. Then, Spenser opened her eyes. Her belly churned with a sudden sense of momentum that propelled her forward.

"Rachel mentioned to her friend Madison that she felt like she was being watched everywhere—at home, especially," Spenser said. "And we assume that Rachel's stalker was in her room and collected some trophies."

"Okay, but what does that mean?"

Spenser didn't answer but walked across the backyard, leaving Amanda to catch up. She opened the back gate and stepped into the forest that lay behind the house. The silence of the woods was so absolute that it had a physical weight. As she stood there among the wide trunks of the trees, the hair on the back of her neck stood up, and Spenser got that sensation of being observed. It was like there was something out there with them. It was at that moment she understood why people might latch onto a myth like the Okwala. She couldn't deny it anymore.

But that wasn't why she was out there. Spenser wasn't interested in hunting down a legend or trying to disprove a children's tale. She was out there for one reason. She was out there to get answers about a missing girl. To find her. And to find the human man who'd taken her.

"Sheriff, what's up?" Amanda asked.

Spenser gave herself a little shake, pulling herself out of her head before she got lost up there and started to overthink everything. If she let that happen, she was going to complicate something that should be straightforward.

"Keep it simple, stupid," Spenser muttered to herself.

Spenser's eyes roamed the forest floor, not sure what she was looking for but confident she'd figure it out when she saw it. For several long minutes, she studied the world around her. She searched for the piece of the puzzle that would bring the whole picture into focus. That would give her theory some life.

And then she saw it.

Lightning shot through Spenser's veins. Her skin tingled, and every hair on her body stood on end as she studied it for a moment. That sense of momentum that roiled in the pit of her stomach accelerated and pulled her along even faster. Spenser turned and looked at the back fence of the Kehoe house, then back up at it again, her theory solidifying in her mind.

"Are you okay, Sheriff?" Amanda asked.

"Yeah. I'm fine."

"Can I ask why we're out here?"

Spenser turned to Amanda. "Rachel told Madison she was sure somebody was watching her. Especially when she was at home."

"Right. But you also said she was paranoid about something that happened in her past."

"But we have proof she wasn't simply being paranoid—"

"Unless she was and nobody broke into her room, and she just misplaced her things, like Madison suggested she often did."

"What if she wasn't being paranoid, though?"

Amanda frowned. "I'm just playing Devil's Advocate here, but so far, your idea of a stalker and somebody so obsessed with Rachel they had to possess her is just a theory. We haven't actually found any evidence yet that your theory is correct, and that this isn't just a crime of opportunity. We haven't found any proof that somebody didn't just see Rachel out there and then tried to kill James and abduct her for… reasons I'd rather not talk about."

Spenser grinned. "By your logic, we haven't found any concrete proof it wasn't the Okasha who snatched her either."

Amanda chuckled. "You're never going to stop throwing that back in my face, are you?"

"Probably not," she replied. "But my theory isn't just a theory anymore."

"How do you figure?"

Spenser raised her arm and pointed to the deer stand that was perched high in the tree. Amanda stared at it for a moment as if not understanding what she was seeing. But then realization dawned on her, and she groaned.

"That deer stand is cleverly hidden, but I'll bet you my entire salary from now until I retire that if we climb it, we're going to find it has a direct sightline to Rachel's bedroom," Spenser said.

"There are a lot of hunters in the area."

"I don't see a game trail around here," Spenser countered. "And it seems a little too coincidental that this deer stand just happens to overlook the bedroom of a girl who was sure she was being watched and who was later abducted."

Amanda took a moment, her eyes flitting from the deer stand to the back fence of the Kehoe house and back again. Spenser could see her turning it over in her mind. But not even a skeptic and self-designated Devil's Advocate like Amanda could deny the fact that it was far too great a coincidence to actually be a coincidence. She finally turned back to Spenser, her shoulders tense and her lips a tight slash across her face.

"I'll call Arbery to come process the scene," she said.

CHAPTER TWENTY-SIX

It was her first day off the cane, and Spenser was doing well. Better than she had in a while. Ryker, though, insisted on bringing her to the office and picking her up later. No need to overdo it and have to go back on the cane, he'd said. It was adorably overprotective.

"Thanks," she said. "You can just drop that over there."

"You got it," he replied.

Ryker set the large box of donuts they'd picked up on the way into the office on the counter in the break room while Spenser hung on to the smaller one. A few of the morning shift deputies wandered in, said good morning to them both, grabbed a donut, and then headed out again. Lane Summers grabbed a maple bar and then leaned against the counter. As if sensing she wanted to talk, Spenser gave Ryker a smile and a peck on the lips.

"I'll see you tonight," she said.

"Be safe," he replied.

"Always."

He paused with a slight frown. "Be safer than that."

Ryker gave her another quick kiss, then said goodbye to Lane before turning and heading out of the office. Spenser watched him go, her heart fluttering. She loved that he still had that effect on her.

"You're a lucky woman, Sheriff," Lane said.

"I'm aware," Spenser replied. "Trust me."

"And he's a lucky man, too."

Spenser chuckled. "I'm aware of that, too. What's up, Lane?"

"Just wanted to give you an update. We kept an eye on them as you asked, and I'm not sure how those idiots managed it, but that mob Johansen and Hurley whipped up yesterday somehow avoided shooting each other out there in the woods," Deputy Summers said. "We had to arrest a few of them when they got into a brawl at the Whistle Stop later on, but at least they didn't accidentally kill somebody. We've got three still in the drunk tank sleeping it off."

"Thank God for small wonders," Spenser replied. "Anyway, give the guys in the drunk tank a few more hours, then cut them loose."

"No charges?"

"No. Not worth the paperwork," Spenser said with a snort. "Thanks for the update, Lane. Good work out there. Keep it up."

"Thanks, Sheriff," Summers chirped.

Spenser continued through the bullpen, making sure to stop and say good morning and check in with all her deputies. Communication was important to morale. She always wanted her deputies to know they were being heard and could talk to her without hesitation. She wanted to run her department with respect, not through the fear and favoritism her predecessor seemed to employ during his tenure. And so far, she'd seen positive returns.

She stepped into the conference room, finding Amanda and Jacob at their usual spots. They were hunched over their laptops, working away, and glanced up when she walked in. Spenser set down the box of donuts and coffee she was carrying, and as usual, they descended on it like a swarm of locusts.

"Bless you," Jacob said and took a swallow of coffee.

"You're here early," Amanda said around a mouthful of blueberry fritter.

"I was anxious to get started. We've got a lot going on," she replied. "Anybody call the tip line with leads on the sketch we put out?"

"We got one call from somebody who said the man in the sketch looked like Bill Gates and another who said it was their math teacher at Taft, Dan Downs," Jacob said.

"I checked. It's not Dan Downs," Amanda added.

"Any other calls?"

"Nothing you want to hear," Amanda replied. "And all I have to say is that there are a lot of disgustingly perverted kids in this town."

Jacob smirked. "Amanda and Lane apparently have quite the fan club of teenage boys."

"I'm not really all that shocked," Spenser said with a laugh.

"Oh, don't go assuming you didn't get a couple of perverted messages, too, Sheriff," Amanda said. "Jacob, play the one that came in this morning—"

"No. Don't. Thank you," Spenser said.

She was disappointed but not really surprised that they hadn't gotten much from the tip line. The sketch was about as generic as she'd ever seen. With a frown on her face, Spenser leaned back in her chair and let it all percolate in her mind. Finding the deer stand had been significant. It's likely that was where Rachel's stalker had been observing her from. She'd told everybody she was being watched, and Spenser believed somebody had eyes on her.

"Jacob, there are a lot of hunters in the area, right?" Spenser asked.

He scoffed. "Hundreds."

"How much does one of those tree stands go for?"

"The low end is a couple of hundred dollars, and the higher end ones can go for more than a grand," he answered.

"The one we found behind the Kehoe home… what does something like that cost?"

Jacob put the pictures they'd taken of the deer stand up on the monitor and tapped the end of his pen against his lips as he studied it for a few minutes.

"I'd say that's a mid-level stand," he said. "I'll do some digging to confirm, but I'd guess that one is going to be somewhere between four and five hundred bucks.

"I'd have to imagine only a serious hunter would put out that kind of money for one of those things," Spenser said.

"Or somebody very committed to stalking Rachel," Amanda said.

"That one looks a bit older. That thing is four or five years old, maybe? He could have bought it used," Jacob offered. "Unless your guy has been stalking Rachel for that long, I'd say unless he picked it up second-hand, he bought it before he crossed paths with her. I mean, unless he was stalking her when she was a teenager?"

"Yeah, that's even creepier. Thanks for that," Amanda said.

"It's possible, but unlikely. I don't see our guy waiting that long to take her. The nature of his obsession compelled him to act. I don't see him waiting years to do it," Spenser said. "I'd say you're right, Jacob. He owned that stand before he had any idea who Rachel Kehoe was."

"Is it unique enough to track the sales?" Amanda asked.

"It's definitely not unique," Jacob said. "The company that makes that one has made a whole line of them—has been making lines of them for more than twenty years. They sell hundreds, if not thousands, of these things every year. They sell them all across the country, so unless we can figure out where he bought it, that's not really a viable avenue."

"Unless…" Spenser started, then tapered off as she gave her words time to coalesce.

"Sheriff?" Amanda prompted.

"Jacob, is there any way you can put together a list of licensed hunters in the area, then cross reference that against a list of people who've bought that model of deer stand?" Spenser asked.

"I mean, I can try. But I'm kind of skeptical that I'm going to be able to get the sales information for that stand."

"And if you can run another search… maybe try to match the sketch against the photos in the hunting license database?" Spenser asked.

"Shall I also convince the sun to rise in the west tomorrow?"

"If you're up to it, sure."

"Boy, you don't like to make things easy on me, do you?" Jacob said.

"I have faith in you," Spenser said. "You're the best at what you do, right?"

He guffawed. "Throwing my words back in my face is against the rules."

"I'm the boss; therefore, I make the rules around here," she teased.

Dr. Arbery stepped into the conference room, his posture ramrod straight, wearing his usual uptight expression. Despite his prissiness, Spenser liked the man. And she respected his work. But Arbery always looked at her and the way she ran the department disapprovingly. He wasn't a man who liked coloring outside the lines and viewed those who did as somehow wrong or deviant.

Spenser had hope for the man, though. Somewhere deep down, she was sure he enjoyed the loose atmosphere and the camaraderie she fostered. If he didn't enjoy it on some level, why would he continue to work for her? It certainly couldn't be for the money. A man of his talents could have his choice of jobs at a far higher salary than she was able to give him.

He tapped the folder he was carrying against his open palm, a small frown playing across his lips. "Is this a good time, Sheriff Song?"

"Of course. Yes, please," she replied. "What is it, Dr. Arbery?"

"We finished analyzing what we found out on the deer stand, which wasn't very much," he said. "We did manage to pull one print. Unfortunately, it was a partial, and it was smudged at that, so we didn't have enough points of comparison to make a successful match in the system."

"Damn," Spenser muttered.

"We did find more strips of burlap at the scene," he said. "We studied them, and they appear to match those we found at the original campsite."

"Burlap strips," Spenser mused. "Any idea what they're for?"

Arbery shook his head. "No clue, Sheriff."

Spenser tapped her pen on the table and considered it for a moment before she shook her head. She had nothing.

"Well, I'd surmise the burlap strips tie the deer stand to our original crime scene. We're likely looking at the same offender in both spots," Spenser said. "Okay, was there anything else out there of note at the deer stand, Dr. Arbery?"

He cast a glance at Amanda. "Well, there were no odd animal tracks or unexplained fur at the scene, so we can probably safely cross the Sweetwater Devil off our list of suspects since I have yet to hear a version of that silly tale where the beast uses a deer stand."

Jacob choked on his donut as he tried to suppress a laugh while his sister's face flushed a bright shade of scarlet. Amanda looked into her cup of coffee, unable to meet his eyes, though Spenser could see the rueful curl of her lips. Apparently, Arbery did have a sense of humor.

"Nice one, Doc," Jacob said. "I give that dig a nine-point-five."

Arbery turned and, without another word, walked out of the conference room.

"A silent assassin, that one," Jacob teased.

"Sheriff, do I have the power to fire people?" Amanda asked.

"You most certainly do not. I'm starting to like that guy."

"Me too," Jacob said.

"You both suck. You both need to know that," Amanda said.

"We're well aware," Spenser teased.

"Okay, so the deer stand is a bust," Amanda said, trying to steer the conversation back on topic. "What is our next move?"

"Well, while Jacob is trying to get the purchasing information on the deer stand, we can help him out by pulling all the hunting license photos and comparing them to our sketch," Spenser said.

Amanda groaned. "That is going to be brutal."

"Nobody said this would be easy."

"True enough," she replied.

Spenser leaned back in her chair again and frowned. "I just wish I could figure out what in the hell those burlap strips were for."

CHAPTER TWENTY-SEVEN

"I HAD NO IDEA JUST HOW MANY LICENSED HUNTERS there are in the area," she said.

Ryker chuckled. "Yeah, we've got a few around here."

"The awful thing is I have no idea if we're doing all this for nothing. That sketch is so vague, it could be any of them."

"And don't forget there are plenty of people around here who never applied for a hunting license. The guy you're looking for might not even be in that stack."

Spenser groaned. By the time Ryker had picked her up and gotten her home, her eyes were crossed. She and Amanda had spent hours locked away in the conference room, comparing their sketch to photos from the hunting license database. Their suspect was so vague and bland he resembled dozens of the pictures they'd looked at. But none of them were close enough to definitively say that was their guy.

"I didn't even consider unlicensed hunters," she said. "Shoot me now, please."

"Yeah, not everybody is down with paying fees to do something they say is their God-given right, I'm afraid," Ryker replied.

Standing beside him, Spenser took a sip of her wine and leaned against the railing on the back deck. In the yard below, Annabelle and Mocha chased each other, tongues lolling and tails wagging as they wrestled in the soft grass. Ryker had made a wonderful dinner, and though she was a thousand percent better, physically speaking, Spenser still hadn't gotten her wind back quite yet and tired easily. After a long and grueling day at the office and now a good meal, she was just about ready for bed.

Ryker had the rest of her things moved up from the cabin while she was at the office, so she was officially moved in. And for the first time since he'd first asked her, Spenser didn't have the slightest bit of trepidation about it. For the first time since he'd asked her to move in, Spenser was settled with her decision. More than that, she was content. Even happy.

"So, the deer stand didn't pan out, huh?" he asked.

"Not really. I mean, from one standpoint, yeah. The burlap strips at both locations show a very possible connection, maybe even direct correlation, but it's still unclear."

"Any idea what the burlap is for?"

"Not a clue."

"Bindings?"

Spenser shrugged. "Maybe. Hard to say right now."

There was a faint tickle in the back of her mind like an echo of recognition. She'd rolled it around her mind about it for a while, trying to dredge it up from the back of her mind, but it hadn't come, so she'd stopped. She'd decided to let her subconscious work that knot for a little while. Some of Spenser's biggest breakthroughs came when she wasn't trying to force them to come.

"You all right?" he asked.

Spenser nodded. "Just tired. I haven't quite gotten my stamina back."

"Marley said it's just going to take a little time."

"Yeah, I get it. I'm just ready to be back to one hundred percent already."

"Need to kick in some doors, do you?"

Spenser grinned. "Relax. It's going to be a while before I'm ready for that. I'm wiped out just from staring at pictures all day."

"Is it selfish to say that it gives me comfort that you're safely tucked away in your office looking at pictures all day?"

"Yeah. That's pretty selfish," she replied with a laugh.

"Well then, I guess I'm selfish. And I'm okay with that."

Spenser rolled her eyes. "You're such a jerk."

"I do what I can."

They stood together in silence for a moment, sipping their wine and watching the dogs romping around together in the yard. Ryker turned to her, uncertainty on his face.

"How are you now that we've got all your things here?" he asked.

"Good. Really good."

"Yeah?"

Spenser leaned over and gave him a gentle kiss. "Yeah. This is going to be good. For both of us."

"It will be."

"I'm falling asleep on my feet, though," she said. "I need to clean up the kitchen, then take a shower and get to bed."

"You go on and take a shower. I've got the kitchen."

"You cooked that amazing meal. I'll clean the kitchen."

"Tell you what, next time I'm recovering from a terrible stab wound, I'll let you clean up the kitchen for me. Until then, go shower. I've got this."

Spenser drained the last of her wine and gave him another kiss. "Thank you. You really are too good to me."

"Yeah, I know," he teased. "But you're worth it."

"I'll see you soon?"

"I'm pretty sure you're going to be asleep by the time I get to bed."

"I'll try to stay up, but honestly, I might be."

He kissed her forehead. "Don't try. Get some sleep."

Spenser carried her empty glass in the kitchen, guilt stabbing her heart about leaving him to clean everything after he'd cooked for her. But she was wrung out. She was grateful for such a thoughtful and considerate man in her life. She walked down the hall toward the bedroom and glanced at the pictures on the wall as she passed by them. Something tickled the back of Spenser's mind as she passed one particular photo. She stopped, then backed up and looked at it again.

It was a picture of Ryker with his team over in Afghanistan. They were in their desert-colored fatigues and posed in front of the ruins of an old, historic building. Behind them was a breathtaking view of the snow-capped peaks of the Hindu Kush mountain range. They were all geared up, holding their weapons at the ready, with stern and intimidating expressions on all their faces. Ryker never talked much about his experiences overseas, and she never pushed him to open up. For many combat veterans, it had been incredibly traumatizing, and she never wanted to force him to open that Pandora's Box of nightmares.

They all looked so young in the picture, but even then, Spenser could see the haunted shadows in their faces beginning to form. She could see the start of the deep, indelible scars they would forever carry. How could they not? They were kids playing at war, seeing the unimaginable while being ordered to do the unthinkable. Of course, that sort of experience would leave a trauma that lingered and echoed throughout the rest of their lives, at least, for those who'd survived.

As she looked at the men in the photograph, the quiet whisper in the back of her mind began to grow louder. The gentle tickle became an insistent prodding. Spenser gritted her teeth and tried to listen, trying to understand what the voice in her head was telling her. She let her eyes roam the picture, certain that was what had triggered the murmuring in her mind. There was something in the photo that had tripped a recollection. Spenser took in the faces of the men, the mountains in the background, their weapons, their uniforms—

Spenser's eyes grew wide, and her heart skipped a beat or twelve as a surge of excitement flowed through her veins.

Understanding gripped her in an iron fist as that sense of forward motion pulled her along once more.

"That's it," she gasped. "Of course."

Spenser ran to the office and grabbed her laptop, quickly opening the lid to wake it up. The wait seemed interminable, so she used the time to take a series of slow breaths, doing her best to ground and center herself. As certain as she was that she'd stumbled onto the answer, at the moment, it was just a theory. Untested and unproven. She had been doing the job long enough to know that what seemed like a sure thing could turn into a dead end in the blink of an eye. Until she was certain, she needed to temper her expectations and control her emotions.

"Hey, what are you doing?" Ryker asked as he stepped into the office. "Thought you were going to bed?"

"I couldn't sleep right now if I wanted to."

"Uh oh. I recognize that look."

"What look?"

"Dog on a scent."

"You and Amanda," she said with a chuckle. "I don't have a look."

"I hate to break it to you, but you do. You absolutely get this face when you're onto something," he replied. "So, what is the scent you've stumbled onto?"

"I know what the burlap strips are."

"The what?"

Spenser's computer came up, and she quickly typed it into the search bar, waiting impatiently for the results. When they did, she called up the images and turned the screen so Ryker could see it.

"The burlap strips. They're from a ghillie suit," she said.

CHAPTER TWENTY-EIGHT

"WELL, I'D SAY YOU SOLVED THE MYSTERY OF THE Okasha," Jacob said.

Amanda stared at the screen in disbelief. The ad photo showed a figure holding a hunting rifle dressed in the company's forest-themed ghillie suit among the wide tree trunks and low-hanging pine boughs of a sylvan environment. It covered the person inside it head to toe and was designed to blend into the forest around it. In the dark, the loose strips of fabric that dominated the suit and helped it look like a natural part of its surroundings could likely be mistaken for the stringy hair of the mythical beast. The bulkiness of the suit made the person inside it seem larger than they were. Spenser could see why, in the dark, under heightened emotional circumstances (and a solid dose of THC), somebody might see a monster instead of a man in a suit.

"What do you think?" Spenser asked.

"It looks like the descriptions of the Okasha," Amanda finally said. "It looks just like what James described seeing out there."

"A ghillie suit," Jacob said. "I never would have figured that one out."

"How did you get there, Sheriff?" Amanda asked.

"I was looking at some of Ryker's pictures from when he was overseas last night and recalled seeing one in some military movie I saw once. It just popped."

"That's a nice pull," Amanda said.

"Very nice pull," Jacob agreed.

"Now we need to find out who has one."

"That might be tougher to pull," Jacob said.

"I've got to assume this isn't a common item," Spenser said. "And from what I saw last night, they're not cheap, either. There probably aren't a lot of people around here who have one. I mean, that's a little hardcore, even for dedicated hunters."

"Fair," Jacob said.

"Other than Flick's, what other shops outfit hunters in town?" Spenser asked.

"There's half a dozen different outfitters," Amanda answered. "And that's assuming our guy didn't buy his suit in one of the surrounding towns. That's going to add another dozen shops."

"At least," Jacob said.

"Well, I guess we've got our work cut out for us then," Spenser said. "Jacob, give us a list of the outfitters in and around town. Amanda, we're going to divvy up that list and then hit the bricks and start knocking on doors."

"Good, old-fashioned legwork, huh, Sheriff?" Amanda asked.

"Good, old-fashioned legwork," Spenser confirmed.

"Let's get to it."

"Glad to see you don't have an angry mob in your parking lot today," Spenser said.

The man behind the counter was in his sixties with a healthy beer gut, wiry white hair, and a beard that hung to his chest. Barney Flick's cheeks were rosy, and he had a bright smile, making him look like an offseason Santa Claus. Spenser had run down her half of the list Jacob had given her and had come up empty. None of them had sold or special-ordered a ghillie suit. Flick's was her last shot at coming up with anything actionable. She just hoped Amanda had better luck on her end.

Flick's Sporting Goods should really just be named Flick's Things That Can Kill You Store. Guns of every flavor, compound bows, crossbows, a frightening array of knives—which made Spenser shudder as the memory of Alex Ricci sticking one in her flashed through her mind. There was a small section with other recreational sporting equipment—soccer balls, basketballs, baseballs, and bats. But other than that, the rest of the store was filled with weaponry. It was clean and well organized, making it easier for people to find things to kill other living beings with.

"Yeah, those boys do get themselves wound up, don't they?" he replied.

"That they do."

"We're all just lucky they didn't run off and shoot nobody in the woods as keyed up—and liquored up—as some of them were."

"We're all very lucky."

"Ain't there nothin' you can do about that kind of thing?"

Spenser shook her head. "Unfortunately, they have a right to gather and speak. And so long as they're licensed hunters, I can't do anything about them carrying weapons either."

"That seems a shame. One of these days, somebody's going to get hurt."

"I agree. But we have a Constitution, and I'm sworn to uphold it, as well as the current laws of this town and state. My hands are somewhat tied."

"I'm as freedom lovin' as the next fella, but that seems backward," he said. "It's crazy that you gotta go and clean up after the fact instead of doin' somethin' about it before it happens."

"Tell me about it. Being a cop is sometimes like being a janitor. We just follow along and sweep up the crap others leave behind."

Flick laughed out loud, his voice deep and thunderous. "I know that's right. Anyway, for what it's worth, you're doin' a bang-up job around here, Sheriff, and I'm gonna be votin' for you instead of that greasy, slick-backed, carpetbaggin' worm Rafe Johansen."

"I really appreciate that, Flick."

"So, what can I do for you, Sheriff?"

"I need to ask you about ghillie suits."

He looked a little taken aback. "Ghillie suits?"

"Yeah, they're suits designed to look like—"

"Yeah, yeah, I'm familiar with what they are. But why are you askin' about them?"

"I assume they're not common items, so I just need to know if you've sold any in the last, say, five years or so?"

"Oh no, I don't stock them. Ain't sold any."

"You've never special ordered any?"

He shook his head. "Nah. Not me. I never had any requests for 'em. Hunters around here don't really seem to be that invested in camouflage beyond your typical camo gear. Way too bulky and hot to be runnin' around in the woods anyway."

"Yeah, that makes sense," Spenser said. "So, where would somebody get ahold of one?"

"These days? Online, I reckon. That'd probably be easiest," he said. "The quality ain't always the best—a lot of these companies put out trash products made of cheap materials. But if somebody ain't worried about that, they'd probably go that route. Or they could make one themself. Ghillie suits ain't that hard to make. But again, it might not be the best quality."

Spenser hoped that wasn't going to be the case. If their offender had ordered a ghillie suit online, there was virtually no chance of tracking it. She was putting a lot of their eggs into one basket, but they didn't have much of a choice. She was sure they were on the right path—for the first time, she was absolutely certain they were on the right path—but they had very few ways to prove it.

"What if somebody wanted a better-quality suit? One that was durable and built to last? Where would they go for that?" Spenser asked.

"Army surplus stores, probably. That's where you're usually going to find stuff like that. And the quality is usually better. Plus, it's used goods, so it's gonna be cheaper," he answered.

Spenser frowned. She still wasn't familiar with all the stores in town, but she wasn't sure if they had an army surplus store in town or not.

"You're gonna want to talk to Georgie Mitchell," Flick said.

"And who is Georgie Mitchell?"

"Sergeant George Mitchell. Former tanker. Did a few tours in the Middle East. His family's been here for generations," he replied. "He's got a surplus store of sorts out in the Heap. He's a good guy, but he's an … acquired taste."

"What do you mean?"

"When he came back from the war, he wasn't quite right. Not all there," Flick responded. "Like a lot of the poor souls who went over there, he came back broken. But I seem to recall he had a couple of ghillie suits in stock. If anybody has one, it's gonna be him. Or he might be able to point you in the right direction, anyway."

"That's terrific. Thank you for your help, Flick. I appreciate it."

"Anytime, Sheriff. Keep up the good work out there."

Out past the artsy district of town called Little Paris was the Heap. It wasn't a very big piece of town, consisting of just three large salvage yards. It was where the town's old cars and appliances went to die and were cannibalized by the do-it-yourself crowd. On a low hill above the other two salvage yards sat Mitchell's Junk. And on the grounds of the salvage yard was Mitchell's Surplus, which was housed in what had been a large barn in a former life.

The air was dusty and carried an odor that was half barnyard, half mildew, and must. And like the junkyard behind the barn, it was crammed full of stuff that looked like it had been thrown inside haphazardly and in no discernable order. There were no marked aisles. There were just racks and shelving units strewn about all willy-nilly. She figured the layout made sense for this area of town.

"Afternoon, Sheriff."

The voice came out of nowhere, making her nearly jump out of her skin. Her heart racing, Spenser turned to see a large man, six-three at least, stepping out from behind a shelving unit that held a collection of wicked-looking knives. His graying hair was cut short in a military style, and his dark eyes were narrow, flashing with suspicion. He was broad-shouldered and fit with a square jawline and a body that looked like it had been carved from stone. The man had quite obviously kept up with his exercise regimen in his civilian life.

"You move quietly for such a large man," Spenser said.

"I was trained well," he said.

"George Mitchell, I presume?"

"Sergeant Mitchell," he replied. "Why are you here?"

"I just wanted to ask you a few questions, Sergeant."

Spenser's pulse started to race when she noticed the .45 on his hip. The holster strap was unbuckled, and he was ready to go. Mitchell's body was taut. He stood ready for action, like a snake coiled and ready to strike at the slightest hint of provocation. He stood casually, but his hand hovered near his weapon, his glare as icy as it was suspicious.

"Are you here as a representative of the Deep State?" he asked.

Spenser stared at him for a beat, not sure how to answer that question at first. She did her best to avoid making any sudden movements or do anything to alarm the man in any way. He was a ticking time bomb, and the last thing she wanted to do was set him off.

"No, Sergeant Mitchell. I don't involve myself in federal matters. I'm just here to ask you some questions about a town matter," she replied.

"Is this about the missing girl?"

"It is."

"She's gone, Sheriff. The Okasha doesn't leave survivors."

He said it with such conviction that Spenser could tell he believed in the legend, and there would be no convincing him that Rachel Kehoe wasn't taken by the beast. She needed to pivot to another line of questioning. Maybe if she didn't mention the abduction and focused on something else, she'd get somewhere with him.

"Have you ever been told what the Okasha truly is, Sheriff?"

"What is it?"

"An interdimensional being."

"I'm sorry, it's a what?"

"A being that can travel from one dimension to another," he said. "The Okasha ain't really the Okasha. It's just one member of a race of these interdimensional beings called the Yunco."

Spenser was starting to see what Flick had meant about the Sergeant not being entirely all there and holding some strange beliefs. She wondered, though, if it was a result of the combat he'd seen or a preexisting condition. It didn't ultimately matter. She wasn't there to talk about legends and interdimensional beings.

"Is that so?" Spenser asked.

He nodded solemnly. "The shadow government—the ones who are actually running this country behind the scenes—has known about these beings for a very long time. They've met with them many times and are currently working with them."

"Working with them? To do… what?"

"Whatever the shadow government needs them to do. Assassinations, political abductions… I have it on good authority they were involved with the Kennedy assassination."

"I hadn't heard that," Spenser said, trying desperately to find a way to get this conversation back on track. "Listen, Sergeant Mitchell, I'd really love to hear all about this—"

"You would?" he asked.

"I would. Another time. Right now, I'm kind of on a running clock, and I need to ask you some questions about a very terrestrial nature. Boring questions, actually. But questions I very much need the answers to."

He seemed to loosen up at the prospect of getting to share his beliefs with her, and the corners of his mouth lifted upward slightly, softening his otherwise stony appearance.

"What can I help you with, Sheriff?"

"Well, it's my understanding that you may have sold a ghillie suit?"

"Sure. I've sold six of them in the last five years."

"Wow. That's very... specific."

He shrugged and pointed to an empty clothing rack she hadn't noticed before that bore a handwritten sign that read, "Ghillie Suits."

"I got six five years ago—two snow, one desert, three forest," he said. "They're all gone now. Therefore, I've sold six in the last five years."

Spenser looked around the cluttered shop and had a sinking feeling that brought a frown to her lips. "Sergeant Mitchell, I don't suppose you have receipts for the sale of those ghillie suits?"

"Of course I do. I'm a very organized man, and I run a tight ship."

Finally. Some potentially good news.

CHAPTER TWENTY-NINE

Jacob and Amanda howled hysterically as Spenser related her conversation with Sergeant Mitchell. She'd done her best to get the receipts and get out of there, but she'd been sucked into an hour-long chat about the cooperation between the shadow government and the interdimensional beings known as the Yunco, of which, the Okasha was one. It was, by far, one of the strangest conversations she'd ever had in her life.

"If you really consider it, it makes a certain amount of sense," Jacob said. "I mean, the idea of a shadow government running the country, not these interdimensional beings working with them."

"It sounds like you found your soulmate, big brother. Kind of sounds like you two would get along famously," Amanda said.

"Be sure to bring your own tin foil hat, though," Spenser said.

"I am so glad you took that bullet instead of me," Amanda replied. "I am positive I wouldn't have been able to handle that with as much grace as you did."

"I'm not sure I handled it with all that much grace."

"You listened to him rattle on about these far-out, wackadoodle conspiracy theories for an hour," Jacob chimed in. "I'd say you handled it with some grace."

"It's not like I had a choice. He wouldn't give me the receipts until I let him share his truths with me," Spenser responded. "Still, it's kind of sad. I mean, he's a combat veteran who's retreated into this strange, fantasy world. It doesn't seem like he has anybody to take care of him. He could obviously use some help."

"Maybe you can have Ryker talk to him?" Amanda offered. "As a fellow combat vet, maybe he can relate and might want to help."

"That's actually not a bad idea," Spenser said.

"Hey, I'm full of them," Amanda chirped.

"She's full of something," Jacob teased.

Spenser took a long draw from her bottle of water and waited for them to settle down. Once they had, she leaned forward.

"Okay, let's get on track here," she said. "Amanda, did you get any hits from the shops you went to? Anybody buy ghillie suits?"

Amanda shook her head. "Nope. None of the stores I visited even sell them. And nobody special ordered them. It looks like Mitchell is the only game in town."

"Assuming they didn't buy them online. If they did, we are absolutely boned," Jacob said.

"We'll jump off that bridge when we come to it. So, for the sake of argument, we're going to assume they didn't. At least for the moment," Spenser said. "Which means, we've got the names of the six people who bought ghillie suits from Sergeant Mitchell."

"All right, so what are we going to do with them?" Jacob asked.

"The first thing I want you to do is run those six names against the hunting license database," Spenser said.

"That's a much easier ask," Jacob said. "Give me a couple of minutes, please."

Jacob hunched over his computer, and his fingers started to fly over the keyboard. Spenser took another drink of her water and waited as he worked, silently crossing her fingers that this lead was going to pan out. She wasn't sure what she was going to do if it didn't. If their offender wasn't in the database or hadn't bought one of Mitchell's six ghillie suits, she was going to be sunk.

"Okay, it looks like we have six matches," Jacob announced. "Herm Glaser. Zach Ansille. Craig Donner. Tim Porter. Simon Elbert."

"That's a good start. All right," Spenser said. "What can you tell me about these guys?"

Jacob pecked away at his keyboard. The monitor on the wall lit up, and six DMV photos were shown on the screen.

"Of the six men pictured here, two of them—Zach Ansille and Tim Porter—bought their ghillie suits from Mitchell five years ago, but they no longer live in the state of Washington."

"That would seem to preclude them from our suspect list," Amanda said.

"It would seem to, yes. Very good, little sister." The photos of the two men on the screen darkened. "That leaves us with four who are currently still in the area."

"And what can you tell me about them?" Spenser asked.

"Herm Glaser, forty-three, is an attorney who has an office in Seattle but lives here in town. Wife, three kids, no record, and he seems to be squeaky clean in every way," Jacob said.

"Can you print out his photo for me?" Spenser asked.

"On it," Jacob said.

The printer on the table started to whir, and a moment later, the photo she'd asked for slid out and into the tray. Spenser grabbed it.

"Next?" Spenser asked.

"Craig Donner, age thirty-seven, lives in Westerton and works as a mechanic there, too. Not married, but his socials show that he's engaged. Has a couple minor arrests in his background. Looks like he's been in a couple of bar fights, but nothing too serious," Jacob reported.

The printer whirred again and his photo slid out. Spenser grabbed it and set it down on the table next to the first one.

"Simon Elbert, forty-four years old. Lives in town, works as a general handyman and has a side hustle making custom furniture; however, that business doesn't seem to be overly successful," Jacob said. "He's had a couple minor run-ins with the law. Nothing big, just a couple of drunk and disorderlies. Seems like he likes to drink."

Elbert's picture slid into the tray. Spenser grabbed it and lined it up next to the other two.

"And last but not least, we have Don Haverton. Thirty-nine, divorced, father of two. It doesn't look like he has custody of his kids, and his ex-wife has a restraining order out against him that alleges domestic violence," Jacob reported.

"Sounds like a charmer," Amanda said.

"He doesn't have steady work and, instead, seems to do odd jobs, and lives in a trailer over in Greenwood," Jacob said. "If I were to lay money, I'd say this is our guy."

His picture slid out of the printer and Spenser lined it up next to the others. After that, she pulled out the flyer with their composite sketch from the folder on the table and set it just below the photos. Standing up, she took a step back and looked at the pictures, comparing it to the sketch on the flyer. Jacob and Amanda joined her, and the three of them stood there for a few minutes, silently studying the impromptu lineup.

"What do you think?" Amanda asked.

"Honestly? The sketch bears a resemblance to all four of them. And none of them," Spenser replied.

"I'm so glad I'm not the only one who sees that," Jacob said and chuckled.

"Great. So, we're not going to be able to eliminate any of them," Amanda groused.

"No. We won't."

Amanda turned to her. "It sounds like you have an idea."

"I do."

"Care to share, Sheriff?"

"We're predicating this whole abduction on the theory that one of these four was so obsessed with Rachel that they stalked her. That they watched her closely," Spenser said.

"Right. I'm with you so far."

"At some point, their paths had to cross. We've been banging our heads against the wall trying to figure out where that was—"

"And we've come up empty."

"The Kehoes might be able to fill in that blank for us," Spenser said. "I'm going to take these photos over and see if they recognize any of the men. Maybe they'll be able to tell us where Rachel crossed paths with her stalker and where the obsession started."

"And this is why they pay you the big bucks, Sheriff."

Spenser laughed. "While I'm gone, keep digging. I want to learn everything I can about these guys when I come back. If one of these clowns is our guy, I want to be sure of what we're walking into when we go scoop him up."

"On it," Jacob and Amanda said in unison.

"Good. Then I'm off to hopefully get an ID."

"Not to be the doomsayer, what happens if none of these four is our guy?" Amanda asked.

Spenser grimaced. "Then, to borrow a phrase from your brother, we're totally boned."

CHAPTER THIRTY

It had only taken Spenser a couple of phone calls to find the Kehoes, who were staying with Mrs. Kehoe's sister in Millbrand. She'd offered to come out there to update them on the developments with their daughter's case, but they'd told her they were already heading home and would meet her there. True to their word, they were already home when Spenser pulled the Bronco to the curb in front of their house.

"Thank you for meeting with me," Spenser said, setting her messenger bag on the floor next to her as she perched on the edge of the loveseat.

Brock and Denise huddled together on the larger sofa across from her. Drawn and pale, they clutched one another's hands. They both looked wrung out. They had matching dark half-moons beneath their bloodshot, watery eyes, and they both appeared to have dropped significant weight in the past week. The stress of Rachel's disappearance had obviously been taking a physical as well as emotional toll on them.

Pacing behind them, though, arms folded over her chest, was Veronica, Rachel's fiery little sister. She, too, looked as if she hadn't been sleeping much, but rather than drawing inward and withering away like her parents seemed to be doing, she looked angry. And scared. Veronica's cheeks were flushed, and her narrowed eyes, while bloodshot and shimmering with unshed tears, burned with a white-hot rage.

"First of all, I just wanted to check in with you to see how you were all holding up," Spenser began. "I'm sure this can't be easy—"

"How in the hell do you think we're holding up?" Veronica snapped.

"Roni, stop," her mother admonished her.

"Why should I? Rachel's been gone for like a week now, and the sheriff here still doesn't have the first damn clue where she is," the girl railed. "She's been out to dinner with her boyfriend plenty. You saw her sitting on her butt playing lovey-dovey with that freak on the hill over at Vinnie's the other night, Mom. You told us so yourself."

Veronica stopped pacing but didn't lower her arms. Instead, she turned the full intensity of her rage onto Spenser. Rather than challenge the girl or defend Ryker from her cruelty, Spenser let her have her say. Let her get it all out of her system. That much fear and anger was corrosive and had probably been percolating in her stomach for days now. She imagined it had to be hard for a girl her age to deal with her sister being taken and having no answers. Spenser just wanted her to purge it all from her body.

"Roni, you can either be quiet and respectful or you can leave the room," Brock said, his voice low and tight.

The girl threw her arms into the air with a disgusted snort then stormed away. A moment later, a door at the back of the house slammed so hard, it shook the walls around her. That explosion was followed by hard metal music being played so loud, that Spenser felt like she'd stumbled into the pit at Ozzfest.

"We're sorry about her," Brock said. "This has been tough on Roni."

"And I'm sorry she said that about you and Mr. Makawi," Denise said softly. "You have a life beyond your job, and you're entitled to it. I just—"

"There's no need for either of you to apologize. I can't imagine how difficult this has been for all of you. And I'm sure seeing me having dinner the other night didn't do a lot to inspire confidence in you. I just want to make sure you understand my whole department has been working around the clock to find Rachel and bring her home. We have been doing everything we can, chasing every lead, and developing evidence to make that happen."

Fighting back her tears, Denise leaned against Brock as if drawing strength from her husband. He wrapped his arm around her shoulder and pulled her to him tighter while battling his own emotional turmoil. Spenser was frankly glad to see them leaning on one another. She'd seen far too many families blown apart by situations like this. When emotions run high, people tend to either stick together, binding themselves to one another, or they pull away and fragment.

Statistics of marriages surviving the loss of a child showed a great many families fell into the latter category. A depressing number of marriages couldn't survive the strain of losing a child. Spenser wasn't counting Rachel out and still believed they were going to find her. She took heart in seeing the Kehoes coming together rather than turning on each other.

"And have you found any leads, Sheriff? Can you tell us who took our little girl yet?" Brock asked, his voice hoarse and scratchy.

"Actually, we have a solid lead, but I'm going to need your help."

Still clutching each other's hands, the Kehoes leaned forward, their eyes suddenly flashing with renewed hope. Spenser silently hoped and prayed this was going to pan out.

Spenser reached into her messenger bag and pulled out the file she'd put together. She didn't yet have enough to justify pulling the potential suspects in for a lineup, and frankly, she didn't want to tip them off that they were even looking at them yet, so she'd had the photos of the four men put into six-packs—a photo array of six men with similar features and appearances. Law enforcement used six-packs to prevent any allegations of leading or tampering with an ID in any way. It would be a pure, untainted ID.

Spenser laid the quartet of six-packs on the table in front of the Kehoes then sat back. She watched them looking at all the photos for a moment without saying anything, giving them a little time to absorb it. Finally, Denise raised her head, her eyes shimmering, and her cheeks flushed scarlet as she was battered by waves of emotion.

"Is one of the men who took Rachel here? Is one of them—"

"Denise, I just need you to tell me if any of the men in these photographs look familiar to you."

"Sheriff, are you looking at one or more of these men?" Brock jumped in. "Did one of them take our little girl?"

"I'm afraid I can't tell you anything specific at the moment. I must protect the integrity of our investigation and can't lead you in any one direction. I just need you to confirm whether any of the men in these photo arrays are familiar to you," Spenser explained.

He clearly wasn't happy, but he nodded, seeming to understand. He quietly encouraged his wife to look at the photos closely, and together, they picked up the arrays and studied the faces of the men. Spenser watched them. She studied the way their eyes flitted from one photograph to the next, absorbing every detail and nuance of the faces they were seeing. She watched them closely, waiting for that hit of recognition. Praying that it would come.

And then it did.

Brock tapped on the picture of a man in the third six-pack. "Him. This is Simon Elbert."

Spenser had to keep from pumping her fist as a flash of excitement rocketed through her, sending her pulse soaring. She took a beat to stuff it all down, though, doing her best to remain calm and steady. That was just one part of what she needed.

"And how are you familiar with him, Brock?" Spenser asked.

"Simon's a woodworker and he's pretty handy with things," Brock replied. "He's been doing a lot of work on the house for us. He's pretty much building that additional room on his own."

"Are you saying he's the one who took our daughter, Sheriff?" Denise asked.

"I can't see that. He's a little slow and, sure, he's a little odd, but he's a good guy," Brock offered.

"I'm not saying he's the one who took your daughter. Right now, I'd just like to sit him down and ask him some questions," Spenser said.

"What kind of questions?" Brock asked.

Spenser needed to give them something but didn't want to say too much. She didn't want to get their hopes up or falsely demonize an innocent man.

"We have evidence that whoever took your daughter has been watching her—"

"What sort of evidence?" Brock asked, his face aghast.

"We found a deer stand up in a tree behind your house," Spenser replied. "It's got a clear sight line to Rachel's bedroom, and we're certain that whoever took her had been watching her for quite some time. This wasn't a spur of the moment abduction."

A choked cry burst from Denise's mouth and Brock pulled her close again. She buried in her husband's chest as her body shook with her sobbing.

"He's been in our house. He's been around this family for a while," Brock said. "He never seemed to pay any undue attention to Rachel. He never said much of anything, really. Like I said, he's a little slow and he's odd, but he keeps to himself."

"And I'm not saying that he is definitely our guy. But your ID in conjunction with some of the other evidence we've developed warrants a conversation with him," Spenser replied.

"What sort of other evidence, Sheriff."

"I'm afraid I can't get into the details with you," she responded. "I'm sorry, but it's critical that I protect the integrity of this investigation."

He nodded but was clearly frustrated. He wanted more. Spenser, though, couldn't give him what he wanted.

"Again, it's important that I stress to you that Simon Elbert may not be the man we're looking for. We're going to have a conversation with him, but it's critical that you don't assume the worst. Do you understand?"

He again nodded. "Yeah. I get it."

"Good. Now, when was the last time you saw him?" Spenser asked.

"It's been a few weeks," he replied. "We had to stop the work on the house—permit issues. I told him I'd give him a call when we were ready to go again. We got the permit thing cleared up, and I called him a few days ago and am still waiting for him to call back. He does a lot of work on the side, so it didn't strike me as out of the ordinary or anything—"

"Has he not called back because he took our daughter?" Denise asked.

"Again, we can't presume anything. It could be as simple as him having taken some out-of-town work, like your husband suggested. I'm going to track him down and have that conversation, and when I do, I'll keep you both updated. Until then, please sit tight and don't mention this to anybody. The last thing we need is for somebody to stir the pot and turn this thing into a town-wide witch hunt."

Spenser said that with Rafe Johansen in mind. He was a man who would try to capitalize on anything to whip people into a frenzy. And if it got out that she was looking at Simon Elbert as a possible suspect, she had no doubt Rafe would stir up his base of gun-toting fanatics with some red meat, fan the flames, then turn them loose. And she'd been around long enough to know that posse would soon become a lynch mob.

"Please. Keep this to yourselves for the time being," Spenser implored.

Brock nodded. "We will.

"Okay. Good," Spenser said as she got to her feet. "Then I need to get to work."

She headed out of the Kehoe home, pulled along by that growing sense of momentum that made her almost giddy. An ID didn't prove guilt. It didn't prove anything. And there was still a hell of a lot more work for her to do. But Spenser was certain, that after spinning her wheels for days, she was finally on the right track. It was a critical first step.

And that was something she could work with.

CHAPTER THIRTY-ONE

"Wow. I would have bet good money that the guy they picked out of the six-packs was going to be Don Haverton," Amanda said.

"Yeah, same here. I'm kind of surprised," Jacob said.

"He's a wife-beater. Low-hanging fruit," Amanda added. "We probably should have known. It's rarely the low-hanging fruit."

"It's low-hanging fruit for a reason," Jacob said. "The same reason clichés are clichés."

Spenser studied the photo of Simon Elbert sitting on the table in front of her, the bantering between Amanda and Jacob just background noise. Six-five with a heavyset build, Simon Elbert was a physically imposing man. She imagined how he would look in his ghillie suit, in the dark, coming at her and suppressed a shudder. It had to have been terrifying, and Spenser could see exactly why James Burnham believed the Okasha was coming for him and Rachel.

Elbert had a shaggy mop of dirty blonde hair, dark, narrow eyes, thin lips, and a weak chin with a pronounced cleft. Yet, even at forty-four years old, Elbert had chubby cheeks and a youthful baby face. There was an intensity in those dark eyes, though, that gave Spenser pause. He looked quiet and unassuming—even Brock Kehoe had mentioned that Elbert was slow, suggesting perhaps that he may have had a developmental disability.

As she studied his features, Spenser wasn't so sure that he was slow. She wasn't convinced he had a developmental disability. There was something in his eyes, a certain cold edginess that made her think he was a lot smarter than people gave him credit for. She'd seen it before in some of the monsters she'd chased. She learned a long time ago that being quiet and keeping to yourself didn't equate to stupidity. Spenser had found, more times than not, that those who sat back and watched, those who closely observed others, and always played their cards close to the vest that were the most dangerous.

"Jacob, what else can you tell me about Simon Elbert?" Spenser said. "Dig into his history. I want to know what we're up against here."

"Already ahead of you on that one, boss," he said.

"Let's have it."

"All right. Simon Elbert graduated from Taft High School and, according to his records, was a very above-average student. Got good grades, tested well, and apparently has an IQ that's one-thirty-plus. Very smart guy, apparently," he said.

It confirmed what Spenser was already thinking about him. He wasn't slow or stupid. He was quiet and measured. That, in her opinion, made him dangerous.

"Okay, go on. What else do we know about him?"

"After high school, he joined the Air Force, did six years, then rotated out. From what I found, his service wasn't exceptionally distinguished or anything like that," Jacob answered.

"Well, I'd say the fact that he served at all is pretty distinguished," Spenser said.

"Fair enough."

"What did he do after?"

"Not much. It looks like he worked a string of menial jobs, bouncing from one to another," Jacob said. "He's doing general handyman stuff now. He also has a side hustle making custom furniture, though it doesn't look like that's his main source of income."

"Family?" Spenser asked.

"He's got a sister who still lives in the area—Lydia. Both parents are deceased," he said, then grimaced at what he saw on the screen.

"What is it?"

"Elbert's father murdered his mother, then killed himself," he replied. "This was when Simon was fourteen years old—Lydia was twelve. They went to live with an aunt after that, who passed just a few years back. Natural causes, if you're keeping score."

"What about his record?" Amanda asked.

"Drunk and disorderlies. A couple of them after he rotated out of the service," he said. "Nothing since. He's been clean."

Amanda was staring at her computer screen. "He doesn't have much of a social media footprint. He's got a Facebook account, but he hasn't posted anything to it in years. I can't find any other socials for him."

"Other than the Kehoe's ID, is there anything else connecting him to Rachel?" Spenser asked. "Does he maybe have hidden social media accounts? Or is there anything from her socials that set off any red flags?"

"I haven't found any hidden social media accounts for him, but I'd be able to tell you more definitively if I had a look at his phone or computers," Jacob said.

"As for Rachel's socials, she's a beautiful girl, so she's got a lot of creepers on her pages. Most of them are really gross," Amanda responded. "But I didn't see anything that set off warning bells. I didn't see anything that made me think she was being stalked."

"Which means he either doesn't do social media or he's savvy enough to not make it obvious," Spenser mused. "I'm betting it's the latter. He's obsessed with her, and I think because she's all over socials, he was keeping tabs on her that way as well. He just has enough discipline and self-control to not let himself be seen."

"You might be right. But I'd sure like to get ahold of his electronics," Jacob said.

"Ditto that. I'm sure it's going to be a gold mine."

"Is there anything else I need to know?" Spenser asked. "Does he have any weapons registered to him?"

Jacob tapped away on his keyboard for a couple of minutes, then nodded. "Yeah. He's got a Colt .45, an AR-15, and a Mossberg 12-gauge shotgun all registered to him."

"Fantastic," Amanda muttered. "I have to wonder how many other weapons he's got that he never bothered to register."

"The good news is that he can only use one at a time," Spenser said.

Amanda chuckled. "That's a valid point. So, what's our next move?"

"We've got a warrant for Elbert's house, so let's go and take a look."

"Should we saddle up some backup?"

"He's not going to be there," Spenser said. "He's going to be wherever he's got Rachel."

Amanda frowned, and Spenser paused, recalling the conversation she'd had with Ryker when he'd asked her to stop taking unnecessary chances. When he'd asked her to learn to delegate and not be the tip of the spear every time, this would probably be one of those times when a little discretion really might be the better part of valor.

"Get Lane and Miguel geared up—vests and long guns," Spenser said. "We'll brief in the parking lot then roll out."

"Good call, Sheriff."

Spenser smiled as she got to her feet. "See you out there."

Simon Elbert lived in his family home. It was a small cottage-style house that had definitely seen better days. The paint was faded and chipping, and many of the windows were cracked, if not broken out completely, with plastic sheeting and cardboard covering the holes. Spenser and Amanda stepped lightly up onto the sagging, creaking porch after sending Deputies Summers and Bustos around to the back of the house. Spenser was almost certain Elbert wasn't there, but she was taking appropriate measures, just in case.

Spenser keyed open her mic. "Summers, are you and Bustos in position?"

"In position, Sheriff," Summers responded.

"Keep your eyes open. We're about to breach."

"Copy that."

Spenser stood in front of the door and raised her foot to kick it in but winced as a sharp jag of pain shot through her. Amanda put her hand on Spenser's shoulder.

"Hold that thought, Sheriff," she said.

Amanda reached out, grabbed the doorknob, and turned it. Spenser snickered softly, realizing it was unlocked.

"Work smarter, not harder," Amanda said.

"Yeah, yeah, yeah," Spenser muttered.

They drew their weapons and stood on either side of the door. Spenser's body tensed, and the adrenaline began to flow like a furiously rushing river. She gave Amanda a nod. She was ready. Amanda gave the door three hard raps.

"Sheriff's department!" she called out and shouldered the door open.

Their weapons leading the way, they stormed into the house low and fast, careful not to cross each other's line of fire. At the same time, Summers and Bustos came crashing through the back door and into the kitchen that lay beyond the arch that separated the room she and Amanda were standing in.

"Clear!" Summers called out.

"Front room, clear," Spenser said. "Fan out and clear the rest of the house."

Amanda, Summers, and Bustos spread out and began checking the rest of the rooms, their calls of "clear" echoing through the house. Spenser holstered her weapon and looked around the living room. Elbert wasn't in the house, just like she knew he wouldn't be. Spenser was positive Simon Elbert was with Rachel wherever he'd stashed her. His obsession wouldn't allow him to leave her side. Not until he was done with her.

"House is clear, Sheriff," Lane said as she stepped into the room.

"This place is a pig sty," Bustos remarked.

Elbert clearly wasn't much for housekeeping. Or furniture. There was one large, threadbare sofa in the living room that looked like it had been there since his parents were still alive, and a battered old recliner. The nicked and scarred coffee table was littered with old bags of food, moldering pizza boxes, and beer cans. A thick layer of dust coated every surface in the room, and the carpeting was stained and matted. A stench like rotting meat hung heavy in the air.

"He's not here," Lane said, frustrated and upset.

"Believe it or not, it's not necessarily a bad thing," Spenser responded.

"What do you mean?"

"It means that he's very likely still with Rachel, which tells me she's still alive," Spenser said. "She might be playing along with him. Whatever she's doing, she hasn't broken that fantasy he's got in his mind yet. That gives us a chance to find her and bring her home."

Before Lane could reply, Amanda's voice echoed from the back room, sharp and alarmed. "Sheriff, you're going to want to see this!"

Spenser turned and rushed to the back of the house, finding Amanda in the last room at the end of the hall. And the moment she stepped into the room, Spenser felt her heart drop into the pit of her stomach. On the wall across from the door, Elbert had taped dozens of pictures of Rachel, all of them candid shots taken when it didn't seem like she was even aware that she was being photographed. Some of them had been taken outside of her school, others while she was out with her friends, and still others from a vantage point that could have only been from the deer stand in the tree behind the Kehoe house. A table sat against the wall below the photos, and on it sat the trinkets he'd taken from Rachel's room, including five pairs of her panties.

"Jesus," Spenser gasped.

"It's a full-on shrine," Amanda said. "You were right, Sheriff. He's obsessed with her. We need to find this guy. Fast."

"All right, have Lane and Miguel stay and lock this place down," Spenser said. "And call Arbery. Have him come out and process the house. Tell him to look for anything that might be able to help us find him."

"Copy that," she replied. "What about us?"

"We're going to talk to Elbert's sister. Hopefully, she'll have some idea where he is," Spenser said. "If we find him, I guarantee we're going to find Rachel."

CHAPTER THIRTY-TWO

ELBERT'S SISTER, LYDIA, LIVED IN THE NEIGHBORING TOWN of Greenwood in a small, one-and-a-half-story brown-shingled Cape Cod-style home with a large, American flag hanging from a bracket on the column out front. A CPA, Lydia ran her independent accounting and wealth management firm from her home office. A small shingle hung outside the door of the offset garage. It was a very nicely kept, tastefully landscaped home in what looked like an upper middle-class neighborhood, with a black BMW X5 parked in the driveway.

"What do we know about Lydia?" Spenser asked as she pulled to a stop at the curb.

Amanda consulted her tablet. "Widowed. Her husband was in the army and was killed in action overseas. One daughter, who is a freshman at Washington State—Lydia's alma mater. She's got a master's degree in accounting and finance and operates her own accounting and financial management firm. She apparently does very well, too."

"It looks like it."

"A quick look at her socials shows she's got a wide friends group and has a very active lifestyle. She's quite the fashionista and connoisseur of wine, apparently," Amanda reported. "She prefers reds, if you were curious."

"I wasn't."

"Just reporting the facts."

Spenser harrumphed. "So, she's basically the polar opposite of her brother."

"Yeah, pretty much."

"Okay, let's go talk to her."

They climbed out of the Bronco and headed up the walkway to the front door. Spenser knocked and took a step back, doing her best to appear as non-threatening as she could. A moment later, the door opened. Six feet tall with hair the color of sand that was pulled back in a ponytail that fell to the middle of her back, Lydia Elbert stared at them with cool, mocha-colored eyes. She was a lean, fit woman with perfectly applied makeup, and was dressed in a designer navy blue pantsuit with a cream-colored blouse beneath the blazer and a string of pearls around her neck.

If she was surprised to find Spenser and Amanda on her porch, she did a good job of hiding it. Her icy gaze didn't waver, and her expression was blank and unmoving. She gave off all the warmth of a glacier. It was a complete one-eighty from the smiling, jovial woman in the photos she'd posted to her social media pages.

"Yes?" she asked.

"Good afternoon, Lydia Elbert?"

The corners of her mouth pulled down slightly. "Shaughnessy. Elbert is my maiden name."

"Of course, I'm very sorry," Spenser replied. "I'm Sheriff Spenser Song, and this is Undersheriff Amanda Young."

She eyed their badges. "You're a little out of your jurisdiction, aren't you?"

"We are. But we informed Sheriff Early we were coming to speak with you," Spenser replied. "He gave us his blessing."

Her perfectly sculpted eyebrows rose slightly. "Speak with me? About what?"

"Your brother."

A loud, frustrated sigh burst from her mouth. "What did he do this time?"

"May we come in and talk to you?"

Lydia hesitated as her eyes flitted from Spenser to Amanda and back again. Her brow was furrowed, and her lips were creased into a frown. But she finally stepped aside.

"Come on in," she said.

The house was nicely put together without being ostentatious. It was obvious Lydia was doing fairly well for herself, but she wasn't overly performative about her wealth. As she led them down a hall and into a dining room, Spenser noticed the pictures of a tall girl with honey-blonde hair and dark, intense eyes displayed prominently. She saw a folded American flag in a triangular case sitting atop a credenza with photographs of her late husband in uniform and a shadow box that featured his medals hung on the wall just above it. It wasn't difficult for Spenser to see that family meant everything to Lydia.

Except for her brother. She didn't see a single picture of Simon anywhere. Although there were a few pictures of her parents in frames, obviously her love of family didn't include Simon. She'd erased him from her life, figuratively and physically.

"Your daughter is beautiful," Spenser said as she gestured to a photo on the wall that showed the girl at what appeared to be her prom.

"Oh. Yes. Thank you. I'm very proud of her," Lydia responded. "Please, have a seat."

Spenser and Amanda sat down on one side of the large, elegantly carved dining room table while Lydia sat down across from them. The woman's laptop sat open. A couple of files were stacked neatly on one side of it, and thin tendrils of steam drifted from the mouth of the mug that sat on the other side. She'd obviously been working when they interrupted her. The table was beautiful. It was handcrafted and, recalling that Simon was a woodworker, Spenser wondered if he had made it for his sister at some point before she'd erased him from her life.

"Can I offer you some coffee or water?" Lydia asked.

"No. Thank you. We're fine," Spenser said.

"All right. So, what can I do for you, Sheriff?"

"When was the last time you spoke with your brother?"

She blew out a loud breath. "It's been years, honestly. The last time I saw Simon was Christmas, two years ago. He... well... he was drunk and made a scene, and I asked him to leave. I told him that I didn't want to see him again until he'd gotten his life sorted out."

"No phone calls? Nothing like that?" Amanda asked.

Lydia shook her head. "No. Nothing. What is this about? What has Simon done now?"

"You've asked that twice now—what has he done now?" Amanda started. "We know he had a couple of drunk and disorderlies, but those were years ago. Does he have a more recent history with the police that we don't know about?"

"Nothing serious. But the police here in town have let me know they picked him up on nuisance complaints a couple of times. Because I've got a good relationship with the police department, they let him off with a warning and didn't file any charges against him," she replied. "This was a year ago or so. I never spoke to Simon about it. I washed my hands of my brother a long time ago."

"What sort of nuisance complaints?" Spenser asked.

"They found him looking in a woman's window once. The other time, she'd called the police when he wouldn't stop following her around."

Spenser nodded. His obsessions didn't begin with Rachel, just as she'd thought. She was merely the latest in a line of fixations that gripped him. It spoke to Simon's mental instability. He obviously had some issues, which was likely what Brock Kehoe had picked up on in Simon, rather than any perceived mental deficiencies.

Lydia sighed again and buried her face in her hands. Spenser could see the woman's face and ears turning red but didn't think she was crying. The woman took a couple of beats, then sat up. Her cheeks were dry, but she looked like she was going to be sick. Spenser got the feeling she was holding something back. Whether it was because she didn't want to get involved or because, even though she had washed her hands of him, she was still trying to protect her brother, Spenser wasn't sure. The more she studied the woman, though, the more certain she became that she was holding onto a piece of information that could prove critical.

"What is it, Lydia?" Spenser asked. "I feel like there's something you want to tell us."

The woman quickly picked up her coffee mug and took a drink. Her hand was shaking and she suddenly looked uncomfortable. Spenser wanted to give her a little space and let her come to it on her own. If she pushed the woman too hard, Spenser was afraid she'd shut down entirely. But she didn't have time to play games. The clock was ticking on Rachel Kehoe.

"Lydia, what is it you're not telling us? Please," Spenser said. "There is a young girl's life at stake right now and—"

The woman's eyes grew wide and her mouth fell open. "What? What did my brother do?"

"We believe he abducted a young woman," Amanda said. "He beat her boyfriend nearly to death, and he's taken her somewhere."

Lydia covered her mouth with her hand, her face quickly draining of color. She swallowed hard and tried to gather her wits about her.

"He… abducted a woman?" she asked, as if in disbelief.

"We believe so, yes," Spenser confirmed. "We found evidence that he had been stalking this woman for quite a while."

Lydia hesitated and stared into her coffee mug. Spenser thought the woman seemed like she was weighing whether to tell her what she knew or not. As if sensing that Lydia was wavering, Amanda spoke up.

"He had a shrine to Rachel in his bedroom—surveillance photos, items he'd lifted from her bedroom. He even stole pairs of her panties," Amanda said bluntly.

A look of pure disgust crossed Lydia's face. If there had been a piece of her heart and mind intent on protecting her brother, learning what he had been up to seemed to have torn that down. Without a word, Lydia got to her feet and walked out of the room. Amanda shot Spenser a questioning look. Curious to see what was going to happen next, Spenser shook her head and motioned to give the woman a minute.

Lydia walked back into the room a few minutes later and set a photo album down on the table. She opened it and flipped to a page before turning it around and sliding it over to Spenser. There were two photos beneath the plastic covering on the page—Lydia and a young girl with honey-blonde hair, cornflower blue eyes, and delicate features. Spenser turned to Amanda.

"Look familiar?" she asked.

Amanda's face was colored with surprise. "My God. She looks just like Rachel."

Swallowing down the distaste that marked her face, Lydia cleared her throat. "This was my best friend, Enid. We were both thirteen when this picture was taken. Simon would have been fifteen at the time."

"What happened, Lydia?" Spenser asked.

"My brother became fixated on her. Obsessed, I suppose you could say," she said, her voice soft and filled with shame. "He followed her around, stole things when she spent the night—panties among them. Enid and I found his shrine to her, and it freaked her out so bad, she stopped speaking to me. And when he didn't stop stalking her, Enid's parents moved her away, sending her to live with relatives in Texas about a year after that."

Spenser and Amanda fell silent, absorbing what Lydia had just told them. Spenser wasn't entirely surprised. This kind of psychopathy tends to develop in a person's adolescent years. In Simon's case, that psychopathy was likely compounded by the trauma of his parents' murder-suicide. Lydia's friend Enid had obviously imprinted on Simon's brain. He'd probably believed there was some shared connection between him and Enid—a connection that didn't exist anywhere but in his own mind. But it had been intense.

After the fallout from the situation with Enid and whatever backlash he'd faced from it, Simon had probably managed to sublimate those feelings. Had learned to redirect his obsessions elsewhere. But when he ran into Rachel Kehoe, a spitting image of that girl who'd originally triggered his psychopathy, he couldn't hold himself in check any longer. He couldn't stop fixating on her and had, at some point, decided that he wasn't going to let Rachel get away like Enid had. Simon was going to have and keep her at all costs. That was when his plan came together, and he ultimately came crashing down on her that fateful night out at Mossy Flats.

"My brother is very smart, Sheriff. But ever since our parents… died… he's had issues. Severe emotional issues. I've done everything I can for him, but nothing I've done has actually helped. He seems to prefer to live like he has been," she said, her tone saturated with regret. "I cut him out of my life because I couldn't live in the past with him any longer. I needed to move forward with my own life. I… I feared he might do something like this, but there wasn't anything I could do. There wasn't anything…"

Her voice trailed off, and she fought back the deep emotion that colored her face. Her eyes grew red and watery, and, despite her efforts, tears rolled down her cheeks.

"Lydia, this is not your fault. There isn't anything you could have done to stop this," Spenser said gently. "This isn't on you."

She shook her head. "I should have—"

"Sheriff Song is right," Amanda added. "There is literally nothing you could have done to stop your brother from taking Rachel. Nothing at all."

"But you can help us get her back," Spenser said.

Lydia raised her watery gaze. "How?"

"Does he have any property or a cabin somewhere that's not registered in his name?"

"No. He doesn't have the money for that," she said. "If not for our parents leaving the house to us when they died, he'd be homeless."

"Okay, can you think of anywhere he likes to go to be alone?" Spenser asked. "Can you think of someplace that's off the beaten path where he might go when he needed to get away?"

Lydia frowned and turned away, seeming to be thinking hard. The torment and guilt on her face were hard to look at, and Spenser felt awful about opening these old wounds inside of her. But a young woman's life was at stake, so she was determined to do whatever it took, even if it meant stirring up the old, painful ghosts in Lydia's life, to get her back.

"When we were kids, Simon always used to like hanging out in the old silver mines out past the Ghostlands," she said. "I don't know if he still does. I mean, that was a really long time ago. But I remember him telling me that he liked to go out there to be alone."

Spenser exchanged a glance with Amanda. The old silver mines were the perfect place to hide out and stash a woman you'd just abducted. They were off the beaten path, far away from civilization, and there wasn't a lot of foot traffic out that way. Spenser wanted to kick herself for not thinking of the silver mines sooner. Of course, she didn't think anybody had really thought about the old silver mines for decades.

Except for Simon Elbert.

"Thank you, Lydia," Spenser said.

"Please," she said. "Don't hurt Simon. He's troubled, but he's not a bad person."

"We're going to do everything we can to bring this situation to a peaceful resolution for everybody involved. We don't want to hurt your brother," Spenser said. "But you also need to know that much of how this plays out is going to be up to him. But we will do our very best to make sure this doesn't go sideways for any of us."

As Spenser and Amanda got to their feet, Lydia's gaze fell, unable to meet their eyes any longer. She buried her face in her hands and began to sob quietly. The moment they were out of the house, Amanda was on the phone, pulling as many deputies into the office as they had on duty, telling them all to gear up and get ready. Spenser was ready to get this show on the road and to bring Rachel home alive and unhurt.

Despite her assurances, that they would do this as peacefully as they could, Spenser knew the endgame for this kind of offender. When they were caught and had no way out, it usually involved a hail of bullets. She just hoped she could limit the damage to Simon alone.

CHAPTER THIRTY-THREE

Spenser, Amanda, and half a dozen of her deputies stood in the Ghostlands, a place on the far edge of town famed for being the party place for the town's youngsters. It's where generations of Sweetwater Falls' most notable families came to get their drink on, well away from the prying eyes of the town's adults. Once upon a time, it had been the silver miners' cabins, with half a dozen structures still standing… though just barely. They were rotten and decrepit, and despite looking like a strong wind might blow them down, they somehow remained upright and had for a lot of years.

"All right, we're looking for Simon Elbert, who, we believe, abducted Rachel Kehoe," Spenser said. "His sister thinks he might be hiding out here in the old silver mines."

"But there are a dozen mines. Maybe more," Deputy Jerry Kruger said. "How are we going to know which mine he's in?"

"We don't. So, we're going to have to search each and every cave out there," she answered. "But you've all been assigned a partner and a section on the maps Amanda is handing out now. Stick with your partner and to your assignment. No freelancing, guys. None. I am not going to tolerate anybody going cowboy out there. Am I understood?"

"Yes, ma'am," they chimed in unison.

The search was going to be a tedious, laborious, and most worryingly, incredibly dangerous task. She had no doubt that Simon knew every inch of the caves out there and had every possible tactical advantage. And there was no more dangerous animal than a dangerous animal who'd been backed into a corner. She was scared for her deputies. But there was a girl in trouble out there, which meant there was a job to be done. They'd all signed up for this job, knowing a time might come when they'd have to put their lives on the line. That time was now.

"You're all paired up for a reason. Nobody goes alone," Spenser said. "Stay on comms. I want everybody checking in constantly. And if you see something, sound the alarm and wait for the cavalry. Don't engage alone. Am I clear?"

"Yes, ma'am," they all responded in unison.

"Make sure your vests are strapped on tight. Keep your heads on a swivel and watch each other's backs," Spenser said. "Any questions?"

Nobody had any, but Spenser could see the tension in all their faces. It wasn't often they had to gear up and go after a dangerous character, and although Spenser had trained them all and continued to drill them all on emergency procedures relentlessly, there was a world of difference between training and real-life action. They didn't get a lot of the latter in a town like Sweetwater Falls. But it was exactly why they should all be glad that Spenser had spent the amount of time she had on getting them ready for it.

"Remember your training, guys. This is exactly the scenario we've been doing it for," Spenser said. "All right. You have your assignments, so let's head out. Be careful. Everybody, and I mean everybody, comes home tonight. Understand?"

Another chorus of "yes, ma'am" echoed through the trees around them. Spenser's stomach tightened, and her mouth was dry, but she couldn't put it off any longer.

"All right. Let's head out," Spenser said.

The deputies paired off with their assigned partners and headed off into the woods. Amanda stood beside Spenser, watching them all go. Her heart thundering in her breast, Spenser tried to swallow down the thick, greasy feeling of nausea that welled up in her throat.

"It's going to be okay," Amanda said. "You've trained everybody well."

Spenser grunted, cradling the shotgun in her arms, and took a moment to quell the maelstrom churning inside her belly. Drawing a deep breath, she held it and counted to ten before exhaling.

Together, they set off, following one of the trails that led to the east. They were assigned to the number two and four mines that sat about a mile and a half from the Ghostlands. Spenser felt a lot better, but she wasn't quite at a hundred percent yet, so getting there was going to be a bit of a challenge. But she gritted her teeth and pushed through the lingering discomfort. She would be damned if she wasn't out in the field with her team, not when they were that close to finding Rachel Kehoe and bringing her home.

Her only concern was in what condition they would be bringing her home. While she thought all signs pointed to her still being alive, she knew that when you were dealing with somebody as emotionally disturbed as Simon Elbert, she couldn't assume anything. She recalled a case where a man had murdered his wife and children and then lived with their bodies for more than a week. It was only a neighbor, alarmed by the smell of decay, who'd alerted the police.

"How are you holding up?" Amanda asked quietly.

"I'm good enough."

"Just be careful," she said. "Pace yourself, Sheriff. If you need to stop and rest—"

"I don't. Keep going."

They walked for another ten minutes or so before entering a clearing. Just ahead of them was the opening for mine number four. Officially speaking, it had been closed down decades ago. A few rotting wooden boards, meant to keep people out, still hung over the mouth of the mine. Most had been torn off long ago by kids who enjoyed exploring mysterious caves like the mines.

After a pair of teenagers had gotten lost deep in the mines, Spenser had issued a warning about staying out of the mines, but there was no practical way she could prevent people from going in if they wanted to. The kids had been found, but she knew others hadn't been so lucky. She'd heard more than a few stories about people going into the mines just for a bit of adventure or perhaps hoping to find some of the silver rumored to still be inside, who'd never come out again.

Every now and then, a few would-be treasure hunters would discover the remains of those who'd gone before them and weren't as lucky. And yet, despite the number of people who'd been swallowed up by the mines and had never been heard from again, people continued to go adventuring in the winding labyrinth of tunnels. All Spenser could do was shake her head.

As they cautiously approached the mouth of mine number four, Spenser's belly tightened. The hair on the back of her neck stood on end, and tendrils of electricity tingled across her skin.

"Amanda, get down!" she shouted.

The younger woman immediately threw herself behind a large rock as a shot rang out. It hit the rock with a sharp ping, sending chips of stone raining down on Amanda. Spenser hunkered down behind the wide trunk of a pine tree, her shotgun at the ready, and looked at the darkened mouth of the mine.

"Amanda, are you all right?" she called.

"I'm good. I'm good," she replied.

"Call in the cavalry."

"On it."

Spenser slowly leaned out from behind the tree and then quickly ducked back when she heard a click. Simon took another shot at her. The bullet hit the tree she was hiding behind with a dull thud. The distance to the mine was too great for her shotgun to be effective, and she felt like she had more control with her sidearm anyway, so Spenser leaned it against the tree then pulled her Glock out of her holster, flipped off the safety, and chambered a round.

"Simon Elbert, I'm Sheriff Song," she called. "It's over. Come out with your hands up."

"No," he shouted. "Go away."

"Simon, you need to let Rachel go—"

"I love her, and she loves me. Leave us alone!"

Spenser licked her lips. She needed to confirm the girl was still, in fact, alive.

"Rachel, can you hear me?"

The seconds ticked by without a reply, filling Spenser with a cold sense of dread.

"Rachel?" Spenser called again.

"I'm here—"

Rachel's voice was cut off by the sharp sound of skin meeting skin, which was followed by a scream filled with pain. He'd slapped her. The sound of her voice, though, lifted Spenser's heart, and when she glanced at Amanda, still hunkered down behind the large rock, the younger woman was smiling and flashed her a thumbs up. Rachel was alive.

"You don't talk to her," Simon called. "You leave her alone. You leave us both alone!"

"Simon, Rachel's parents are very worried about her. They need to see her. They need to know that she's all right."

"Enid is fine! Tell her parents that Enid is fine, and she wants to stay here with me!"

The fact that he was calling her Enid showed Spenser how deep into his delusion Simon really was. He didn't see Rachel as a replacement for the woman he'd fixated on so long ago. He believed she was the woman. It made the situation a little more volatile and unpredictable than Spenser would have liked. He was living in a fantasy, and their arrival threatened to shatter that for him. And if Simon's fantasy bubble was to suddenly be popped, and he was thrust back into reality, she feared he might lash out at Rachel.

The chatter on the radio from the deputies crashing on their position told Spenser they were still five minutes or more away. She was afraid they didn't have five minutes. Every second Simon was forced to deal with them and confront reality, it threatened to shatter his illusion. She waved her hand to catch Amanda's attention and when the woman turned to her, Spenser raised three fingers, telling her to go to their private radio channel.

"We're running out of time," Spenser said. "We need to move."

"We don't have backup."

"They're still minutes away. We might not have time to wait."

Even from her vantage point, Spenser could see Amanda's face tighten. She knew what Spenser was saying was right. She just didn't like it.

"What are you thinking?" Amanda asked.

"Verbally engage him," Spenser said. "Keep him talking."

"Sheriff—"

"Keep him talking."

"I think *you* should keep him talking—"

Recalling just how large Simon was, Spenser shook her head. Amanda was slight and didn't have much in the way of physical combat training. The last thing Spenser was going to do was send her in to handle a beast of a man like that.

"Keep him talking, Amanda. That's an order," Spenser said.

"Sheriff—"

Without giving her a chance to respond, Spenser shut off her radio and moved off through the trees. Keeping low and moving as fast as she could, Spenser moved from point of cover to point of cover. Behind her, she heard Amanda begin to engage Simon verbally as she'd instructed. By the time she'd circled around through the trees and was approaching the mouth of the mine from behind, Spenser looked out into the tree line in front of her and saw that the rest of her deputies had arrived, taking up positions of cover, weapons at the ready.

"Get out of here and leave us alone!" Simon shouted from the mouth of the cave. "If you don't leave us alone, I'm going to kill Enid then kill myself."

It was a direct callback to what his father had done. Simon's mental illness ran deep. Worse, she knew that he was willing to go through with it. Edging slowly along the rock wall beside the mine's entrance, careful to avoid making a sound, Spenser held her breath. She gestured to Amanda, urging her to keep him talking. The faces of her deputies were grim, and the air around them was heavy, and thick with tension.

"Simon, please. Just come out and let's talk about this," Amanda called. "There's no need for anybody to get hurt. We just want to talk."

"I'm going to count to ten," Simon shouted back. "If you're not gone by the time I get to ten, I'm going to kill Enid and then myself! I mean it now! Don't make me do this. Enid and I just want to live alone in peace!"

Spenser was close enough to hear Rachel's sniffing and soft groans as she recovered from the blows Simon had rained down on her.

"Ten!" Simon shouted.

"Simon, don't do this!" Amanda called back.

"Nine!"

Spenser holstered her Glock, then pulled the small canister of tear gas off her tactical vest and pulled the pin.

"Eight!"

Spenser gave it a silent three count, then leaned out and threw the canister into the mouth of the mine. A loud pop was followed by the hiss of the gas releasing. A moment later, as gas drifted out of the mine's entrance, she heard Simon hacking and coughing wildly. She turned the corner and found him just inside the entrance, hands to his eyes, trying to fight off the gas.

Spenser grabbed him by his wrist and bent it backward. He howled in pain but the weapon in his hand tumbled to the ground, hitting the dirt with a dull thud. Moving as fast as a viper, Spenser kicked the weapon out of his reach and then used her momentum to fling him out into the sunlight. She followed him out, determined to put him down, but he recovered quickly and thrust his foot upward. Spenser's momentum carried her straight into his foot, and it caught her flush in the stomach, hitting the exact spot where she'd taken Alex Ricci's blade.

She recoiled as a bright flash of pain tore through her body. Spenser stumbled backward and ended up on her backside, gripping her side, her face contorted with agony. The pain was intense, and the voices of her deputies, all shouting, were muted and fuzzy, and she couldn't make out what they were saying. Through her tear-blurred eyes, she saw the mammoth figure of Simon Elbert, on his feet, advancing toward her.

Pushing through the pain that rocked her, Spenser crab-walked backward, trying to put some distance between herself and Simon. It was then she noticed the sunlight glinting off the long, curved blade in his hand.

"Oh, hell no," she croaked. "Not again."

Moving swiftly and fluidly, Spenser drew her weapon and fired a shot. She watched as the bullet tore through Simon's thigh. A thick crimson spray hit the dirt behind him, and Simon grunted in pain. His face was red, twisted with pain, but his eyes burned with rage. He took another step, and Spenser thought she was going to have to put him down for good, but two large bodies flew in from the right and, with a perfect form tackle, Deputies Woods and Berman swept Simon off his feet and drove him straight into the dirt.

Simon thrashed on the ground beneath them and howled in both outrage and pain, but Woods and Berman were large and well-muscled themselves. They managed to get the big man onto his belly and had his hands cuffed behind his back as swiftly and smoothly as a pair of cowboys roping cattle at the rodeo. Once they had Simon secured, they stepped over and helped get Spenser back on her feet.

"Thanks, guys," Spenser said.

"You okay, Sheriff?" Woods asked.

She nodded. "Yeah. I'm good."

"I think we're going to let Marley be the judge of that," Amanda said.

Spenser gave her a wry grin. "Guys, can you get Simon back to the cars? He's going to need some medical treatment on that leg."

"On it, Sheriff," Berman said.

"Good work," Spenser said. "Everybody, great job."

Clutching her belly and gritting her teeth as she fought off the pain that rippled through her midsection, Spenser turned and headed for the mine. Amanda fell into step beside her. As they approached the mine, they stopped as a figure emerged from the thinning cloud of smoke that drifted from the entrance.

"Rachel," Spenser said.

Moving with a shuffling jog, Spenser reached the girl and, together with Amanda, held her up. She was pale and looked weak. Deep purple bruises marred her porcelain flesh, and she had dark half-moons beneath her eyes. Her clothes were dirty and ragged, she had dried blood crusted at the corners of her mouth and around her nostrils, and she looked like she'd lost ten pounds over the course of her ordeal. But she looked at Spenser and Amanda with an expression of relief and the light of gratitude shining in her eyes.

"Thank you," she whispered. "Thank you."

The relief and joy she felt was overpowering, and, overcome by those emotions, Spenser pulled the girl into a tight embrace. Rachel melted into her, then reached out and grabbed Amanda's hand. The battered girl clung tightly to her and gripped Amanda's hand as if she was lost at sea and they were life preservers. Her thin body shook hard as she cried, and Spenser just held her tighter. With tears in her eyes, Spenser turned to Amanda whose cheeks glistened with her own tears, and they shared a smile, the pain that had gripped her a moment before, totally forgotten.

"Thank you," Rachel whispered again.

CHAPTER THIRTY-FOUR

"How is she doing?" Amanda asked.

Spenser dropped into her chair at the conference room table and let out a breath, happy to be sitting down finally. It had been a long day, and she was worn out.

"They're keeping her for a few days for observation, but Marley says she's confident that Rachel's going to make a full recovery. Physically, anyway. She's probably going to need a lot of counseling to deal with the mental and emotional impact of everything she's been through."

"At least she's alive to get that counseling," Amanda said. "That's a very good thing."

Spenser nodded and leaned back in her chair, enveloped in a sense of warmth as she recalled the reunion between Rachel and her family. There hadn't been a dry eye in the house. The joy on all their faces had been genuine, and it wasn't hard to see just how much they all cared for each other. The job took a lot out of Spenser, and there were more days when she went home feeling like garbage than not, but moments like that restored her soul.

"You did that, you know," Amanda said. "You were on the case right from the jump. You knew we were looking for a man and not some big monster."

"We all did that."

"You knew from the start that there was more going on, Sheriff. You found the deer stand. You made the connection to the ghillie suit. I really don't know that Rachel would have been found if not for you. It just goes to show me that I still have a lot to learn."

Spenser shook her head. "You'll get there. I've just been doing this kind of work a lot longer than you. The more you see and are exposed to, the easier you'll start to see all the different angles. I know for a fact you weren't going to actually be chasing a monster out there. You would have eventually gotten around to making the connections I did. I just had the benefit of experience, not to mention catching a few lucky breaks along the way."

"Yeah, well, we're all lucky for your experience then."

"I can't do my job without all of you guys. That's what a team is, Amanda," Spenser told her. "And in all fairness, Simon Elbert is a big monster."

"Speaking of monsters, you don't have to be afraid anymore, little sister," Jacob crowed. "I've captured the Okasha!"

They turned to see Jacob stepping into the conference room with Simon's ghillie suit in a plastic evidence bag. He held it up and mockingly roared like a monster. Amanda's face flushed, and she turned away, though not before Spenser saw the amused smirk on her face.

"I hate you, Jacob. You're the worst person in the history of the world," Amanda chuckled.

"The worst? I can probably think of a few people worse than me."

"I can't."

Laughing to himself, Jacob hung the ghillie suit up on a rack, making sure it was still in Amanda's eyeline, before sitting down again. As they slung insults back and forth, Spenser looked at the suit. It was made of dark fabric and covered with hundreds of strips of burlap that had things like moss and leaves glued to it, helping it blend into the forest setting. Seeing it up close like that and imagining a man Simon Elbert's size wearing it made it easy for Spenser to understand why James Burnham had believed it was a creature from legend attacking them. In the dark, Spenser probably would have believed it, too.

"I've got to say, this feels good," Jacob said. "I like it when the good guys get the W. I like it even more when getting that W also gives me something to hold over my kid sister's head for the rest of her life."

"I should shoot him," Amanda said. "Prison might not be so bad."

As they laughed together, Alice stepped into the conference room with an uncertain expression on her face.

"I'm sorry to interrupt, Sheriff," she said.

"That's all right, Alice. I was just listening to the kids bickering, so I welcome the interruption," Spenser replied. "What is it?"

"Umm… Mayor Dent just called. She said she needs you in her office. Now."

The tone in Alice's voice, along with the way she was looking at Spenser, made the good feelings evaporate almost instantly. Something was up.

"Did she say what it was about?" Spenser asked.

"No. But I heard through the grapevine that a couple of FBI agents showed up today."

Spenser groaned and rolled her eyes. Her day of reckoning had apparently finally come.

"Okay, thanks, Alice."

"Is everything going to be okay?" she asked.

"Everything's going to be fine," Spenser said with more confidence than she felt.

Amanda's smile vanished. "This is about Ricci?"

"I would assume so."

"Should I come with you?"

"No, it's fine. I've got this," Spenser replied and got to her feet. "I'll see you guys in a bit."

Maggie was seated at the head of the conference table when she walked in. To her right sat Clyde Rea, head of the New York Field Office's Organized Crime Bureau. Seated next to him was a man Spenser didn't know. Spenser paused and took the temperature of the room. It was heavy. And Maggie's face was neutral, telling her whatever this was, it wasn't going to be good.

"Clyde," Spenser said with a nod as she sat down across from him.

"Spenser," he replied. "It's been a while."

"That it has."

Clyde Rea was about her height, with jet black hair he always wore slicked back and sporting a three-piece suit. Today's selection was charcoal gray pinstripes. She could practically see the Pomade glistening in the sunlight that slanted in through the windows. His eyebrows were like two bushy caterpillars positioned above dark eyes that were permanently squinted. He completed the Snidely Whiplash look with a pencil-thin mustache.

The man sitting next to him was tall, probably six-three or so, and rail thin. He had a long, gaunt face, a horseshoe of dirty blond hair, hazel eyes, and a prominent nose with a pair of round, rimless spectacles perched on it. His suit, like Clyde's, was charcoal gray, but he went with a violet-colored tie and matching pocket square, but no vest. When he looked at Spenser, his eyes were flat, his face expressionless. She was tempted to check his pulse to be sure Clyde hadn't brought a living corpse along to this little Powwow.

"So, what can I do for you, gentlemen?" Spenser asked.

"We asked Mayor Dent to observe this meeting, since she is technically your direct superior," Clyde began.

Maggie shot her an apologetic glance, but Spenser shrugged her shoulders, silently communicating to the woman not to worry about it.

"The more the merrier," Spenser replied. "Care to introduce me to your friend?"

"My name is Stephen Minaya, and I am an Assistant US Attorney for the Southern District of New York," he said crisply.

"You boys are a long way from home. I assume it's for something important."

"It is. We're here about Alex Ricci, Sheriff Song," Minaya said.

"I figured as much. What about him?"

"The US Attorney has concerns about his death," Rea said. "And frankly, so do I."

Spenser rolled her eyes as she sat back in her chair and stared at the two men. Something was going on here. She could see it in their eyes.

"What's going on here? What are you guys really after?" Spenser asked.

"Answers, Sheriff Song," Rea said. "We're after some answers."

"Why are you guys suddenly so concerned about a dirtbag like Alex Ricci? It seems a little strange that his death brings the head of the OC Bureau and an AUSA running."

"We want to get your side of the story, Sheriff Song. We want to understand how it is that you ended up killing him."

Maggie remained silent, no doubt instructed by Rea and Minaya to keep her mouth shut under one threat or another. Her face burned red, though, and she glared holes through them.

"Because he attacked me, and I defended myself," Spenser said.

"I understand that is your claim. We have read your incident report," Minaya said. "So, walk us through this. What do you mean when you claim he attacked you? Please, be specific."

Spenser looked from Minaya to Rea and back again, the red flags waving in her head. She took a moment to assemble the facts in her head and try to put them all together. They had an agenda. That much was clear. But what was that agenda? The moment the question floated through her mind, the answer became obvious.

"Are you investigating me?" she asked. "Are you two really trying to build a case against me for Alex Ricci's death?"

Minaya glanced at Rea, some silent bit of communication passing between them before he turned back to her. His eyes were cold, his face expressionless.

"You were very vocal about Mr. Ricci being the one who actually murdered your husband and not his brother, Derrick—"

"And yet, in your infinite wisdom, you folks put him in prison for the rest of his life for it anyway," Spenser cut him off. "Don't get me wrong, Derrick belongs in prison. Just not what you people put him in prison for."

"Do you see how this looks, Spenser?" Rea said.

"No, I really don't."

Rea sighed impatiently. "You didn't agree with the prosecution of your former partner. You blamed his brother, and that brother then turned up dead… by your hand," he said sternly. "Do you see how it's looking now?"

The full scenario finally played out in Spenser's mind. She hadn't thought of it sooner, only because it was so asinine that she didn't waste any bandwidth even considering it.

"So, you're going to try to railroad me the same way you railroaded Derrick," Spenser said. "I see what's going on here now."

"We're not looking to railroad anybody. We're searching for the truth here, Spenser."

She opened her mouth to respond, then quickly closed it again. Something still wasn't adding up for her. Why would they be so concerned with Alex Ricci's death, by her hand or not? He was a parasite. A killer. His death really shouldn't have made waves, let alone waves big enough to bring the head of the OCB and an AUSA running to her doorstep. Not unless…

"Oh my God," Spenser said. "He was an informant. He was working with you guys."

Rea and Minaya both shifted in their seats and looked suddenly uncomfortable. They shared another silent bit of communication before Rea spoke.

"Yes. He was. We had been working with him for several years, and the intel he provided led to some major arrests," he confirmed.

Spenser sat back in her chair and stared at them in disbelief. It all made sense now. He was a major asset for the Bureau, and because they lost track of him and he ended up dead, they all had egg on their faces and needed to take a head in return. Her head, specifically. She took a beat to absorb it, then sat forward again.

"Yeah, well, you two should have put a leash on your dog because he's been hounding me for a while now. This is what happens when you work with a cold-blooded killer like Alex Ricci. This isn't on me. This is on you," Spenser said.

"Spenser, he was our informant and our responsibility, and we're taking his death very seriously. Mr. Ricci was a very valuable asset," Rea told her.

"And we take vigilante justice even more seriously," Minaya said.

"So, let me get this straight… I've been very outspoken in my belief that Alex and not Derrick murdered my husband and then murdered him to get even. Is that about right?"

"It's a theory we're looking into," Minaya said.

"There's a few problems with your theory," Spenser said.

"Such as?"

"He came here. To Sweetwater Falls, all the way on the other side of the country," Spenser responded. "I didn't go to New York and gun him down on Fifth Avenue. He came here. He came here to my home and attacked me in my driveway."

"We understand that is your assertion," Minaya said. "Can you prove that he attacked you?"

"Would you like to see the scars he left on me?"

Maggie's cell phone buzzed with an incoming text message. The two men turned to her with annoyance on their faces. Giving them a withering glare, she picked up her phone and read the message. Setting the phone down, she fixed them both with an icy, cold expression.

"I have something that may answer all of your questions, gentlemen," she said.

"Mayor Dent, we're not here to—"

"I thought you were here for the truth?" she asked.

Minaya started to reply, but his words were cut off when the conference room door opened. Spenser felt a flush of warmth as Ryker strode into the room. He gave her a wink and then turned to the two men, his face hardening instantly. He stood beside

Maggie, set his laptop down on the table, opened it, and hit a few keys.

"I don't know who you are, but this is an official proceeding," Minaya said.

"My name is Ryker Makawi. I own the cabin that Sheriff Song has been renting, and I have the surveillance video of the night Alex Ricci laid in wait and then attacked her as she arrived home."

Rea and Minaya both opened their mouths, perhaps to object, but they never got the chance. With the video playing, Ryker turned the screen to them. They watched the video. Watched Ricci appear out of nowhere to attack her and the fight that ensued. Spenser had been so blindsided and back on her heels that she hadn't even thought of the video cameras outside the cabin.

"I'll make sure you both get a copy of this video," Ryker said. "For the official file."

As the video ended, the two men slumped back in their chairs, seemingly deflated. They exchanged a glance, both of them apparently realizing the case they'd been trying to build against her was now DOA. They needed a head for their failure to control their informant, but thanks to Ryker and Maggie, they weren't going to be able to take hers.

"All right," Rea said as he closed his notebook and got to his feet. "Thank you for your time. I'm glad we could get this all cleared up."

"Please make sure to send us a copy for our files, Mr. Makawi," Minaya added. "And if we have any more questions, we'll be in touch."

"You do that," he grumbled.

The two men couldn't get out of the conference room fast enough, retreating with their tails between their legs, the narrative they'd been building in flaming ruins all around them. When the door closed behind them, Spenser jumped to her feet and ran to Ryker, throwing her arms around him. He scooped her up and spun her around, laughing along with her. She gave him a kiss as he set her down, and Spenser gave Maggie an equally enthusiastic hug.

"You guys saved my butt," Spenser said.

"You didn't do anything wrong," Maggie replied.

"They were sure going to make it seem like I had, though."

"Scumbags," Ryker growled.

Spenser's expression sobered. "Seriously, though, thank you both. As we've seen, they have no problem railroading people to cover their own butts, so I'm profoundly thankful to you guys for not letting them get me. Thank you for having my back."

"We protect our own, kid. You know I've always got your back," Maggie said.

"There's no way in hell we were going to let that happen to you."

Spenser intertwined her fingers with Rykers and gave his hand a firm squeeze, that sense of being safe and protected washing over her once more. Emotions, thick and deep, welled up within her, and Spenser's eyes stung as tears of gratitude spilled down her cheeks. Maggie gave Spenser's arm a gentle squeeze and offered her a smile.

"Now, since those nice gentlemen made it clear that I'm your direct supervisor, I'm ordering you to take the next week off," Maggie said.

"Maggie, I—"

"Not up for debate. You need to go relax and unwind and, most importantly, finish letting your body heal up."

"Like I said, I'm fine. I promise."

"And like I said, not up for debate," Maggie said, then turned to Ryker. "Think you can do something with her for the next week? Tie her up and throw her in your basement for all I care. Just do not let her work and make her relax."

The corner of Ryker's mouth quirked upward. "Yeah, I think I can manage that."

"Good boy," she said. "Then I'll see you in a week."

Spenser objected weakly as Ryker took her by the hand and led her out of the conference room. By the time they got to the parking lot, Spenser's attitude started to change, and she found herself looking forward to an entire week with nobody and nothing else but Ryker. Mostly. She wasn't good with idle time, but when Ryker flashed her that smile that melted everything inside of her, she was willing to give it a go.

"So? What are we going to do for the next week?" she asked.

He tipped her a wink. "You'll see."

CHAPTER THIRTY-FIVE

THEY SAT IN FRONT OF THE FIRE, WARMING THEIR HANDS. Spenser nuzzled closer to him and laid her head on his shoulder, enjoying the moment. After a long day of romping and running around like maniacs, Annabelle and Mocha were stretched out, snoring away in the large, six-person tent that Ryker had put up. He poured her a glass of wine and handed it to her, then gazed at her with a warm and affectionate smile.

"Thanks for being open to going camping with me," he said. "I was afraid you were going to shoot me down."

She looked up, gazing in wonder at the sky through the branches of the canopy overhead. The heavens sparkled dazzlingly, looking like millions of diamonds had been scattered over a canvas of black velvet. She'd never seen so many stars and found it breathtaking.

"I'll admit, I've never been much of an outdoorsy kind of girl. I've never actually gone camping before—I don't like the dirt and the bugs," she said with a laugh. "But honestly, this is nice. It's really nice."

"It was the s'mores, wasn't it?"

"They certainly didn't hurt," she replied. "But the company is pretty good, too."

He leaned over and gave her a kiss, and she relished the warmth of his lips lingering on hers. For the first time in a long time, Spenser felt healed. Not physically. Not from the wounds Alex Ricci had inflicted upon her. She felt emotionally healed. Even spiritually. For the first time since Trevor had died, she felt whole. Complete. It was something she didn't think she would ever feel again. But it was yet another first in the long line of firsts she'd experienced with Ryker.

"How are you feeling?" he asked.

"Tired. A little sore. But honestly? I feel really good."

"Do you think you're going to hear from those Bureau clowns again?"

She shook her head. "You and Maggie made them look like idiots. They've already got enough egg on their faces, and I doubt they'll come back for a second helping. They desperately need a scalp, but you closed the door on them taking mine. So, thank you."

"Like Maggie said, we've got your back. Always," he replied. "I just worry they'll try to come at you from a different angle."

"I know how those guys think, and after you gave them definitive proof, that their informant tried to murder me, they'll pivot and find somebody else to blame. They're all about covering their butts as quickly and efficiently as possible. You burned them once, so they're not going to waste more time by giving you a chance to do it again. Trust me. This is over."

Ryker raised his glass. "Then to the end of the Ricci saga in your life, once and for all."

"I'll drink to that."

Spenser tapped her glass against his, and they sat in silence for a few minutes. The crackle and pop of the fire were the only sounds. The world around them was quiet as Spenser gazed heavenward, admiring the stars. She felt like she was among them, floating along in deep space. She closed her eyes and soaked it all in.

"I can see why you come out here to get away," she said. "It's nice. No phones, no computers, nobody pulling you in a thousand different directions."

He nodded. "I like to come out here when I need to clear my mind. Being out among nature always grounds me and helps me find my center."

"I think I can get used to it."

"Even with all the dirt and the bugs?"

"Well, you've set up a pretty nice campsite. It's hardly like camping in the dirt at all."

"I told you I'd take care of you."

She raised her gaze to him. "You do. You take care of me really well. You always do, and I'm grateful for it."

"We take care of each other."

"It feels like it's more you taking care of me than the other way around. You're always making dinner and planning dates—"

He pulled a face. "Taking care of me isn't always about making dinner or planning dates. You take care of me in a thousand other ways. You've helped me overcome a lot, Spenser. You've helped me become a better man. That's taking care of me, too."

"I'm glad you think so."

"I know so."

She pulled him down into a slow, lingering kiss that filled her heart and soul with a heat that warmed her from the inside out. His eyes glittered in the light of the fire like the stars above them.

"This really is a perfect night," she said. "Thank you for this."

He opened his mouth to respond, but the snapping of a branch out among the trees stopped him before he could speak. Spenser turned and tried to peer through the darkness of the forest but couldn't see a thing. The hair on the back of her neck stood up as goosebumps prickled her flesh.

"What was that?" she whispered.

"Maybe it's the Okasha," he said.

She elbowed him. "That's not funny."

"It's a little funny."

"Like not at all."

"One of these days, you'll have to accept that there are things in this world that can't be explained with science or logic," Ryker said.

"You told me you don't believe in the Okasha."

"That doesn't mean I don't believe there aren't things in this world that defy explanation," he countered. "There are a great many things that I have no explanation for."

"Like giant Bigfoot-like creatures in the woods?"

He shrugged. "I accept there could be creatures in the woods we can't explain."

"If you're trying to make me feel better, you're failing spectacularly."

Ryker's laugh was cut off by another branch snapping, followed by what sounded like heavy footsteps moving in the darkness among the undergrowth. Spenser's stomach lurched, and her heart pounded so hard, she feared it would bruise her from the inside as what sounded like deep, heavy breaths echoed through the air around them. Ryker's body tensed, and he reached into his bag, pulling out his .45. Ryker was not the kind of man who feared anything, so seeing the mild concern flash across his face was enough to throw Spenser into a near panic. He put his hand on her shoulder and shook his head.

"Don't move," he whispered, his lips brushing her ear.

Mocha and Annabelle whimpered from the tent. Both of them were standing, their hackles raised, staring into the darkness. Though they growled and bared their teeth, neither seemed especially keen on plunging into the woods in search of whatever was moving among the trees. They were afraid. And for good reason, because whatever was out there sounded large, and Spenser silently cursed herself for not bringing her Glock. But she really didn't think they were going to have to fight off the wildlife.

"Is it a bear?" she whispered.

Ryker shook his head. "No. Whatever's out there is on two legs."

"How can you tell?"

"The way it's moving. You can tell the difference between something moving on four legs versus something on two."

"Then what the hell is out there?"

"I have no idea."

A low growl drifted from the darkness, the sound of it chilling Spenser to the bone. Her heart raced, and nervous sweat slicked her body as she hunkered down, waiting for whatever it was to emerge from the darkness. Her logical mind rejected any notion that there was a monster lurking in the woods. Rejected the very idea of the Sweetwater Devil. But her paranoid, terrified, reptilian brain sent images of the large, hairy, red-eyed, fanged beast flashing through her brain.

Spenser heard another deep growl, but then the footsteps crashing through the undergrowth seemed to be moving away from them. It was only then that Spenser let out the breath she had been holding and realized she was shaking like a leaf in a strong breeze. She continued staring into the darkness, trying to see through the gloom to what was out there. She didn't believe in mythical creatures or paranormal entities and knew there had to be a logical explanation for whatever it was they were hearing. There just had to be.

Just before she turned back to Ryker, desperate to share a laugh about all this and find that logical explanation with him, Spenser heard another low growl that drew her attention. And as she stared into the inky shadows between the trees, she saw what looked like eyeshine, as if the fire flashed off a pair of deep ruby-red eyes in the darkness.

The blood in her veins turned to ice, and her mouth was suddenly drier than the Sahara Desert. Feeling like she was on the verge of a panic attack or maybe total heart failure, she turned to Ryker with her eyes wide.

"Did you see that?"

"See what?"

Spenser turned back to point to what she'd seen in the darkness, but there was nothing except the inky pools of shadow again, leaving her to wonder…

AUTHOR'S NOTE

Thank you for joining Spenser Song on another exciting adventure in Sweetwater Falls! I feel I really put her through the wringer this time around—recovering from a brutal attack while dealing with missing campers, a legendary creature, and the Bureau breathing down her neck. Talk about a full plate! But that's what makes Spenser so special; she faces everything head-on, no matter how overwhelming it gets. I hope this adventure pulled you in and captivated you till the very end!

Before you go, let me give you a glimpse into what I have in store for Spenser next. In the upcoming book, she's diving into a chilling cold case that's been haunting Sweetwater Falls. When a grieving mother pleads for the truth behind her daughter's tragic death, Spenser is drawn into a web of lies, high school secrets, and a decades-old grudge that could tear the town apart. There's plenty more to uncover and I can't wait to share it with you!

If you're yearning for another riveting mystery to dive into, I highly recommend checking out my best-selling new release PRISON BREAK, part of my Blake Wilder series. With the Black Cell unit dissolved and a chaotic prison break to deal with, Blake's got her hands full. Shootings, escaped convicts, carjackings, murders—it's a whirlwind of mayhem. Can she handle it all this time?

I always aim to deliver the best reading experience for you. Your feedback helps me understand what delights you and where I can improve. If you enjoyed this adventure, please consider leaving a review. Your feedback helps other readers discover the series, fuels my motivation to keep writing, and is an integral part of shaping this series.

Thank you once again for your continued support. It is because of YOU that I have the motivation to keep going and keep delivering the stories you love.

By the way, if you find any typos or want to reach out to me, feel free to email me at egray@ellegraybooks.com

Yours truly,
Elle Gray

CONNECT WITH ELLE GRAY

Loved the book? Don't miss out on future reads! Join my newsletter and receive updates on my latest releases, insider content, and exclusive promos. Plus, as a thank you for joining, you'll get a FREE copy of my book Deadly Pursuit!

Deadly Pursuit follows the story of Paxton Arrington, a police officer in Seattle who uncovers corruption within his own precinct. With his career and reputation on the line, he enlists the help of his FBI friend Blake Wilder to bring down the corrupt Strike Team. But the stakes are high, and Paxton must decide whether he's willing to risk everything to do the right thing.

Claiming your freebie is easy! Visit
https://dl.bookfunnel.com/513mluk159
and sign up with your email!

Want more ways to stay connected? Follow me on Facebook and Instagram or sign up for text notifications by texting "blake" to 844-552-1368. Thanks for your support and happy reading!

ALSO BY
ELLE GRAY

Blake Wilder FBI Mystery Thrillers

Book One - The 7 She Saw
Book Two - A Perfect Wife
Book Three - Her Perfect Crime
Book Four - The Chosen Girls
Book Five - The Secret She Kept
Book Six - The Lost Girls
Book Seven - The Lost Sister
Book Eight - The Missing Woman
Book Nine - Night at the Asylum
Book Ten - A Time to Die
Book Eleven - The House on the Hill
Book Twelve - The Missing Girls
Book Thirteen - No More Lies
Book Fourteen - The Unlucky Girl
Book Fifteen - The Heist
Book Sixteen - The Hit List
Book Seventeen - The Missing Daughter
Book Eighteen - The Silent Threat
Book Nineteen - A Code to Kill
Book Twenty - Watching Her
Book Twenty-One - The Inmate's Secret
Book Twenty-Two - A Motive to Kill
Book Twenty-Three - The Kept Girls
Book Twenty-Four - Prison Break

A Pax Arrington Mystery

Free Prequel - Deadly Pursuit

Book One - I See You

Book Two - Her Last Call

Book Three - Woman In The Water

Book Four- A Wife's Secret

Storyville FBI Mystery Thrillers

Book One - The Chosen Girl

Book Two - The Murder in the Mist

Book Three - Whispers of the Dead

Book Four - Secrets of the Unseen

Book Five - The Way Back Home

A Sweetwater Falls Mystery

Book One - New Girl in the Falls

Book Two - Missing in the Falls

Book Three - The Girls in the Falls

Book Four - Memories of the Falls

Book Five - Shadows of the Falls

Book Six - The Lies in the Falls

Book Seven - Forbidden in the Falls

Book Eight - Silenced in the Falls

Book Nine - Summer in the Falls

Book Ten- The Legend of the Falls

ALSO BY

ELLE GRAY | K.S. GRAY

Olivia Knight FBI Mystery Thrillers

Book One - New Girl in Town

Book Two - The Murders on Beacon Hill

Book Three - The Woman Behind the Door

Book Four - Love, Lies, and Suicide

Book Five - Murder on the Astoria

Book Six - The Locked Box

Book Seven - The Good Daughter

Book Eight - The Perfect Getaway

Book Nine - Behind Closed Doors

Book Ten - Fatal Games

Book Eleven - Into the Night

Book Twelve - The Housewife

Book Thirteen - Whispers at the Reunion

Book Fourteen - Fatal Lies

A Serenity Springs Mystery Series

Book One - The Girl in the Springs

Book Two - The Maid of Honor

ALSO BY

ELLE GRAY | JAMES HOLT

The Florida Girl FBI Mystery Thrillers

Book One - The Florida Girl

Book Two - Resort to Kill

Book Three - The Runaway

Book Four - The Ransom

Book Five - The Unknown Woman

Made in the USA
Columbia, SC
02 September 2024

41490113R00137